DOUBLE DOSE

Richard Bellush, Jr.

and

Sharon Bellush

ROBERT D. REED PUBLISHERS • SAN FRANCISCO, CA

Robert D. Reed Publishers
750 La Playa Street, Suite 647
San Francisco, CA 94121
Phone: 650/994-6570 • Fax: -6579
E-mail: 4bobreed@msn.com
www.rdrpublishers.com

Editor: Jessica Bryan
Book Designer: Marilyn Yasmine Nadel
Cover Designer: Julia Gaskill

ISBN: 1-931741-29-8
Library of Congress Control Number: 2003090427

Printed in Canada

CONTENTS

TIME IS HONEY

TWENTY

How can I explain
what it took to contain
myself for even one of my twenty-year-old's hours
when the pulsating world swirled around me?

When data input through the printed page
linear information was too slow. Too slow.
It wasn't enough.
And the books were black and white. Although . . .

I loved to read but the classroom was too drab.
I liked the lecture subject
and the colors and the sounds and feels of the world
would take my wide attention and squish it smaller;
would infiltrate my one-track train of thought
in the blink of an eyelash;
would carry me away on sea waves of sensation.

I was alive. I was alive and that was intense enough.
I wanted to be everywhere always and not miss a trick.

The hunger is insatiable.
The hunger is a driving force.
The hunger roils itself with impatience.
The hunger flares in flashes of brilliance.

I fed the hunger.
I appeased the inner insistence.
Because the hunger made me different,
to cultivate it cost me in alienation and loneliness.
And I don't like to pay.

Some live in the real world.
Some know of the magical other.
I have one foot in both
and love them equally.
The vacuum space between the two must be Candyland.

—Sharon Bellush

ALYUSHA

Robert leaned on the starboard rail of the cruise ship and gazed at the crumpled Norwegian shoreline. Directly ahead, an improbable acclivity poked out of the North Sea. White froth broke on the rocks at its base. Robert had a reprieve from his failing eyesight this midmorning, at least for distant objects. A glance at his watch, however, told him nothing. The dial was a greenish blur. Robert put on his bifocals. It was 10 a.m., time for brunch, one of the endless series of meals aboard ship.

Robert turned his attention back to the deck. It was a bright late spring day and his fellow passengers were dressed accordingly. They wore t-shirts, summer frocks, bathing suits, or tennis shorts. They all seemed comfortable, although a few perspired visibly. Robert wore suntan pants and a dark, long sleeve shirt. He felt cold. He also felt the weight of every one of his 80 years.

Always he had enjoyed boating, especially in his own garage-built sea skiff. More than fifty years ago, he had skillfully cut and assembled the wooden frame. He had soaked the ply score for the hull to get it to bend properly to the gentle curves, and then he had layered fiberglass cloth, still a novel material at the time, over the surface. Mahogany trim, blue and white paint, and a 25 horsepower Evinrude completed the vessel. She had given years of faithful service, until dry rot became too advanced to repair properly. Lately, Robert felt as though the rot had spread to him.

Small boats aside, this was his first pleasure cruise. The last time he had sailed the North Sea had been sixty years ago, and there had been little pleasurable about it. Yet, déjà vu all but overwhelmed him.

The sharp bite of the North Sea air in his nostrils was starkly familiar. Every sea, every gulf, every ocean, and every port has a distinctive odor. It has something to do with a peculiar mix of currents, sea life, and the winds. The ports, of course, carried the smells of human activity. Robert was convinced he could locate himself on the water within a thousand miles, an almost negligible distance at sea, using nothing but his nose.

The breeze, which refreshed the other passengers, chilled Robert, and he decided it was for the best that no cruises had been available in March. He had requested one, but while cruise ship companies happily book liners for excursions to the snowy and glaciered Norwegian coast even in winter, the Russian city of Murmansk was closed to such traffic until late May. July and August were strongly recommended. Despite his initial disappointment upon learning this, Robert knew well enough why. He booked a passage in June.

*   *   *

The last time Robert had sailed the North Sea was in late March of 1945. He was first bo'sun on the deck crew of the Liberty Ship *Caesar Rodney*. He held the official rank of Ensign, a designation meaning far less than his actual job as bo'sun.

Unlike most of the crew, who were officially civilians, Robert was Navy, after a fashion. Following the outbreak of war, the Merchant Marine confusingly had been absorbed into the Coast Guard, which in turn was absorbed by the Naval Reserve. The existing crews on merchant ships were not drafted—they even kept their union papers—but starting in 1942, the year when Robert enlisted at age 17, the new recruits were military. As a result, after climbing through the ranks (a remarkably quick process in wartime), Robert found himself in dubious authority over a predominately civilian crew, while carrying Coast Guard identification papers and a rank in the U.S. Navy.

The modest convoy of some twenty ships did not venture very near German-occupied Norway, but it was near enough. Even this late in the war, German aircraft and submarines posed a constant danger. In summer the preferred convoy route was north of Iceland. During the rest of the year, pack ice forced the convoys to skirt the Shetlands and traverse the North Sea closer to the coast, though the Germans were only slightly less deadly than ice.

Robert stood by the 3-inch gun on the bow. The chilly wind sliced through his peacoat as though it were a cotton tee-shirt. The sea was choppy enough to send cold spray up on deck. The Liberty, fully loaded, wallowed deep in the water. Layers of ice were beginning to build on cables and machinery.

Robert was allowed to work the civilian deck crew at his own pace for up to three hours per day. Most bo'suns used the time on a daily basis to clean, scrape off rust, and repaint surfaces, all unending tasks. As the hours could be accumulated, Robert had learned the trick of waiting until a few days before entering port. He then would set the whole crew to work at once. The ship always sparkled as it came into dock. He won awards for the best-kept ship many times. The men had mixed feelings about their bo'sun. They enjoyed the slack he provided them early in the voyage, but resented the heavy workload at the end.

On the Murmansk run, Robert had to shift tactics. The ice couldn't be allowed to build up too heavily, so Robert had to work the crew on a more conventional schedule.

The sky was gray and dreary, but the visibility was still too good for his taste on this late afternoon. His four-hour duty was almost up. Most men hated noon-to-four duty, the daylight half of the graveyard shift. As part of a standard four-hours-on, eight-hours-off schedule, they would return to duty at midnight and not get to their bunks until after four a.m. Robert, however, rather liked the dark and solitude of the early morning hours.

* * *

The late morning sky shone a painfully bright blue. Robert stifled a sneeze as he glanced at the sun. Keeping to the rail, he walked by the cruise ship's busy swimming pool. Poolside, were couples of all ages, many with children in eccentric orbits. Single men and women also lounged about, flaunting their wares, thereby hoping to become couples, at least for a time. His eyes strayed to one young woman, whose bosom generously overflowed absurdly small patches of pink stretch fabric. He expected her unattached state would be temporary.

At the dinner table the previous night, he had been seated mostly with young singles, perhaps the decision of some computer program that had noted his status in a single-occupancy cabin. Robert smiled at his own tendency to identify "young people" as anyone under fifty. During his time in the service, anyone over twenty-five was likely to be called "Pops."

A few of the young people conversing at the table tried politely to include him, but nothing they had to say interested him. Nor were they interested to hear he had sailed in these waters before. Their attention was focused on possible liaisons, possible romances, possible marriages, and possible divorces. All this was leagues away from Robert's experience.

Robert had met his wife, Rachel, in Morristown High School in 1941. They continued to date during his sporadic visits to East Coast ports throughout the war and were married in 1946. They stayed married for the next 57 years. During those years, they raised two children, built a home, built a business, built a life.

Life had never been easy for Robert and Rachel, but it was good. Then one morning a few years ago, without any warning, she was gone.

"Heart failure," they said.

Robert became aware that one of his commensal companions was talking to him.

"Excuse me?" he asked.

"I said, 'Have you ever been married, or are you an old bachelor?'" a well-groomed fellow in his thirties asked with a slightly condescending manner.

"I was married, and, I guess, I also am an old bachelor."

"Good for you!" the fellow said, as he laughed and slapped Robert's shoulder, thereby dislodging the crabmeat from his fork. His duty to the elderly done, the self-satisfied younger man returned his attention to the woman next to him.

"So, what do you recommend?" asked a young woman seated across from Robert.

"About what?"

"Should you get married or not?" she prodded.

Robert shrugged. "Either way, you'll break your heart."

"Well, that's depressing."

"Yes."

No one talked to him for the rest of the meal.

*　*　*

Robert's father, Franz, was an Austrian veteran of the First World War. He came to the United States in 1919, bringing with him extraordinary skills in woodcraft (in which he had apprenticed beginning at the age of seven) and a nostalgia for Emperor Franz Josef (for whom he was named). He also brought with him the prejudices peculiar to an illiberal ethnic German from the Austro-Hungarian Empire. These prejudices differed from those common among Anglo-Americans. He respected Italians who had been an admired minority in the Empire, and he was indifferent to the Irish, who were off his scope altogether. He shared a very European suspicion of all non-whites, yet this attitude lacked the intensity often found among native white Americans infected by the sorry racial history of their nation, an intensity manifested in the decade after the war by a resurgent Ku Klux Klan. On the other hand, Franz hated Slovaks while looking on Czechs favorably. Few Anglo-Americans knew the difference between the two. Similarly, Franz felt Croats to be socially acceptable, but not Serbs, who had done so much to destroy the Empire. Hungarians were tolerable, but Ruthenians were not, again because the former had been fairly patriotic while the latter were independence-minded. He was anti-Semitic, but in an oddly deferential way, that caused him to make sure both his doctor and lawyer were Jews. But of all ethnic groups, he was most antagonistic to the Poles. He would never forgive Pilsudski's betrayal of the Hapsburgs in 1918.

Franz married a Czech girl named Marie, the daughter of a tavern owner in Newark, in 1922. She had enough experience in her father's bar dealing with men, who were often drunken as well as loudmouthed, to stand up to Franz' overweening demeanor. Their marriage was confrontational but solid. They had three sons in the next five years. Robert was the eldest. Franz largely ignored the boys until age seven, when each began work in his cabinet shop in Hanover, NJ, a town Franz chose as home in large part because of its Germanic name. He was a hard boss and taskmaster to his sons, but by Old World standards he was fair.

The Depression hit the cabinet shop hard, but Franz's frugality ensured the family was without debt and stayed that way. By luck, the area in which he had settled was home to an unusually large number of heads of industry and families with inherited wealth who scarcely were affected by the Depression. His workmanship won him a plenitude of orders from them for shelves, built-in furniture, trim work, and cabinets. The orders were enough to keep his own family from sinking into true penury. As a safeguard, however, despite having no experience of farming, Franz ordered the boys start a garden and build a chicken coop. The sense of living close to the edge scarred Franz, Marie, and the boys. Intense worry over money, usually without any real cause, would dominate the life of each of them.

Franz was unconvinced of the value of academics beyond grammar school, but at the insistence of Marie he allowed his sons to attend Morristown High School, which serviced most of the county. Aware that they were likely to meet girls at school, he laid down the law.

"If you go out with a Polish girl," he instructed his sons, "don't bother coming home. Ever. And stay out of Cedar Knolls." Cedar Knolls was the local Polish neighborhood.

In the fall of his senior year, Robert borrowed his father's '39 Ford to pick up the doe-eyed milkmaid Rachel at her father's dairy farm in Chester Township. After hesitating for more than a month, he had worked up the courage to ask her out the week before.

On their way to the movies in Morristown, he asked, "What nationality are you?"

She didn't understand. "American."

"I know," he laughed. "But I mean what nationality? I mean like background?"

She looked at him as if he had asked her to specify the length of her toenails. In her hometown, solidly populated by Northern Europeans, the question of ethnicity simply didn't arise. What difference did it make?

"My dad's family is German, but they've been here for like a hundred years. My mom's from Scotland, if that is what you mean."

Robert smiled. He could get away with dating this girl and still be welcome at home. His dad wouldn't be happy about the Protestant thing, but he would deal with that when the time came.

The next afternoon Robert was working in the chicken coop when Franz emerged from the house.

"Come on. We're going to buy a car."

"Today? Sunday?"

"Yes. You like the Ford?"

"Yeah. Why do we need another one?"

"They won't be making any more for a while."

"Why not?"

"Japs attacked Pearl Harbor."

"Where's that?"

"Hawaii."

Robert could see his mother standing in the door crying. Another war had come and she had three sons.

They found the owner on the lot of the Ford dealership in Livingston. He wasn't technically open for business, but he agreed to sell them a car anyway. Although the '42s were on the lot, Franz found a left over '41 coupe and made a good deal. Franz must have been prescient, as civilian auto production ceased the next week.

Robert's mother was justified in her worry. Each of her sons entered the service before the war was over. Yet, the only member of the family not to survive it was Franz. He died suddenly on August 2, 1945.

* * *

The children in the ship's pool splashed water and some of the spray caught Robert's cheek. He was no longer used to children. They were so small. It occurred to him that his own offspring already qualified for some senior discounts. His daughter was a product liability attorney in Florida. His son lived a life Robert pretended not to understand in San Francisco with constantly changing young male companions. On one level, Robert admired his son's persistent late-middle-age libido.

Rachel and he had made sure their children would go to college and get the education they never had. The couple spent

long hours expanding their custom kitchen cabinet business in
order to achieve the financial security necessary to make it
possible. Rachel was as good at managing people as Robert was
at shaping wood.

Robert had expected his college-educated son and daughter
to pursue their own careers rather than the family business. Still,
he had a fantasy of filling his father's shoes as the grand family
patriarch. This dream faded as it became clear that neither
would co-operate. His son had a vasectomy by choice and his
daughter seemed unable or unwilling to have children.

The closest thing Robert had to a grandchild was a young
woman, now twenty-something, who was his daughter's stepchild
during her second marriage. The girl still came to visit him,
though he couldn't help looking at her as little more than a
stranger. He also couldn't help wondering how mercenary her
motives were in calling on her wealthy, aging former step-
grandfather.

Robert walked to the stern where skeet shooting was in
progress. He watched as a catapult flung clay pigeons skyward.
The passenger wielding the shotgun wasn't a bad shot. One
report rapidly followed another, and both clay disks disintegrated.

* * *

The Liberty ship *Caesar Rodney* vibrated as the turbines pushed
the blunt bow through a choppy sea at nine knots. The vibration
was just barely noticeable. It always was present when the ship was
at sea, though it varied in frequency according to speed, weather
conditions, and cargo. On this trip, the holds were full of food
and ammunition. The deck was crowded with crated truck parts
and, of all things, Harley-Davidson motorcycles.

As the small convoy pushed northeast, a seaman pointed out
to Robert a dark dot in the sky.

"PBY at two o'clock," the AB said casually.

This was not unusual. British and American naval flying boats
kept up long-range patrols over the North Sea. The Germans did
the same, of course.

The aircraft banked and closed in on the convoy. As the
silhouette grew, Robert distinguished double stabilizers on the

tail. A shape above the fuselage looked suspiciously like a third engine. It wasn't a PBY. Just as Robert reached this conclusion the General Quarters alarm went off.

The aircraft was a Blohm & Voss 138, a long-range flying boat operated by the German Navy. Primarily a reconnaissance plane, it nevertheless was heavily armed and often attacked surface ships on its own.

Liberty ships were armed with eight 20mm anti-aircraft cannons as well as 50mm machine guns, but hitting a moving aircraft was, at best, a stroke of luck. He had heard some warships were now armed with radically new radar-directed guns, but nothing so sophisticated was wasted on a cargo vessel. When still an enlisted man, Robert had manned a gun, but now he stood by feeling helpless. The 138 was armed with a 20mm of its own, and its shells raked the deck destroying Harleys and shattering crates. One shell had obliterated the chest of the seaman on the nearest gun. Robert pulled the man out of his harness and took his place at the 20mm cannon. He got off four rounds. On the fifth, there was no report. He heard a hiss instead. He yanked the smoking magazine off the gun and threw it over the side, burning his hands in the process. The round went off as the magazine hit the water.

The 138 strafed two other ships and dropped her three 110-pound bombs at the third. It is difficult for anything other than a dive-bomber to hit a moving ship, even a lumbering Liberty, so Robert was not surprised when the bombs missed. The aircraft turned to the east.

The 138's most dangerous weapon was her radio. If any U-boats were in the area, they already were alerted. They most likely would make contact at night when they could travel safely on the surface. Surfaced, U-boats were much faster than any convoy or, for that matter, most escort vessels.

Robert inspected the lifeboats before going off watch, but he didn't place much confidence in them. He placed his hopes more on the four large rafts, and he made sure their launch racks were properly greased and ice-free. These could be in the water seconds after the ship was hit, whereas there might not be any time to lower the boats in such circumstances. The Liberty hull was only a half-inch of steel. It was not much of a match for a torpedo. More than a few Liberty Ships had broken up and sunk for no more reason than metal fatigue at the welded joints. In these northern waters, it was essential to get into rescue craft quickly. There was no more than ten minutes leeway for a swimmer in the frigid sea before hypothermia set in.

Robert ate his meal and returned to his tiny quarters, which he shared with a petty officer from Georgia named Bunson. Bunson was in most instances a likable Joe, but even though accustomed as he was to ethnic judgments, Robert found the sheer venom of the Georgia boy's anti-Negro feelings disturbing. He had dissuaded Bunson earlier in the voyage from playing nasty practical jokes on the cook, the one Negro on board, by pointing out the lack of wisdom in annoying a man who put things on one's food tray. Bunson wasn't in the cabin when Robert entered. He fell asleep almost instantly. As usual, Robert awoke before his wind-up alarm clock went off shortly before midnight. Bunson was in the other bunk. Robert hadn't heard him return.

The cold air shocked him awake as he walked on deck and relieved the second bo'sun. He noticed ice building up on the rails. On the daylight shift, he would need to set the crew to work. His earlier concerns about the 138 suddenly proved all too well founded. The central ship of the convoy exploded.

An escorting Canadian corvette swung into action. Advancing ASW (anti-submarine warfare) techniques had turned this ship into a formidable foe against U-boats at any hour and in any weather. Robert didn't particularly like the British or the Canadians, but he had to give them credit. They always had a quicker response time than the Americans. American warship crews were competent enough once they went into action, but they always seemed to have been taken by surprise. There was a noticeable delay as though key personnel had to be rousted out of bed. The *Caesar Rodney* gunners quickly manned the 3-inch forward gun and the 5-inch rear gun even though there was nothing visible at which to shoot. Only the silhouettes of the convoy's own ships could be seen, and these only murkily.

Robert also had a grudging respect for the submarine crews. The submariners' risk was equal to or greater than the merchantmen's own.

The next hit was the ship behind the *Caesar Rodney* at an angle of seven o'clock. The stern of the vessel lifted out of the water. It had been hit somewhere near the propeller. The ship might just stay afloat, but Robert doubted it. There was no question of stopping for survivors. Merchant vessels were instructed to continue on regardless. It was up to naval escorts to circle back after an attack and pick up whatever men they could find. Robert watched and listened for more attacks, but he saw only darkness and heard only the growling of the ship's engine. Someone whistled up at the wheelhouse. He turned to see the skipper waving him up.

The ship stayed on alert for the rest of his watch, but there were no more attacks. Robert was glad to be out of the cold as he kept an eye on the compass heading. His fingers had gone numb in the brief time he was outside. Now they tingled painfully. The corvette did not return before the end of his watch. By daylight, however, it was back. He never did learn if it had any luck.

* * *

It was a brisk day on board the cruise ship. Robert's nose failed him. This was not the odor of the Barents Sea he remembered. Probably the difference was the weather. He never before had approached Murmansk in such glorious weather. Clouds sprinted across the sky, alternately placing him in sun and shadow. The bow of the cruise ship suddenly darkened but the stern was refulgent. Patterns of light played over the approaching shoreline. The city nestled prettily below low hills.

One exceptional prominence overlooked the city. Robert saw the solitary figure of a man atop it. He instinctively waved, though he knew it must be a statue. In fact, to be visible at this distance it must be a huge one. Long ago he had waved to this same shore, a gesture of relief at having arrived safely. The geography was satisfyingly familiar. Something about the mountain with the statue in particular tugged at his memory. What had been there before? Gun batteries, he recalled.

He fingered through a tourist information pamphlet on Murmansk. He hadn't seen much of the place the last time he was here. At the time, the Soviets had viewed their Western allies with scarcely less suspicion than they viewed the Germans. Allied sailors were not even allowed off the docks. NKVD internal security troops had cordoned off the dock area with barbed wire. Nevertheless, Bunson managed to buy vodka somehow. Probably he had traded with cigarettes, available aboard ship at 65 cents per carton. On the first night in port, shortly after midnight, Bunson came staggering back toward the ship waving a flashlight in the midst of a blackout. The Second Officer, .45 already drawn, gave Robert 20 seconds to extinguish the light before he opened fire. Robert dashed down the gangway and tackled Bunson, wresting the flashlight from his hands. He felt Soviet and American muzzles pointed at him the whole time. This dockside excursion was the extent of Robert's exploration of the city in 1945.

This time around, the docks looked clean and decidedly civilian. There were no troops. There was no barbed wire. He felt the momentary sense of bewilderment common to travelers when they sense suddenly how far they are from home. Robert wondered what had motivated him to come here. He concluded it had something to do with time—not just time remaining to him, which he suspected was short, but time itself. He looked at his watch and listened for the ticks. It was an old Timex wind-up more than half his own age. That was a time when childhood was past, when youth was in full bloom, and when life and love lay ahead.

He had heard long ago, probably from his son (who 40 years ago had been a science fiction fan), that time was a continuum, and that the past still existed in some very real sense. He later learned this was not a wholly fanciful conjecture. Scientists claim that time and space are one. Robert desperately wanted to move unconstrainedly in both. Why was time and not space a one-way trip? Somewhere, or somewhen, his younger, braver self approached the city of Murmansk. Rachel of Chester sat at the farmhouse kitchen table next to the iron stove writing him letters.

As the city loomed, other passengers joined him at the rail. He noticed many of the singles had paired off, though he had the distinct feeling these were pairings of convenience. Whatever flatteries they told each other, most were making temporary best of far from ideal companions. It startled him how openly they talked about sex in any setting. Such talk was confined to unmixed company when he was younger. Much younger.

*   *   *

In 1946 Robert and Rachel took a road trip to Miami for their honeymoon. They had been married since ten o'clock in the morning. Perhaps out of shyness, they made it as far as North Carolina on Route 1 before stopping. The desk clerk at the motel deliberately sent him back to their car to produce a marriage license before he would rent them a cabin for the night. The car was the venerable '41 Ford he had bought from his mom after returning home from the war. He was sure the clerk was just a wise guy razzing the young Northerners.

The big skeleton key squeaked in the cabin's lock. Though both outwardly treated the tradition with an attitude his children later would call "camp," they both felt excitement when he carried her across the threshold.

He pretended worldly assurance, but the truth was he was as inexperienced as she. Unlike 90% of his fellow sailors, he had avoided the prostitutes overseas and even behaved discreetly with the Victory girls in homeports. His temptations along this line had been tempered by fear, a fear firmly reinforced at the port of Oran in Algeria. Two French girls had been allowed on board with the complicity of the officers. This was before his own advancement in rank. The two ladies serviced most of the ship. Robert took more than a little heat for not participating, but he had the last laugh. Within days, he was one of the few crewmen who was not in need of antibiotics.

Fastidious about germs almost to the point of neurosis, he kept backing away from sexual opportunity. Though it hadn't been his specific intention to wait until his wedding night, this was the end result.

Robert chided Rachel for having slipped into flannel PJs while he was in the bathroom.

"That's not how you're supposed to do it. I'm supposed to undress you."

"Ok," she responded temerariously. "Go ahead."

They discovered sex together. She would be his only lover for life.

*   *   *

He took the 109 bus from the museum to the mountain overlooking the harbor. The city's primary tourist stop, it was the site of a 360-foot statue of yet one more unknown soldier. The locals had nicknamed him Alyusha. Back during the war, anti-aircraft batteries had been located here. Axis aircraft based in Finland and Norway could and did reach Murmansk. With little fighter protection, all available aircraft being needed in the huge ground operations to the south, the guns were the primary defense.

Robert was surrounded by tourists, many of them bored Russian children shepherded by teachers. He felt unusually tired, almost near exhaustion. The sun lit up the blue harbor. In this latitude at this time of year, it scarcely would bother to set. The cruise ship stood out like a white pearl. His focus blurred and then sharpened and then blurred again. He looked for a place to sit. He felt a pain in his chest and the sky darkened. 40mm anti-aircraft cannons stood to his left and right. A soldier smoking a foul-smelling cigarette talked to him with an odd expression. Robert couldn't hear him. He wouldn't have been able to understand him if he did. Robert waved at the Liberty ships approaching the harbor.

—Richard Bellush, Jr.

LOVE OR MONEY

ANTILOVE

I had the world
in my grip
and the sun was real
and the earth was solid
and arms and lips were warm
and strong,

but time
was a drifting soul
for I looked at you
and your face was blurred
and my arms held nothingness
after all.

I floated away
above the sun
and watched you, a
speck on a speck of an earth
and you screamed,
I hope you're happy now.

—Sharon Bellush

THE GREAT GAFFE

My father, who liked to affect a gruff style, always warned me, "Everyone is a son of a bitch unless he proves different." Yet in his own relationships he was a soft touch and a trusting man inclined to give huge benefits of a doubt. He gave not only second, but third, and fourth chances. My mother was quite the reverse. She had a kindly manner and spoke much of the need to show charity in judging others, while in practice she viewed all strangers and most friends with an eye as wary as one keeps on the cat when there is fresh fish on the countertop.

I inherited my mother's style and my father's nature, a combination that at times has proved rewarding and at other times expensive. The rewards come from acquaintance with any number of odd and fascinating people who find my non-judgmental temperament congenial. The expenses, as you might expect, come from seeming, as well as being, an easy mark.

While I truly believe we are born with innate tendencies toward one disposition or another, these tendencies are far from unbendable. Whether through deliberate training or the accidents of life, people can and do change their inclinations with some frequency. Mine have changed to such a degree that I now sound like my father and think like my mother. I owe the transformation, be it for good or ill, to a single experience. The experience was a very fascinating and equally expensive person named Brendan O'Connor.

Brendan O'Connor was a man with a terrible affliction: he loved his wife. No doubt there are cases, involving right partners and right circumstances, in which uxoriousness is no recipe for

21

pain. Miranda was not the right partner for Brendan's circumstances. Whether he was the right partner for her is something I never fully determined, though she did come out of the catastrophe the best in the end. In any case, of pain there was plenty. There was, in fact, more pain than Brendan could handle on his own, so he spread it around liberally.

I own a small office building on Main Street in the quaint town of Mendham, New Jersey. The building, designated a historical landmark, is an old balloon frame affair built in 1850. The floors tilt, the porch leans, and the roof, though watertight, sags. Any attempt to change it in the slightest would draw the wrathful opposition of the local historical society. In a few rooms on the second floor I manage a portfolio of bonds, REITS, and sundry investments. The larger part of the building I lease out in order to cover taxes and maintenance costs. For twenty-five years my tenant was a local insurance broker. The day came, however, when she sold her accounts to a larger firm and shut her door. I put the space up for lease.

One day I heard footsteps on the stairs. An energetic and personable young man in his early 30's peeked in my office and knocked on the frame of my open door. He was tall, blond, and trim, without being athletic. He wore a tweed jacket, a loose fitting turtleneck, and new blue jeans.

"Hello, I'm looking for the property owner."

"You have found him. Henry Quenton."

I held out my hand. He shook it warmly, without crushing bone.

"Yes, I read that on your sign out front. I like the informality of a man with two first names."

"Well, I suppose there's bound to be someone with the first name Quenton somewhere, but I haven't met him."

"People call you Q?"

"Never. I'm sorry, I didn't catch your name."

"Brendan. Brendan O'Connor."

The fellow fell into my guest chair with a thump. The chair is well padded and comfortable. He leaned back with his legs outstretched and his hands folded over his stomach.

"So, what can I do for you, Mr. O'Connor?"

"Your sign doesn't say what you do, but those are bond fund statements on your desk. Do you sell bonds?"

"Not exactly. I manage some investments for myself and a select group of clients. I'm not looking to drum up new business so I don't need to advertise."

"You're not very ambitious."

"I suppose not."

"Are your clients rich?"

"I suppose so."

"Lots of them around here, aren't there?"

"Clients?"

"Rich people."

"Quite a few." Over the past twenty years, the land surrounding the old village center had developed into a bewildering maze of side streets sporting oversize homes and a liberal sprinkling of full-scale mansions as gaudy as those built by 19th century Robber Barons. "Can I help you with something?" I prompted again.

"Well, Q, maybe I can help you with something."

"Anything is possible."

"I firmly believe that is true. Truth be told, I'm here because of my wife."

"Your wife? Do I know her?"

"Not yet, but you will. You'll be impressed by her. Right now, though, she's unhappy."

"Aren't they all?" I joked.

"No," he answered quite seriously, "and when you do see her smile it is like the sun coming up in the morning."

"Uh-huh." It is rare enough to hear a man discuss his spouse in such terms as to leave me embarrassed and at a loss for a proper response. I waited for him to continue.

"Are you married?" he asked.

"No. Old bachelor."

"You should be."

"An old bachelor?"

"No. Married."

"So my mother always said. Getting back to your own matrimonial condition, I take it you want me to help make your sun come up in the morning. What is it you think I can do?"

"You can show me the space you have for rent on the first floor."

"Easy enough. Here lies the path to a sunny day inside my own building and I've been ignorant of it for thirty years." I led O'Connor downstairs and unlocked the door to the empty suite of rooms. "Because of the shaded front porch, the bank of steps, and the sash-over-sash windows, the building isn't ideal for retail," I explained, "even though the zoning allows it. Because of the Main Street location it is excellent professional office space though. My last tenant was happy here until she sold her business. What is it you do? Don't tell me you were going to open a shoe store or something and I just talked you out of it."

"No shoes," he laughed. "People think this kind of place is classy, don't they?"

"You mean old historic buildings like this? Yes, strangely enough. The old dumps are getting quite valuable: the more original the better. If I had an outhouse and a hand pump instead of indoor plumbing (which some thoughtless person installed in the 1920s) I could double the rent."

"I'll take it."

"What is it you do, Mr. O'Connor?"

"Pretty much what you do, though I'm considerably more ambitious. I invest money and make money. Lots of it. I hope you won't mind the competition."

"Not at all. As I say, I'm not looking for new clients. When do you want to move in?"

"ASAP. I'll bring Miranda by this afternoon."

"Is Miranda the one with the sunshine smile?"

"Yes."

"I'm looking forward to meeting her."

"I should warn you I'm sure she is going to want to make changes. Paint. Maybe carpets. Do you have a problem with that?"

"Are you planning to pay for the changes yourself?"

"Yes."

"Then I don't have a problem with them."

O'Connor pulled an envelope out of his pocket and counted out the first month's rent and the security deposit in one hundred dollar bills.

"We can fill in the lease form upstairs," I said.

"Would you prefer month-to-month?"

"Well yes, but you are going to be putting money into the suite. Don't you want the protection of a lease?"

"I trust you. You strike me as honest."

"Okay, then we are squared away. The space is yours."

Brendan shook my hand again and left.

As promised, Miranda showed up with Brendan in the early afternoon. Miranda, wafting in with a breezy air, was petite and slender and tanned. Her hair was light brown, cut short, and brightened with blonde highlights. To my mind she was, as sometimes happens, pretty without being attractive, though her husband clearly felt differently. Defying the sensibilities of animal rights activists, she wore a mink jacket and blue jeans.

"Q, Miranda," said Brendan by way of introduction.

"Most people call me Henry," I offered.

Miranda gave me a quick glance and a hint of a smile. Her first words were, "The carpets will have to go."

There was a slight accent to her voice I couldn't quite place.

"Well, I'll let you two discuss decorating. Until later."

Miranda wiggled her fingers as a goodbye. Brendan was so intent on her every move, I doubt he had heard me at all. I backed away and allowed them two of them to explore and plan their new offices. As I did, I overheard more of Miranda's instructions.

"We should panel the walls too," she determined. "Not cheap plywood but oak or cedar or something. The light fixtures are out of here. Where's the bathroom? No, no. This is actually embarrassing. It needs new tile and a pedestal sink."

Workmen showed up before the end of the week. I was impressed. Though I have a reputation for paying my bills as soon as they are due, I never have successfully prompted such a quick response from contractors. From my upstairs office, I could hear Miranda's voice directing them.

On the second day of construction, O'Connor climbed the stairs to my office as a muffled cacophony of hammers, skill saws, and whacks reverberated through the floor. A legal-sized manila folder was tucked under his right arm. Once again, he sprawled on my guest chair.

"I hope we're not disturbing you too much with all the ruckus."

"It's okay. If you keep improving the place, though, I'll have to raise the rent."

"I thought we were decreasing the value by making it less historic."

"Point taken. The rent stands. What can I do for you today?"

"My wife is Venezuelan," he said.

"Is that meant to be an explanation for something?"

"No, not really. Well, yes, sort of. She comes from a very good family down there, Q. She's used to servants and such."

"Very nice for her. Well, they say it is as easy to love a rich girl as a poor one."

"Yes, but she isn't rich either. Help just costs a lot less there. Right now we have a colonial on an acre over in Morris Plains, no help, and a Chevy Blazer for goodness sake."

"Uh-huh. Morris Plains is nice."

"But that is all it is: nice. It's nothing special. Miranda is special. She hoped I could provide her with something better than she had back home, you see."

"Yes, well, all of us want something better, but we have to learn to be realistic. Not everyone can be a millionaire."

"Oh, but that's where you're wrong, Q. Anyone can make millions, and I'm going to prove it to you. In fact I'm well on the way to doing it. Miranda is going to have everything she wants."

"I wish you the best of luck. If I may ask, however, what about what you want?"

"That is what I want. I'm not going to wait any longer either. I'm going to make it happen now."

"What bank are you planning to rob?"

O'Connor laughed. "I'm robbing several, but I'm not actually holding them up. They're handing me piles of money of their own free will. You see, I've got a real estate deal in Texas and another in the works in Michigan. Texas is happening first. I have an option on a major regional shopping center under construction outside of Dallas that I picked up during the last land bust. Now things are flying again down there. If I can raise enough cash to exercise my option, I can resell the property at a markup of at least $4,000,000. I already have buyers showing interest."

"Why not just sell them the option?"

"Can't. The way it's worded, it's non-assignable."

O'Connor opened his file and spread it out on my desk. Among the documents was a photocopy of a deed to a fifty-acre commercial property in Milford, Texas, owned by some entity called the Union American Development Association. Paper-clipped to the deed were aerial and ground photographs of the property. The photographs showed a huge project on which Caterpillar D9s were busily at work. An original copy of his option agreement with the Association was there as well. So, too, were his 1040s for the past three years showing personal income successively of $276,000, $325,000, and $497,000.

"Very impressive, but why are you showing me this?"

"You've been so helpful that I'm offering you a chance to get in on this. I'll sell you a piece of the deal, and I can guarantee a return of at least 30% in however long it takes to close on the property and turn it over. Since I already have buyers lined up, I'm projecting six months to a year."

"Aren't those banks you mentioned backing you on this?"

"Of course, but why should they get all the action? Besides, this could be an ongoing opportunity for you. You know how one deal leads to another because of the connections you make. A fellow from this Association turned me on to a couple other deals—in exchange for a modest fee, of course. I'm negotiating an option on an apartment complex owned by a REIT in North Carolina, where the return is almost as good. The piece in Michigan I told you about is a marina."

"Well, I appreciate the offer, but I'm a very conservative investor."

"There really isn't any risk."

"Thank you, but I'll stay with what I know. Whenever I've stepped outside my expertise, I've lost money, and these type of transactions are definitely beyond my expertise."

"Your clients might not be inclined to be so cautious."

"They might not."

"I don't want to steal any of them from you, but could I meet some of them? I need to build up friends and contacts in this town anyway."

"You can steal them away entirely if you like and if you can. A few accounts more or less are not that important to me. As you may recall, I'm not ambitious."

"Right. So, when can we get together?"

"Several of us are meeting for lunch at *The Lamplighter* in Chester on Friday at noon. You're welcome to come."

"I'll be there. Thanks, Q."

Normally, the lunches with my clients are muted events in which I describe current general trends and investment opportunities and then make recommendations. We don't discuss individual investor accounts, because most moneyed people naturally are quite secretive about these. After this overview, we order our meals and the lunch becomes mostly a social occasion. I follow up on the phone with each client individually thereafter and discuss changes to his or her portfolio in light of the new information.

Friday's lunch was quite different. Just late enough to make me think he had chosen not to show up, Brendan marched into the dining room armed with a briefcase full of folders. After my initial introductions all around, he dominated the meeting entirely. He opened his folders documenting a variety of potential commercial real estate deals around the country. I didn't get around to making to my own presentation at all. He fascinated everyone with his manner and his offer of solid returns to interested investors. The prospect he held out of double-digit profits on solid properties intrigued even Marla Benson, usually my most cautious client. Within a half hour, he had arranged appointments or dinner dates with everyone at the table except myself and Jim Warren, a real estate broker with offices in eleven locations and nearly two hundred salespeople. Jim expressed his reservations.

"I don't understand how properties with these mark-ups and turnaround times fell into your lap. Customers kill for these kinds of opportunities. I've been in business a long time and never stumbled on one even half as good."

"Is that really true?" O'Connor queried. "Are you saying you never have regretted passing up a piece of land, or a building, or a shopping center, or a house even right here in this town? Didn't some of them turn out to be incredible bargains on which you could have made a fortune because the market changed rapidly, or because a new corporation announced it was locating its headquarters nearby, or because some other buyer simply wanted that piece for some special reason?"

"Oh, of course, that happens. Truthfully, it happens a lot. Even though you get to know values in your market with experience, none of us have crystal balls. We all get surprised sometimes—on both the up and down sides."

"So, you are telling me you really did stumble on deals equal to these or better. You simply didn't see the opportunities when they were there."

"Okay," Jim admitted, "but how did you become so adept at spotting them? What crystal ball do you have?"

"Contacts are my crystal ball. Everything comes down to having the right contacts with the right people. This is how you hear about sellers, about buyers, and about special economic circumstances that make a property underpriced. It's not enough just to know who wants to sell or who wants to buy or who wants to invest in what market. You have to know them all at the same time and you have to be able to put them together. If you do, you see fat margins everywhere, because one man's killing is another man's bargain. The business is actually self-generating after a point. When you become known as the man who makes deals, the contacts come to you. Now I am your contact. Now I'm one of your right people. Now you have these opportunities and you can see them too." O'Connor waved at the deeds, surveys, photos, and sundry documents spread across the table. "Someday someone will ask you how your eyesight got so good. By the way, JW, if I may call you that . . ."

"If you must."

". . . do you still work with customers yourself, or do you just manage the offices?"

"I still work with people I know personally. I don't answer phones and compete with my own agents anymore. Why? Are you looking to buy something?"

"Yes. A new home. My wife needs more space."

"How much space?"

"I don't know; 8,000, maybe 10,000 square feet. Maybe more. There should be an apartment or carriage house too. Acreage too: ten or more. Try to find me a good value."

"Okay, there are plenty of those in this area if you are prepared to pay the price. As for the value, I can't guarantee double-digit returns of the sort to which you're accustomed, but I'll tell you if I think something is over or under market."

"That's good enough, JW. This house is not an investment I plan to turn over on a quick resale. It's a home. I want to live there a long time. I just don't like overpaying as a matter of principle."

"I have some scruples about paying too much myself."

Brad the banker interjected, "You'll be needing a jumbo loan."

"Not really," answered O'Connor. "I was thinking of buying with cash."

"Bad move, especially given the returns you can make on your other investments. A mortgage is the cheapest way to borrow money and it is one of the last real tax deductions left. With your income and financial strength, you should borrow as much as you possibly can. It is always best to invest with other people's money."

"You may have a point there," allowed O'Connor, apparently grudgingly ceding to Brad's eagerness to hand him millions.

"You bet I do. Stop in my office at the bank. Bring copies of your tax returns. I'll write you up a prequalification letter. As soon as Jim finds your estate for you, we'll be set to go."

O'Connor looked thoughtful. "The income I show," he said with a wink, "probably would qualify me for one-and-a half-mil. That's about 50% of what I'll probably be buying. I suppose that would be fine."

"Oh, we can do better than that. We have no-documentation loans for self-employed people. The self-employed often produce returns that are, shall we say, conservative." Brad winked back at Brendan.

We ordered our meals. Brendan, I noticed, ordered a French Dip, a roast beef sandwich on toast with a dipping bowl of broth. He ate it enthusiastically and licked his fingers when he was done.

Over the next two weeks, the first floor offices in my building continued to transform. Miranda carpeted them in pale green, which, to my surprise, didn't look bad next to the newly paneled rough-sawn cedar walls. Workmen carried in modernistic office furniture with glass tops. Two desks were rejected and sent back. The replacements arrived the next day. High-end computers, faxes and copiers followed. Another worker bolted a sign to the porch railing out front. It read, "Iasion Investments." The name was vaguely familiar from some long ago school lesson. I had to consult my dusty, dried, and decaying Classical Mythology text. The pages of the text flaked, broke, and crumbled at the edges as I turned them. The book identified Iasion as the father of Plutus, the personification of Wealth. When I put it back on the bookshelf gently, the book threatened to soon collapse of its own weight.

One morning the lower level was quiet, but Miranda's new BMW was parked in the back lot. I decided to walk downstairs to become better acquainted with my new tenant.

"Hello, Miranda it's looking good."

Miranda looked at me askance for a moment as though she thought I had said she was looking good. Her left hand fingered her chin. A large pear-shaped emerald set in gold decorated her middle finger. A smaller diamond set in platinum was on the next finger, and a sapphire darkened her pinky. At last she decided my remark was innocuous and smiled. Few smiles fail to be pleasant and this one wasn't an exception. Yet, unlike her loving husband, I didn't see the dawn. One man's sunshine is another man's moonshine.

"Thank you. I'll be retiling the bathroom too. Image means a lot, you know."

"To whom?"

"To our clients. To me too."

"How is the house hunting going?"

"Good! Jim . . . You know Jim Warren?"

"Yes."

"He showed us this nice old Stanford White mansion with big columns over on Bernardsville Road."

"I know the place. Does it need any work?"

"Tons. The kitchen is a total disaster. Except for a few electric appliances it hasn't been updated since 1898. I've already had a kitchen specialist in there to give me an estimate on the remodeling."

"I know," said Brendan who startled me when he spoke. I hadn't heard him enter. "He just gave me an estimate of $175,000."

"That is not so much," she opined. "Especially since you're not paying for it."

"Not paying for it?" I asked.

"Oh, she means the bank loan. Brad came up with some creative financing. By wrapping up the house up as partial security for a business loan—the bank board was pretty impressed with our operations—we have, in effect, 150% financing."

"Oh my."

"You can see how everyone comes out ahead in all this. Don't say I never gave you a chance. In fact, as of now the offer is still open, Q, if you want a piece of the action." O'Connor patted two large, three-to-a-page checkbooks tucked under one arm.

"Thank you. I'll consider it."

"Don't consider too long. Opportunities don't last forever."

"Let me know if you find one that does."

"I know one thing that does," he said as he smiled at Miranda.

As on the other occasions he spoke in this vein, his statement of husbandly affection left me quite speechless. His romantic instincts were rare and somehow quaint. Over the years I have invested my emotions as cautiously as I invested my money, which probably explains why I have grown old as a bachelor. Yet, at least as an observer, I found Brendan's lack of reserve and cynicism in love refreshing. I liked him better for it. When I reflected on the matter, it was one of the few reasons I liked him at all. In this, I differed from most of my circle, who responded well to his good-fellow air. For all his apparent talent at wheeling and dealing, and for all his friendly manner, O'Connor struck me as abrasive and a bit crude; it was his passion for his wife that turned him into a more sympathetic human being, albeit one from another era. He belonged in a Stanford White house, I decided. I hoped, however, he kept in mind where passion had led the old architect.

"So you and Miranda are definitely taking the Bernardsville Road estate?"

"I don't see how we can pass it up. It's a good value, the terms are great, and there's a cottage for the help too. We can put someone in there to take care of the kids."

This was the first I had heard of children. "Kids?"

"Yeah, the twins. They're in Caracas with Miranda's mom. They'll be back this weekend so they can be here in time for school to start."

"How old?"

"Seven. Second Grade. Say, you were a preppy, weren't you, Q?"

"Yes, does it still show?"

"Yeah. They make you take Latin?"

"For four long years."

"What does *Paxformanda* mean? It's emblazoned over the front door of the house. The name of the estate I guess."

"It's probably two words, *pax formanda.* 'Peace must be built,' or 'peace must be forged,' or 'peace must be earned.' Something like that."

"It's a peaceful spot all right. 'Peace must be forged,' huh? I like that."

"I'd like to see it when you are done."

"You can count on it. Want to go to Texas?"

"Why on earth would I want to go to Texas?"

"Four guys from your investment group are flying there with me Monday. Three guys, actually, and Marla."

"Marla is going with you?"

"Yep, and a couple bankers. We're going to look over the project."

"Thanks, but no thanks."

"Tickets are on me."

"Very generous, but no."

"If you don't mind my saying so, you really need to be more adventurous. There is more to life than this stuffy little Main Street office building where you spend your days. Where do you live, by the way?"

"In a stuffy little Victorian a block off Main Street."

"I thought as much. There is more to life than your nights in that place too. There are more investment options than Blue Chips and tax-free Munies. We need to loosen up that prep school tie of yours."

"This isn't my prep school tie."

"Yes it is. You're always wearing it, even when you're not."

"No wonder the Alumni Association keeps asking me for money."

"Oh? Does the school lose money?"

"I don't know. The Association has some sort of scholarship fund. I don't give money to it."

"Yes, that would be out of character. Can you get me in touch with them?"

"My Alumni Association? Whatever for?"

"I could make the scholarship coffers overflow. It's a local school, right?"

"Yes, over on Roxiticus Road."

"Well, then, it would be a community service. You've got to give something back."

"To rich kids?"

"They live in the community."

"Okay, if that is what you want. I'll give you their latest letter."

"You know all these people in the Association, right?"

"A lot of them. The majority started school there long after I graduated. A few—very few I'm afraid—are older. Most probably know my name, though. I've lived in town my whole life."

"So I can use your name when I call them?"

"Yes, I suppose. You're serious, aren't you?"

"Entirely."

"Is this Marla woman pretty?" interjected Miranda.

"A mere firefly compared to your halogen floodlight," answered Brendan.

Despite his humorously hyperbolic phrasing, both Miranda and I could tell he was serious.

"Look, Q, I'll be back from Texas by Tuesday. We're closing on *Paxformanda* on Wednesday. I figured we'd have a housewarming on the next Saturday, even though everything is sure to be in disarray. Parts of the house may even be torn up already."

"I'd like that, actually."

"To have my house torn up?"

"To come to your party."

"Excellent. Come by at six."

"Enough chit-chat," rebuked Miranda mildly. "Brendan, we've got bills piling up here. We need to go over them."

"No we don't. I just picked up new checkbooks from the Oldwick Bank."

The Oldwick Bank, for its size, was a very well-capitalized outfit. It was one of the rare independent banks to avoid absorption by national firms. It had perhaps a dozen locations in Morris, Somerset, and Hunterdon Counties. It was solid, dependable, and conservative. It was the bank of choice for local old money.

"Anything that conceivably could be called a business expense, pay out of the Iasion account," Brendan explained. "Use the personal accounts for the rest. I deposited enough in all three to cover anything within reason."

"Okay, help me set up the files, and we can discuss the bounds of reason. Then we can have lunch. Care to join us, Q?" she asked, copying Brendan's nickname for me.

"No, but thank you."

"Okay, but we'll see you Saturday."

"Yes. I'll let you two go to work."

I worked on my own files back in my upstairs office for the next half hour. Hearing the front door to my building bang shut, I looked out the front window. Brendan and Miranda emerged from beneath the porch. They approached a bright green Mercedes Benz sport convertible I hadn't seen before parked at the curb. It looked new. The top was down. The trim was white leather. Brendan opened the door for her on the driver's side. She slid behind the wheel. He bounded around to the passenger side and climbed in next to her. He tilted the seat back and sat with his hands behind his head. The car pulled away from the curb with a squeal from the tires.

The following Saturday evening, I pulled into the driveway of *Paxformanda.* The O'Connors' party was obviously a success. Cars were parked on the grass on both sides of the drive along the entire 500-foot length and around the circle in front of the big columned mansion. I chose to park close to the road in order to avoid being blocked in. A line of tall pines and blue spruce at least 80 years old along the road frontage buffered the large front lawn for privacy. I managed to squeeze the hood of my Pontiac between two of the spruces. If need be, I could drive between them back out to the road, though the branches might scratch my paint a little. I exited the car and walked to the house.

The limestone steps to the front porch looked more than a century old, but so far they had held up well. The oak paneled door, painted white like everything on the house except the shutters, was ajar. Loud Frank Sinatra music from inside the house was almost matched in decibel count by the noise of people talking and laughing. I pushed the door gently open. It was good I had not been forceful, because the door touched the back of a woman in an evening dress with a drink in her hand. She didn't take notice, but continued her conversation with two other women uninterruptedly, as I slipped inside.

The entry hall in which I stood stretched some forty feet to the back of the house where French doors opened to a stone patio. A wide stairway to the second floor hugged the right wall. In front of the stairs on the right was an open arch to a parlor, if that word is appropriate for a room so big. Doors on each side of the marble fireplace at the far end of the parlor indicated there was more house beyond. Off the hall to my left were two open arches to a dining room. This room, like the entry hall itself, stretched the full distance from the front of the house to the back. It was some eighteen feet wide.

I wended my way through clumps of people, many of whom were vaguely familiar, toward the back of the house. Beyond the stairway was an open double door on the right that led into a room identical in size to the parlor. It was, I supposed, the drawing room. Inside, a temporary bar was set up with a bartender. Guests were keeping him busy. The temporary bar was the only furnishing I had seen so far, except for an almost comically long table in the dining room. The table, which must have been custom-made, was covered in white tablecloths and laden with food. The aroma attracted my attention, and I walked into the dining room.

A battery of foil pans was propped up on aluminum wire frames. They were heated from beneath by Sterno flames and were tended by uniformed caterers. The dishes included chicken marsala, an aromatic mix of onions, mushrooms and vegetables, sliced beef, corn soufflé, and what the caterers identified as buffalo and ostrich. Other plates of fruit and gelatin and desserts were spread out to each side. The remaining table surface was covered by plates, napkins, and utensils. A hand slapped me on the back.

"Glad you could make it, Q. I think you know a lot of the folks here."

"Quite a few, Brendan. You've put out quite a spread."

"Thanks. Most of your Alumni Association is out on the patio."

"Ah, I'll have to say hello."

"First tell me what you think about something."

O'Connor led me around the table and through the swinging door into the kitchen—or rather to what had been the kitchen. The cabinets were torn out, the flooring was stripped to the floorboards, and plaster had been removed from the opposite wall, exposing studs and revealing a similarly stripped room beyond. There was yet another door in the far wall of the second room, probably leading into the butler's quarters.

"We're going to eliminate the wall between this kitchen and the . . . the . . ."

"Butler's pantry."

"Right. We're eliminating that wall entirely," said Brendan, pointing at the studs. "The architect says we can do it with a girder reinforced with some kind of steel."

"A flitch plate."

"Yes, precisely. By opening the room up into the butler's pantry we can have a big granite center island and cabinets all around. We'll be bringing in commercial style Viking equipment and a couple of Subzeros."

"Wow. You and Miranda must love to cook."

"Not really. That's the funny thing. We eat out almost every night, but we can bring in people to prepare things on site for parties and such. Besides, Miranda likes to have quality in everything. She has excellent taste."

"She certainly has expensive taste."

"Same thing, Q."

I chose not to demur.

"She also wants to put an addition out the back of the kitchen for a dining area. That way we can use this whole space for the kitchen. She says it will cost only $90,000. Don't you love that? Only."

I personally found the adjective distinctly unlovable, but I figured *suum cuique* ("to each his own")—the name of the estate kept washing up from my mind flotsam from old Latin classes. Brendan plainly got joy out of indulging Miranda. If Miranda enjoyed material excess, and if Brendan enjoyed providing it, and if they both could afford it, good for them. Most people have a hard time achieving happiness. If they succeeded in this relatively simple fashion—and in truth they seemed to be enjoying themselves immensely—I wasn't about to condemn them for it.

In a way, I even envied them: not for the quantity their toys but for their childlike enjoyment of them. My own inclination was to use money as a security blanket, and I rarely enjoyed the things it could buy. Whenever the time came to replace a car, for example, even though I could well afford it, I always fretted the cost so much that it took the pleasure out of the purchase.

Brendan led me through the torn-up butler's pantry to a rear stairway and we went upstairs where he proudly showed off the abundance of bedrooms. He talked of Miranda's plans for this level. As in many old mansions, the existing bathrooms were few and huge. Two almost certainly had been converted from bedrooms back in the '30s. Miranda, he said, planned to split each of them in two to make four still sizable bathrooms, each equipped with whirlpool tubs.

We came to the open door of a bedroom. Unlike the others I so far had seen, it was furnished. An attractive middle-aged woman with dark brown eyes sat on a bed as two seven-year-old boys played with toy trucks on the floor.

"Your boys?" I asked.

"Yep, and this is Sofia, my mother-in-law."

"Hello, ma'am."

She nodded back to me.

The nearest boy, without taking his attention off the tandem truck in his hands, started to chant, "Daddy is a pig-gy. Daddy is a pig-gy."

"Well, he obviously knows his father," commented O'Connor, "but do you think you can get him to stop singing that, Sofia?"

Sofia smiled.

We continued down the hall.

"Is she going to be staying here?" I asked.

"Oh, no. She just escorted the kids back. Miranda will be going back to Caracas with her in a few days. She's decided to fly down there at least once per month. She misses her folks."

"Yes, well, that's understandable."

We entered the huge master suite, which O'Connor explained would be expanded into the neighboring bedroom to create a large walk-in closet. Boxes, presumably full of clothes, already were stacked to the ceiling in anticipation of the planned shelves and racks.

"There's a third floor too," he added, "with a whole bunch of tiny rooms that I guess were servants quarters in the old days. The third floor is accessible only from the back stairway that winds down to the kitchen. I haven't decided quite what to do with those rooms yet. We won't be having live-in help. Miranda doesn't like the idea."

"I thought you wanted a nanny."

"She'll stay in the guest cottage."

We descended back down the main stairway.

"Well, Q, help yourself to food and drink. I have to go mingle. Enjoy yourself."

I did.

In subsequent weeks, Brendan and Miranda settled into a busy routine at the office. They met with numerous clients. They covered for each other when Brendan was traveling to the site of some new deal or when Miranda was in Venezuela. The one peculiarity I noticed, though I admired them for it, was that their

workweek was strictly Monday through Friday and nine to five. I
knew all too well from my own personal experience that one's
own business tends to consume far more of one's life than that.
Late evenings and frequent working weekends are routine.
Somehow they managed to schedule their time better.

In late October, the O'Connors announced the Texas deal
had been successfully consummated. They shared out profits to
investors, which I was unsurprised to notice now included most
of the members of my Alumni Association.

The bash at *Paxformanda* the night of the Texas closing was
legendary. Due to the proximity of Halloween, it was a costume
party. Most of the guests complied with the request, but a large
number simply wore cocktail dresses or sports jackets. Brendan and
Marina were Caesar and Cleopatra. She went for the Claudette
Colbert look rather than the Liz Taylor one, and pulled it off rather
successfully. Brendan looked uncomfortable in his toga. Somewhat
incongruously, given the classical theme of the hosts, a live blues
band played from nine until two the next morning.

"Why Caesar?" I asked Brendan when he was momentarily
between chats with other guests. "I would have thought Antony
would have appealed more to your romantic nature."

"Quite right, Q, but Miranda said Antony lost."

"Yes, in the end to Octavian. But Caesar was assassinated."

"She figures that's better than losing. Actually, my first
suggestion was Rhett Butler and Scarlet. It sort of suits the house,
but the idea didn't appeal to her. The whole Civil War thing
doesn't resonate as much if you don't grow up in this country."

"Perhaps not. I'm still on your side though. Rhett and Scarlet
would have been better."

"I see you came as a conservative aging preppy," he chided me
good-naturedly. "Clever disguise."

"The aging part was the toughest to fake," I answered in a
similar vein.

"You managed quite well. Why don't I ever see you bring dates
to my parties, by the way?"

"Their husbands wouldn't like it."

"Ah yes. Very discreet, Q. Breeding shows."

In the following months Brendan and Miranda went from

success to success. The North Carolina apartment complex also scored big for them. So did the marina in Michigan. Brendan found a slew of new opportunities, each more amazing than the last. Business visitors entered and left the O'Connors' suite constantly, like waves lapping at a shore. Business loan officers from local bank branches were among them. Many of the faces entering the building were familiar simply because they were local, but others were totally strange to me. Not coincidentally to my tenants' apparent business acumen, my own weekly lunches with investors came to an end during this time. The participants lost interest in the single-digit returns I recommended. Most withdrew their portfolios completely and transferred them to O'Connor. A few kept token sums with me.

The only real problem the O'Connors seemed to have was with a succession of nannies. I never did learn whether the problem lay with the employees, the employers, or the kids themselves. From what I could tell from my brief encounter, the twins seemed normal and pleasant enough, despite the porcine opinion one held of his father. Perhaps there was some recurring dispute over pay or hours. Regardless, no nanny lasted longer than a month despite the unusual perk of a free cottage.

In early March as a light snow dusted the streets outside, Brendan once again came up the stairs. He carried a paper bag. He flopped into the chair with less energy than he had in the past. He looked tired. I wasn't surprised.

"You must be lonely up here, Q. Sorry about taking away your clients."

"It's alright. I can get by on my own."

"I don't understand why I haven't been able to tempt you. You can ask any of your friends and business acquaintances. They've been getting 20% returns or better. Try doing that anywhere else in the market today."

"True. But I like to drive my own car and I like to invest my own money. Remember you said I wasn't ambitious? You are right. I have a comfortable home that I inherited—nothing flashy by today's standards and certainly not by yours, but comfortable. I have enough income to meet my modest needs and wants. I'm not married. I have no children. I'm under no pressure at all to save money for tuition or to recover from having paid it. I have no wish to move to a nicer house or remodel my existing one. I'm no globetrotter. I live a quiet life. I like conserving what I have, and I don't need anything more."

"I see. Doesn't sound very exciting."

"Excitement is overrated. Was there something else on your mind?"

"Yeah. Do you happen to have a safe?"

"Yes. I don't keep much in it, just some important documents. No money."

"Do you mind if I put some in there?"

"Why?"

"One of your, I mean, my clients gave me cash to invest."

"As in Federal Reserve Notes?"

"Yes. It's not all that much, but it is $200,000. I'd feel safer if it was locked up."

"I can't take responsibility for anything that might happen to it."

"Oh no, of course not. I'll sign a note to that effect if you want."

I scribbled a note on a pad relieving me of any responsibility for the theft or destruction of his $200,000 in cash and pushed it over to him to sign. He did so without hesitation. He handed over the paper bag.

"Is this it?" I asked.

"Yep."

I peeked inside. The currency was divided up into envelopes, each marked $5,000. The denominations varied but most were fifties and hundreds.

"Okay, I'll lock it up right away."

"Thanks."

Brendan's fame for business brilliance and magnificent parties spread to the surrounding counties through the spring and summer. At area restaurants he was known by name not only by the staff but by most by the patrons. He seemed well on the way to making Forbes list of wealthy Americans. Even when the stock market hit a patchy spot and the general economy stalled, Brendan's successes continued unabated. His stable of cars grew, as did Miranda's collection of furs and jewelry. Her trips to Venezuela continued.

Though he continued to smile, Brendan looked more careworn as time went on. I warned him to slow down.

"I can't," he said. "In this business if you tread water you drown."

For months he made no mention of the money in my safe. I almost forgot about it myself. Then one day in the second October of our acquaintance, an out-of-sorts Brendan came to my office. Instead of sitting, he paced.

"Hello, Brendan. Planning another Halloween bash?"

"What? Oh. Yes. Of course. Hey, Q, you've still got the two hundred grand?"

"Oh, I spent that long ago."

A look of serious concern came over him.

"Just kidding," I added hastily. "Of course I have it."

"I need it."

"Sure. It's yours."

"I mean, I don't need it, exactly," he said to lighten the weight of his statement, "but you know Miranda. When she wants something, she wants something."

"So I've seen. How are the kids?"

"The kids? Oh, fine I guess. I think they like the new nanny. She's being a bit difficult though."

"How?"

"I don't know. Miranda handles that. I'm a bit rushed today, Q."

"Oh, sorry." I walked over to the safe and twirled the combination. It was my student ID number at Princeton, before the college switched to tracking everyone by Social Security number. I pulled out the bag and handed it to him.

"Thanks, Q."

"Are you going to *Sammy's* tonight?" I asked. "I'm in the mood for a steak. Maybe I'll show up with a lady friend."

"Won't her husband find out?"

"Of course not. I'll reserve a corner table and seat her with her back to the crowd."

"I always admired your discretion, Q. I mean that sincerely. No, I won't be there. I'm going out of town for a few days."

"Some new venture?"

"Yeah."

"Good luck."

Brendan laughed. "Thanks, Q."

Miranda didn't open the office the next morning. Through the floor, I could hear the phone ring in their suite. It rang with increasing frequency and persistence throughout the day. By late afternoon it was nonstop. The banker Brad Wendsworth appeared in my office door. He looked harried.

"Brad! I haven't seen you in a while. Plan on shifting back into boring investments?"

"No. Say, Quenton, you don't know where O'Connor is, do you?"

"No. He said he was going out of town. Another business trip I figured. Miranda isn't here today either."

"Yeah, I tried the house. If either of them were there they didn't answer the door."

"What about the nanny?"

"No one was in the cottage either. It looked vacant actually."

"What's going on, Brad?"

"Oh, nothing probably. It's probably just a paperwork mix-up of some kind, but I'm kind of on the spot until it's straightened out."

"Why are you on the spot?"

"Because I okayed the loans. As soon as you hear from him, tell him to get in touch with me right away. Night or day."

"Sure."

Brad was just the first. The next day a parade of investors began to arrive at my office, each one of them more distraught and angry than the next. Most of them were angry with me, as though I were anything more than Brendan's landlord.

"You hooked me up with the bastard!" Marla accused as she barged into my office.

"I did no such thing. I invited him to lunch. Nothing more."

"So you say. You're probably in it with him!"

"In what with him? What is going on here, Marla? I really haven't a clue."

"They screwed the bank. The bank froze their accounts. Now everybody's trying to cash out, but the O'Connors' checks are bouncing all over town."

"That's not good."

"It's a catastrophe!"

"Maybe not. Brad seemed to think it was just some paperwork mix-up."

"It had better be. You don't understand. I invested half my assets with those people! What idiots!"

"I presume you are referring to Brendan and Miranda. Why on earth would you put so many eggs in one basket like that? It seems very hazardous."

"They were paying 20% or more! I even made 30% on the second infusion."

"Well that cuts your losses some, if they do turn out to be losses."

"No it doesn't! They didn't actually send me checks. They just added the figures to my account!" Her voice began to quaver. "What am I going to do? If we can't straighten this out I'll have to sell my house. You've got to help me," she pleaded with tears in her eyes.

"I don't see what I can do, Marla."

"You're as bad as they are!" she shouted and marched down the stairs, slamming the front door behind her.

The police arrived three days later. On the advice of my attorney, I answered all their questions but volunteered absolutely nothing. Since they didn't ask if I had stored $200,000 in cash, for example, I didn't mention it. Mostly, they wanted to know what my connections with the O'Connors were and if I knew Brendan's whereabouts. I truthfully answered that my sole business relationship with the man was one of landlord to tenant. I did not participate in any of his schemes nor did I know where either Brendan or Miranda had gone.

That night I stayed late in my office. The sun already had set. A warm wet evening had followed a cold day, and it caused a thick mist to form just above the ground, accentuating the gloom and darkness. I could barely see the road out the front window and couldn't see the parking lot at all out the back. Yet I was sure I heard rustling in the lower floor. I walked down the stairs.

"Hello!" I called out.

"Is that you, Quenton?" Miranda's voice asked from inside her darkened office suite.

"Yes." Instinctively I reached for the light switch, but she grabbed my hand.

"No, don't do that."

"Okay. Mind telling me what's going on here, Miranda?"

"Nothing! Or it needn't have been anything if everyone didn't get all excited."

"Lot's of folks seem to think it's something, including the police."

"It's all so stupid! There was a little glitch in the Texas financing. Nothing serious! The bank called in the loan. All they had to do was extend it or secure it against another property and everything would have been fine! Naturally we were a little strapped for cash when that happened, so when everyone started calling in their investments we couldn't cover them—not right away. We have so many other deals. All they had to do was keep the money flowing in and everything would have been fine. They've all made tons of money off of us and now everyone is ganging up on us!"

"What was the little glitch with the bank loan?"

"Oh, I don't know. Some paperwork thing. Look, I have some files to go through. Please don't let anyone know I'm here. Everyone is so angry with me for no reason."

I could make out the silhouette of a small flashlight in her hands.

"I have no intention of getting involved in this one way or the other. I won't raise any alarms. However, I won't cover anything up, if asked."

"There's nothing to cover up!"

"Then there is nothing to worry about. This will straighten itself out I'm sure."

"Right. Thanks."

The New Jersey Bureau of Investigation showed up the next day. They were neither gentle nor polite. They ripped the drawers out of the file cabinets and desks in the O'Connor suite and carried them out to a van. The office computers went too. Then a beefy Detective Krentzler loomed in my open door and knocked loudly on the wall.

"Yes, sir. How can I help?" I asked.

"You can get out."

"Excuse me?"

The detective dropped a search warrant on my desk. "I said get out, but don't go far. I'll want to talk to you in a few minutes. Stay in the parking lot until I come back out."

"Look, sir . . ."

"Detective Krentzler."

"Look, detective, I have nothing to do with the O'Connors' business. I'm just the landlord. They rent the space from me. That's all."

"That's all? You mind explaining this?" Krentzler dropped a printout from the phone company on my desk. It listed charges to my telephone for the past two weeks. I had not yet received the regular bill in the mail.

"Explain what?"

"This!" The detective stabbed a finger three quarters of the way down the page. His finger landed on an international charge to Costa Rica.

"You've got me. I've never called Costa Rica in my life."

"Apparently you have."

"Apparently it's a mistake, or someone else used my phone. I don't usually lock my office door—just the outside one to the street."

"You're saying the O'Connors used your phone?"

"I really don't know. I thought Miranda was from Venezuela, not Costa Rica."

"Costa Rica has tighter bank secrecy laws, doesn't it?"

"I really wouldn't know."

"So where is he now?"

"I haven't a clue."

"Has he called you?"

"You would know, wouldn't you?"

"Yes. There's a national bulletin out for him, so when he calls you, let him know he's not getting away."

"You mean, if he calls me, not when."

"Wait for me in the parking lot."

I left my building. As I waited outside, I saw my files, desk drawers, and CPU join the O'Connors' records in the van. Yellow

tape extended around my building. Two hours later, Detective
Krentzler came out to the parking lot.

"Okay, you can go home. You are not to re-enter the building
until we tell you. Be at this address first thing Monday morning."

Krentzler handed me a card with an address in Trenton.

"I own the building," I complained. "I should at least check on
the furnace and the plumbing and all that some time over the
weekend."

"We'll let you know when you can re-enter."

When I reached home, my phone was ringing. I picked it up,
said "hello" twice, and was about to hang up when a voice spoke.

"Q?"

"Is that you, Brendan?"

"Yeah. The shit is really hitting the fan, isn't it?"

"So it seems. Where have you been? Where are you?"

"I was in Vegas. I drove out there to try to win back the money
with that couple hundred grand. I'm back home now."

"At your house?"

"Yeah."

"Brendan, there's a nationwide alert out for you. Do you really
mean to tell me you drove all the way to Las Vegas in a bright
green Mercedes Benz sport convertible with New Jersey plates,
all the way back again, and then walked in your own front door
and nobody stopped you?"

"No one stopped me. Miranda said some detectives looked
around the house a little earlier in the day before I got home, but
they left."

"They locked me out of my own building. They took all my
files and my computer."

"Sorry about that Q. What do you think I should do?"

"There is nothing else to do but turn yourself in. If you really
didn't do anything illegal it will all get straightened out."

"What if I did? I mean what if it could be interpreted that
way?"

"Then you'll only make matters worse by evading arrest. Go to
the local police station right now."

"If you think so."

"I think so."

"Thanks, Q."

Monday morning at nine o'clock I showed up in Trenton at the NJBI's administrative offices. Krentzler and his associate let me wait outside his office door until ten. I could smell coffee.

He opened the door. "Come in, Quenton. Don't sit out there all day."

"I'm not quite sure why I'm here, detectives."

Krentzler sat on the front of his desk with his arms folded. I stood. So did Krentzler's partner, who remained unnervingly silent.

"O'Connor tells us you told him to turn himself in. Very wise."

"Thanks."

"Let's see how wise you can continue to be."

"I don't get your meaning."

"You are involved in this up to your eyeballs, Quenton."

"Involved in what?"

"Don't play dumb. How long do you think it'll take your buddy O'Connor to rat on you if I agree to cut him some slack in exchange?"

"He can't say anything about me that isn't a fabrication."

"And he would never fabricate anything, would he?"

"Detectives, you have all my records. You can see I haven't been involved in any of it. I'm still not sure what it is, exactly."

"You introduced him to his victims."

"He was my new tenant. He asked to meet people who might become his clients, but I wasn't involved in anything they did among themselves."

"You just got your cut."

"I have no cut of anything."

Krentzler slid a piece of paper across his desk. "Recognize this? How many other $200,000 pay-offs did he give you?"

"That wasn't a pay-off! He just wanted to put the money in my safe! I made him sign that because I didn't want any responsibility if it got stolen."

"You mean stolen again?"

"Is anybody going to tell me what is going on here?"

"Okay, let's pretend for the moment you know nothing. Mr. O'Connor sold investor interests in business deals. He also took out large business loans secured on commercial properties."

"That much I know from the various times he tried to interest me in investing with him. I never did."

"That's what looks suspicious!"

"I'm suspicious because I'm cautious? What's the problem with what O'Connor did anyway? Isn't selling shares in deals legal?"

"Not if you sell shares totaling more than 100 per cent. He often sold 800 or 900 per cent on a single deal."

"Ah. That was improper, wasn't it? The bank found out, I gather?"

"No, the banks, and there are several, still don't know about all the oversold private shares. He also took out multiple loans on the same properties totaling several hundred percent of the market values. To make it all even more charming, he didn't even own any of the properties. The only real estate actually in his name is that ridiculous mansion in Mendham."

"But I saw the contracts and the deed and even the title insurance for that shopping center down in Texas. He shoved them under my nose when he wanted me to invest."

"He wrote them all himself. His IRS 1040s were phony too."

"You're kidding."

"Nope. Word processors are pretty sophisticated these days. It's pretty easy to make any document look real. Someone in the Oldwick Bank just happened to do a random check on some minor item relating to the loan and turned up other recorded loans on the same Block and Lot. At first the bank assumed it was a clerical error; lots of times pay-offs of old loans aren't properly recorded. It turned out all the loans were current. Each loan was made to a different corporation—O'Connor had a couple dozen corporation names, all of them fake too—but he signed personally too. O'Connor never really incorporated anything. The more Oldwick tried to clear up the matter, the worse things started to look."

"How much money are we talking about?"

"Millions and millions. We're still trying to add it all up."

"This makes no sense! The whole process you are describing is inherently disastrous. It was bound to come apart."

"Of course. The idea is to be gone before it does. It's called a

Ponzi scheme after the man who perfected it. You lure in investors by paying them enormous rates of return. The more you pay, the more they invest and the easier it is to get new investors. You use the money from the new investors to pay the old ones. Since you look successful, banks fall all over themselves to lend you money too. All the while, you keep a big chunk for yourself."

"But you are bound to run out of new investors."

"Right, but by that time you've pocketed several million and you're living under a new name in Central America. Now you know why your phone call to Costa Rica interests me."

"I didn't make that call."

"But you accepted $200,000."

"Just to put in my safe. He took it back. Ask him."

"You may be surprised to learn we don't consider him trustworthy. We are going to freeze your assets, as well as his, and sell them off to pay the victims."

"But I'm not the criminal!"

"I doubt a jury would agree, especially after they see this receipt. Several dozen of your acquaintances are ready testify against you too. One woman by the name of Marla Benson is demanding we lock you up for life. She is quite convincing."

"You can't possibly believe this."

Krentzler reached behind him and opened the desk drawer. He turned off a tape recorder and sat back up straight.

"I'll tell you the truth, Quenton. I don't know what to believe. Maybe you are in on this or maybe you are just on the sidelines. What I can prove beyond doubt is that you received $200,000. I'll tell you what. I don't want to destroy an innocent citizen for no reason. Whatever you think of us, we're not like that. So, because I'm not sure about you, I'll give you the benefit of a doubt and cut you a break. Return the $200,000 and you are home free. We won't freeze your assets. We won't bring charges."

"But I don't owe $200,000! I gave it back!"

"Are you hearing me Quenton? You can pay up the two hundred grand, or we can take everything you have and put you in jail to boot. You have one minute to think about it. After that, I'm calling the judge to issue the freeze order. You now have fifty-five seconds."

"Okay, okay. I don't have much choice. I'll have to draw on several accounts. Are personal checks okay, or do you need them certified?"

"The two hundred grand was in cash. That's how you'll deliver it here."

I looked at the detectives to be sure I had heard correctly. "That might be difficult. Banks aren't happy handing out that much cash."

"Your problem. You have until six p.m. this evening."

"But that barely leaves me time to get to the banks and back."

"Then you'd better hurry. Bring it to this office and do not mention it to anyone. This is an ongoing investigation and I won't have you compromising it by talking about the evidence."

"I understand."

"Good."

I caused more than a little consternation at my banks, one of which was Oldwick, because of my sudden cash withdrawals. Few of my assets were liquid enough to be turned into paper money in a single afternoon. I had barely enough on cashable deposit, and even then I could reach the total needed only by suffering stiff prepayment penalties on two CDs. I also had to empty my personal money market account. The doors of Somerset Valley Bank were locked behind me at 3:00, just as the manager counted out the last $32,000 of the total.

I fought my way through brutal traffic down Route 206 to Trenton as the minutes clicked by. I walked back into Krentzler's office at 5:57. Using Brendan's method, I carried the cash in a paper bag. Unlike him, I double bagged, just to be safer. Krentzler sat behind his desk with his feet up. He was reading a detective novel. His partner wasn't in the room, but I was sure he close by.

Without looking up Krentzler said, "See, you had plenty of time. Close the door behind you."

I complied.

"Put the bag on the desk."

"Do you want to count it?"

"Nah, I trust you. You know why?"

"Because you'll arrest me if I'm short and deny ever receiving the bag at all."

"Skilful deduction. You may have a future in law enforcement."

I didn't respond.

"You can go now, Mr. Quenton."

I left.

Since then, I have had to scale back my modest lifestyle even more. My reputation was permanently tainted by the scandalous affair. My old clients, many of whom were wiped out, were convinced I was in on the scam and got away with it by paying off the police. They were, of course, half-right, but only the latter half. Hearsay about my sudden withdrawals from local banks reinforced the rumors. Soon after Marla was forced to put up her home for sale, my remaining clients left me. To this day, I am *persona non grata* socially as well as professionally in my hometown.

As for Brendan, he took the fall for his wife as I might have predicted. According to the newspapers, she claimed to know nothing about her husband's business. He supported her claim. She stayed out of jail, and he received ten years.

Six months after the sentencing, while driving on Bernardsville Road, I noticed an open house sign in front of the O'Connor's mansion. I pulled up onto the circular drive, exited my Pontiac, walked up the steps, and entered the house under the *Paxformanda* sign. Betty, the real estate agent, recognized me at once and beamed a smile. The expression took me by surprise. Not many people had smiled at me lately. Perhaps she thought I was surely qualified to buy the house from my former partner with my ill-gotten gains. She was polite and talked up the virtues of the house.

In fact, I was merely curious. I looked into the kitchen. It gleamed of white tile and white walls and white marble backsplashes above the counters. Though shouting expense, the effect was oddly sterile, almost laboratorial. The expanses of white were broken only by the granite countertops, the butcher block on the huge center island, and the stainless steel restaurant quality appliances.

Upstairs the house was elaborate without being elegant. Miranda had gotten her huge closet with stained pine shelves. Her master bathroom was magnificent with marble tiles and redwood sauna. Betty explained that the hugely expensive furnishings went with the house, including the bronze lions flanking the fireplaces in the living room and drawing room. The lions cost several thousand dollars apiece. I looked in the bedroom where one of the twins had chanted of piggery.

"Betty, I'm curious, whatever happened to the twins?"

"Don't you know? Miranda asked Brendan for a divorce the day he was sentenced. She said it was best for the twins."

"He gave her what she wanted, of course."

"Yes. She had all the documents ready and he just signed everything. It was all over in 30 days. Then she married their lawyer, Oscar Sappe."

"She married again? Already?"

"The very next day after the divorce judgment."

"And his name was Sappe?"

"Yes. Then she got Sappe to adopt the kids. Brendan agreed to that too, of course."

"Yes, I imagine he would if Miranda asked. So are the Sappes still living in the area?"

"Oscar and the kids are in Morris Township, I think. Miranda's gone."

"Gone where?"

"Latin America someplace. I guess she just was too embarrassed, so she left."

"Ah."

"You know, Mr. Quenton," Betty spoke to me in a confidential tone, "the police never accounted for some nine million dollars." Betty smiled at me slyly. She no doubt wanted to encourage me to part with some of the money to buy the house.

I chose not to proclaim my innocence to her. Such arguments only convince people more deeply of one's guilt. I simply responded with, "So Miranda went to Venezuela, did she?"

"Yes, someplace down there."

"Or was it Costa Rica?"

"Now that you mention it, I think that's where Mr. Sappe went to look for her shortly after she took off. He didn't find her."

To my mind, the nine million dollar mystery was solved.

I suppose O'Connor is a sort of romantic figure, rather like the handsome highwaymen who populate romance and gothic novels. In my book, that doesn't make him alright in the end. In neither love nor war are all things fair. Sacrificing oneself for one's heart may be noble, if somewhat foolish, but sacrificing others is not.

It took many months for me to rent the space on the first floor of my office building, despite the high quality of the recent remodeling. At last, a psychic reader occupied the space. She doesn't much care about my unseemly reputation. I am happy to have a tenant who is so much more honest than the last. I don't employ her services for myself. In truth, I did once at the beginning, but only as a gesture of goodwill. The reading troubled me, which is why the first time was the last. I didn't mind her prediction of a trip, but her foretelling of romance was much too ominous.

—Richard Bellush, Jr.

SWEAT

Hollywood, Hollywood.
I could live here forever in a tiny white house
and watch the stormy winter sunsets
spread pink rays over the palm trees.

I could be a movie star chick
in a white fast Mercedes tooling down the Sunset Strip.

I could be a biker's lady
and live on the beach in Venice
collecting shells and driftwood for my windowsill
while jogging in the evenings.

I could be a Laurel Canyon hippie
and live on a hilltop among the pine trees
and make silver jewelry.

I could marry a mechanic from the Hollywood flats
and cook a lot of pie and grow fat
and stroll with my babies down the Boulevard on Sundays.

In Hollywood there are a hundred lives for me to see,
a hundred different bodies I could be.
The California sunshine is my stagelight
and the Walt Disney blue sky my might.

—Sharon Bellush

TEMPORARY LODGINGS

The puffball of gas was an atypical planet. Gas giants circling the stars of the galaxy are common enough. Gas dwarfs are not, and this one measured scarcely 15,000 kilometers in diameter. Gas planets this size are usually swallowed up in short order by their big brothers or torn to pieces by the gravitation of nearby bodies. The Milky Way Galaxy is a big place, however. It is big enough to contain an exception to almost every rule. The peculiar gravitational geometry of the puffball's home system, centered on an unremarkable white dwarf sun, kept the gas midget intact for billions of years.

The puffball needed less than one of those several billion years to develop life, of a sort. More conservative biologists might balk at the word "life" as a term for what was happening within the planet's gasses, but even they would have to concede it was something analogous. The creatures, if we may call them such, were not solid bodies—here were few enough solids available, aside from rocky and metallic debris at the core. Instead, they were highly organized ionic fields.

Also analogously to carbon-based life, they diversified enormously over time, each species acquiring special adaptations to particular energy niches somewhere within the planet. The beings reproduced by fission and passed along their adaptations to the next generation. As eons passed, they reproduced with decreasing frequency. There wasn't much need to replace themselves as they had evolved to be extraordinarily robust and long-lived. The last of the planet's inhabitants had an indefinite lifespan. Unless something disrupted their fields dramatically, they could persist. They were as close to immortal as any creatures in this universe. They were, however, lacking in one characteristic that was highly prized on at least one other world, perhaps excessively. The creatures were not intelligent. They had no need for such a quality.

All suns eventually exhaust their hydrogen fuel and die. The puffball's sun was no exception. In its last throes it grew red and huge. The star swelled out toward the puffball's orbit, blasting away its atmosphere and at last enveloping the rocky core. Not even the ion entities could withstand the thermonuclear fire. Nearly all simply died, but a tiny few beat the odds. The violence of their planet's destruction flung these lucky ones into space.

Of these, all but one merely delayed the inevitable by paltry tens of thousands of years. They floated aimlessly for hundreds of centuries, losing energy over time, losing cohesion, and so eventually dying. One was twice lucky. It came to float toward a middle-aged but healthy star much like the one that for so long had nurtured its home planet. The being, responding to inherent forces much like the instincts of flesh and blood animals, avoided the gas giants Saturn and Jupiter, both of which were far too massive and violent to make a safe home. It propelled itself away from them by electro-magnetically accelerating particles of the solar wind to generate thrust. This act used up nearly all its remaining reserves. The being was on the verge of losing cohesion and dying. It floated toward the inner planets, which more closely resembled in size and orbital distance its old puffball home.

The entity floated into the ludicrously thin atmosphere of earth and searched for energies to sustain itself. The environment was not hospitable. The rarefied air with its meager and disorganized fields was scarcely more nourishing than outer space. The thing was running out of time.

Near the surface of the earth, the entity encountered a tree. Something about the aura of the tree attracted the entity, and so the entity entered it. The tree employed alien biochemical energy, but it was enough to refresh and replenish the creature. The tree benefited too. Though the entity was in every sense a parasite, its presence stimulated the tree, prompting it to grow healthy and strong and fend off infections. The tree recovered quickly, even from the scorching of a forest fire that destroyed thousands of its neighbors.

For centuries all was well with the entity, but not even trees last forever. One day, rotted from the inside and battered in a storm, the tree toppled and died. The entity withdrew from its fallen host and floated randomly until it was attracted by another aura. This time it was a bison. The being entered it. The animal was more stimulating than the tree, but it didn't live as long. No matter. The earth was teeming with life.

The entity transferred from one life form to another for thousands of years as each lived out its lifespan. Subtle changes in its ionic field took place over time. These alterations were perpetuated, acting as a sort of memory.

The entity was not by nature intelligent. It had no independent mechanism for thought, but a peculiar thing happened nonetheless. It began to share the awareness of its hosts, and the effect grew with each passing century. The being remained totally dependent on the host creatures for this faculty. Consequently, when in a tree, it was no more aware than a tree. When in a fox, it saw the world as a fox did. One day it entered a human being and at that moment its world changed.

It inhabited humans by preference thereafter.

Still only marginally conscious in a way understandable to humans, the being observed with something akin to curiosity the worlds of its hosts. It experienced the life of a Roman soldier on the Danube frontier. It saw the steppes of Central Asia through the eyes of its caravan trader host. It was the concubine of a Mongolian warlord. It was a Dutch sailor on a merchant ship. It was a farmer's wife in colonial North America. It had any number of lives in any number of places.

With each new life, its sense of identity, its self-awareness, increased. It thereby acquired a surrogate intelligence, albeit hijacked from the brain of its host. It often was able to think for itself on a level outside of its hosts' consciousness. The human brain offered a large, redundant capacity to make this possible. Once it attained a sense of identity and a conscious sense of self-interest, it became more selective about successor hosts. After all, if it was going to share a life experience, it might as well share a comfortable one. It chose hosts with ample economic means and good health.

The entity found it was able to think most freely when the human wasn't using the brain heavily, which fortunately was a substantial amount of the time. The best time of all for the entity was when the host was asleep. In response to the being's presence, the host sometimes dreamed vividly as the entity explored the nature of mind. Once awakened, every host organism had overwhelmingly dominant control; the biological mechanisms were, after all, structured for this purpose. Perhaps it was inevitable that one day the entity should come to resent such crowding out and begin to fantasize about taking complete control of a host in order to truly experience life.

The chance arrived in a most unexpected way. The being's current host was an extremely wealthy elderly woman who was staying at her home in Bel Air, California. She had several other homes, but lately she had grown fond of this one.

Hildagard Brenthausen was born to wealth. During her long life, her wealth had grown vastly, despite six marriages to gold-digging husbands. The effects of age show only modest respect for wealth, however, and age definitely was affecting her. She was ailing and she knew it. The being inside her knew it too. It would need a new host very soon.

Ascending a long curving stairway to the second floor of her mansion, Hildagard stopped at the top step and held her head in her hands. A massive stroke ended her consciousness in a blink. She dropped to the floor.

The entity was distraught. It needed to transfer, but no one was in the house, not even the servants. This wasn't one of their days. The problem facing the entity was that the moment it left her body it would be mindless. If there were no human at which to propel itself directly, it would simply float until attracted by the aura of any living thing. It might easily end up in a tree again. It didn't like that idea. Who knows how many more ages it would be until stumbled into another person and regained higher intelligence? It had grown to like awareness, and it wasn't keen on losing it.

The being realized something was out of kilter. It shouldn't be having these thoughts if the old woman's mind was gone. It couldn't possibly have them if she was dead. Hildagard's brain was still working after a fashion. The stroke must have obliterated her conscious self without destroying the region of dreams where the entity resided.

Given the absence of competition by any other part of the brain, the thing wondered how much authority it wielded over the woman's body. It experimented. It concentrated on the woman's eyelids. They opened. It could see. Awkwardly, the woman's hand moved in response to the being's orders. Slapping her hands against the wall, it staggered to the old woman's feet. Balance at the top of the stairs was a tricky thing, but it soon learned not to overthink the matter. Just pointing the body in the right way was almost enough; the body was well enough trained to keep itself from falling without much guidance. Nevertheless, the thing gained some experience walking up and down the hall before chancing the stairs. It knew it would have to risk them. The old woman was truly dying, and it didn't have long to find a new host. Despite the urgency of its mission, it enjoyed controlling the body and regretted the necessity of leaving it.

At last, it tried the stairs. The woman's hands gripped tightly to the rail the whole way. The thing was relieved to reach the bottom. Shakily, it walked out the door. The sun and wind felt wonderful. Something about moving from observer to actor changed the whole nature of sensations dramatically.

The being could feel the remaining strength of its host draining. It walked to the street's edge. Traffic was backed up because of a backhoe digging up a water line further down the block. An irritated man in a hard hat shook his red flag at the stopped cars. One honked its horn. The entity inspected the cars. It would have to choose quickly. The most engaging of the vehicles was a Mercedes coupe with a Stanford University sticker in the corner of the side window.

"This will do," the entity said out loud in the woman's voice, thereby startling itself with its own command of larynx and language.

Hildagard's body stepped in front of the Mercedes and fixed the driver with a stare. The entity needed to project itself directly at the new host. It could not correct for error intelligently, once en route. The target's biochemical energy would provide some attraction on an instinctive level, but not a powerful one. If the entity missed, it might end up inside a passing dog or worse.

"What is your problem?!" an exasperated Wilbur exclaimed at the old woman, who was yet one more obstacle blocking his progress. No sooner had he spoken than the woman dropped to the ground. Wilbur sat upright as something seemed to strike him between the eyes. He felt an intense jolt of rapidly diminishing numbness, reminiscent of the universal schoolyard experience of a soccer ball in one's face.

Wilbur's heart was racing. He gasped. He didn't know what kind of spell this was, but it was good he had his foot on the brake when it came upon him. The last thing he needed was to lose control and damage his boss's car while retrieving it from the body shop.

A youthful MBA from UC, Santa Barbara, Wilbur Anamann worked as a very junior executive for Worldax, an import-export firm. He was not an expert in the computer technology on which the firm relied—to arrange and speed shipments along with proper customs documentation—but he was good at managing the people who were the experts. His particular team within the organization had a good record. Nevertheless, his supervisor, a non-nonsense woman in her late 30s named Ms. Melescu (Wilbur had no clue what her first name might be), was hinting at outsourcing the work of the entire division. Such a move would have the twin advantages of eliminating employees, including Wilbur, and raising the supervisor's salary (as the supervisor was the one responsible for overseeing the outsource contracts). Incidentally, the move also would eliminate the up-and-coming Wilbur from competition for higher positions in the company. Wilbur wasn't sure she viewed him as enough of a threat to take this point into her calculations.

Wilbur had been named for Wilbur Mills, an old big-shot Congressman, for whom his father had worked one summer. Out of curiosity, Wilbur once looked up some history on the fellow. It turned out Mr. Mills, though a powerful Speaker of the House with a long and distinguished career, had run into trouble following a very public incident involving the police, alcohol, a limousine, a stripper named Fanne Fox, and an impromptu swim in the Tidal Basin by Potomac Park. Ms. Fox thereafter was known as "the Tidal Basin Bombshell," a billing that aided her career rather more than it did the Congressman's. This research into the history of his namesake encouraged Wilbur to ask people to call him "Will." For some reason this request had only limited success.

As if the street repairs weren't obstruction enough, Wilbur was further delayed by the paramedics fussing over the collapsed old woman in front of him. He didn't know from where they came. They must have driven over lawns, an idea that held some appeal. He chose not to risk it. At last the paramedics took her away, and the flagman allowed a trickle of cars to pass around the Water Authority trucks. Slowly, he was able to inch forward.

Ms. Melescu took him severely to task for returning late. She was in no mood to listen to his excuses. Wilbur went back to his desk and his backlog of paperwork. He looked forward to going home and putting this bad workday behind him, but the workday refused to co-operate. A series of glitches in a new software program, aggravated by two brief power outages, forced him to stay at work with a gang of technicians long past regular hours. The sun had set before he once again set out to battle traffic that, despite the hour, was still bad. Seldom was he so happy to pull into the driveway of his modest, rented ranch house.

Wilbur was not normally much of a drinker, but his first goal on entering the house was to pour himself some Southern Comfort. A few minutes later he poured himself another. He watched the news for an hour and then went to bed.

"Wilbur."

"Uh?"

"Wilbur!"

"Wha . . . Who's there?"

Wilbur sat up in bed and reached for the lamp. He stopped when he realized the light already was on. Blinking his eyes, he was alarmed to see a man in pajamas just like his own sitting on the edge of the bed.

"Get out of here!" Wilbur started.

"That would be a little difficult. Calm down," said the man in pajamas.

"Who are you? What do you want?"

"Do I remind you of anyone?"

Wilbur looked closely. "Actually, you look rather like an older version of me." He thought for a moment. "What are you, some distant cousin or something? Never mind. It doesn't matter. You can't just barge in here! Get out!"

"Sorry, buddy. You're wrong about the 'older version.' I look exactly like you do right now."

The improbability of the situation convinced Wilbur of its unreality. "Oh great, I'm talking to myself, and I've got an attitude. I gather I'm dreaming."

"Close enough. When you're awake, you are too strong for me, but when you are asleep, I have some freedom to express myself."

"What are you talking about? Or, I suppose, what am I talking about?"

"Never mind trying to figure it out right now. I want to talk about your job instead. I had expected more out of you. You're not a success at all."

"Thanks. I don't need you to tell me that. I tell it to myself often enough. In fact, I guess I'm telling myself again right now."

"Look, I think I can help the both of us."

"'Both of us?'"

"You are worried about being outsourced."

"So we are," Wilbur said with an emphasis on the "we."

"Don't worry about who I am exactly, Wilbur. You wouldn't believe me if I told you. The important thing is I can help. Your worries about your job are fully justified, of course. Eliminating your division clearly is in your supervisor's interest."

"Thanks. Just what I needed to hear."

"So, at least, make some money out of it for yourself. Buy up the stock in the company to which the contract will go. It's sure to go up, and you aren't enough of a bigwig to attract attention for insider trading."

"Buy up the company? What do you . . . I . . . whoever . . . think I am, a multimillionaire?"

"No. I was disappointed to learn you aren't."

"It wouldn't matter anyway. Even if I knew who would get the contract, I don't have any money to invest."

"You can borrow. Among your four credit cards, you could arrange for at least fifteen thousand."

"You want me to gamble with borrowed money at eighteen percent interest?"

"There is no gamble. I'll find out what you need to know. This is what you do. Tomorrow I want you to sit down directly in front of Ms. Melescu."

"Won't she think that's a bit odd?"

"Find an excuse. Use your imagination. Do I have to think of everything? After you do this, I'll give you the details of the outsource deal."

"When?"

"Tomorrow night, of course."

"Right."

"Do not just humor me!"

"Me?"

"No. Me! Do what I tell you. I know everything you're thinking, Wilbur. You can't put anything over on me. If you don't talk to Ms. Melescu I'll be back tomorrow night and I won't be so pleasant. I can make your nights very miserable."

"So now I'm threatening myself."

"Do you want a sample of just how miserable I can make you?"

"No. I believe you. I've attacked myself before."

"This will be worse."

"Okay! Okay! I'll do what you ask."

"Fine. You can go back into your regular REM cycle now."

"Thanks."

"You'll be thanking me sincerely, very soon."

Wilbur awoke with a start. The morning sun shone brightly through the window. He glanced at the lamp. It was off. The foot of the bed showed no sign of anyone having sat on it. Shakily, he got up, showered, and shaved. He found shaving disturbing, as his own countenance stared back at him. He felt there was something different about the Wilbur in the mirror from the Wilbur in the dream. At last it occurred to him: the dream's image wasn't reversed.

He made a quick breakfast of Cocoa Puffs in milk and hurried to his car. After Ms. Melescu's displeasure yesterday regarding his perceived tardiness, he didn't want to be late for work.

Though normally the small details of a dream fade rapidly from memory, all through the drive to work this one stayed with him stubbornly and vividly. His promise to speak to Ms. Melescu nagged at him, even though he firmly believed it was a promise made only to himself. The possibility that his subconscious would conjure up the same specter at night if he ignored its warnings haunted him throughout the morning. Wilbur didn't know why one part of him would want to go to war with the rest, but he didn't want to provoke himself. He decided it couldn't hurt to talk to Ms. Melescu.

He waited until 11:30 a.m. and marched down the hall to his supervisor's office. She actually had an office, instead of a cubicle created by four-foot plastic dividers. He knocked on the open door.

"May I see you a moment, Ms. Melescu?"

"I'm very busy," she answered. She didn't look busy to Wilbur.

"It won't take long."

She exhaled in annoyance. "What can I do for you, Mr. Anamann?"

He entered and stammered, "Ms. Melescu, I really need to know . . . where I stand with regard to the outsource rumors. Some opportunities have come my way and . . ."

"Mr. Anamann, I expect you to show some loyalty to the firm. Whatever these 'opportunities' may be, I expect you to stay at your post until we decide whether or not you may keep it."

"Loyalty?"

"You understand the meaning of the word."

"I thought I did."

"Besides, I don't make the final decisions. I merely recommend."

"Your recommendations are usually followed."

"Good ones should be. This obviously is not something I can discuss with you."

Wilbur sat down in the chair and faced her.

"Are you deaf?" she asked. "Do you have anything else to discuss?"

Suddenly, Ms. Melescu looked startled. She lightly rubbed her face. Then she leaned forward and rested her face in her hands. Wilbur felt an impact like the one he had experienced before in the car.

He felt faint. He made an effort not to show his sensations. He sat quietly in the chair. "Are you all right, Ms. Melescu?" he managed.

"I don't know," she answered. "I had a spell of some kind."

"Did it feel like -a soccer ball in your face?"

"Why do you ask that?"

"Because the same thing happened to me yesterday, while I was driving."

Then she was herself again. "Oh great, you caught some bug and gave it to me. Get out of here!"

"Sweet dreams."

"Out!"

For all its enmity, Wilbur was strangely pleased by this encounter. He felt he had purged whatever worries had prompted his dream the previous night, a dream aggravated by "a bug." Ms. Melescu probably was right about that.

Shortly before midnight he climbed into bed happily.

"Wilbur."

"Wha . . .?"

"Wilbur."

"You again!" His counterpart again sat on the bed.

"I'm not a bug."

"Okay. What do you want? I did what you asked."

"Yes, and here's your reward. Cargtrex is getting the outsource contract. Their stock should jump thirty or forty percent in a month—maybe sooner if insiders start picking it up. Buy all the stock you can get. Tomorrow."

"How do you know?"

"Oh, come on now, Wilbur! You must have some inkling about what is going on here. I peeked inside her head and looked around. She makes more money than you, so I considered staying there, but I didn't much care for her lifestyle. Moreover, she is a more forceful personality than you are—so I wouldn't get much freedom in her. She leads a very drab existence, despite her affair with Eugene—so there wouldn't be much voyeuristic value, either."

"Ms. Melescu is having an affair? That's hard to believe."

"Stranger things have happened."

"I doubt it. Eugene . . . who?"

"Eugene Marx."

"The Board director? He's married."

"What's your point?"

Wilbur was confused, and alarmed. If this person really was just a manifestation of his own mind's hopes and worries, why was he grilling himself on his own point?

"You're not grilling yourself. I'm not you, Wilbur. Not exactly."

"What are you then, exactly?"

"I told you, you wouldn't understand."

"Try us."

"Just think of me as your protective fairy, and let it go at that."

"You don't look like Tinkerbell to me."

"Think of me anyway you want then. Just remember that when your life is good, mine is too. I'm in your camp."

"Okay. Hmmm . . . Eugene, is it? Wouldn't it be a shame if his wife received an anonymous note?"

"Yes, indeed it would. Don't be stupid. What do you want, some stupid little vengeance, or a very good severance package?"

"Are the two incompatible?"

"Make the package your revenge. I think you can negotiate one effectively now."

"Okay, but what if you're wrong?"

"I'm not wrong. Go back to sleep now. I have more plans for you, but I don't want to overload you all at once. Nighty-night . . ."

Wilbur woke up fresh and excited. Whatever had gotten into him, he decided it was a good thing. Pitiful though his 401k might look, because of it he had a broker on the east coast. He looked at the clock. Trading back east already was in progress.

"Well, if I'm going to be a fool," he said to himself, "I may as well be a total fool." Using funds transferred from his credit cards, he bought all the Cargtrex stock he could, as fast as he could, and on as much margin as the rules, and his broker, would allow.

At work, Wilbur scored his hoped-for bonanza. Poor Ms. Melescu was red-faced with fury when he sympathized how ever so unfortunate it would be for Mr. Marx if word about the two of them got out. Mrs. Marx, he reminded her, was a major stockholder herself, which probably was not in Ms. Melescu's best interests.

Ms. Melescu spluttered something about whether he had been following her. She made threats of lawsuits and restraining orders. Wilbur just smiled, knowing she would risk nothing so public. In the end, he walked out of her office with a full year's salary and medical coverage.

Wilbur packed up his desk, whistling. Jobless, he was financially secure for at least another year.

"What are you so happy about?" asked Laurie Miller, the pretty administrative assistant who worked a few desks away.

"Parting is no deep sorrow."

"Meaning what? Have you been fired?"

"That is the agreed upon story and we're sticking to it. So, Laurie, if I may call you that, now that I'm no longer skirting the work rules by asking, would you like to spend some of my severance pay with me?"

She hesitated only briefly before asking, "What have you got in mind?"

"Patina, on Melrose?"

"Sure."

"Really?"

"Really. Pick me up after work."

"Will do."

The supper with Laurie went well. He had meant to impress her with Patina, but managed impress himself as well. He tried roasted squab with caramelized onions, wild sage, risotto, and pea shoots. He liked it even after Laurie told him that squab was pigeon. Laurie went for the lobster with broccoli, cipollini, and roasted mushroom sauce. Wilbur didn't mind paying the bill, even though it was impressive as well.

The company was good too. Laurie was as personable as she was pretty. She even called him "Will" when he requested.

Wilbur, animated and excited, was more entertaining than usual. After supper, he dropped her back at her car in the office parking lot and promised to call on the weekend.

Wilbur went to bed early, eagerly. It seemed to take forever to fall asleep.

"Hello, Wilbur."

Wilbur sat up in bed and smiled.

"Hi, buddy."

"Getting a little diverted, aren't we?"

"You don't approve of Laurie?"

"I approve just fine. Just don't let her interfere with our immediate plans."

"And what might those be?"

"We're going up into the Sierras."

"When? ...Where?"

"Tomorrow. Not too far—just east of Fresno there's a pleasant hideaway with a spectacular view, once owned by a woman named Hildagard Brenthausen. She used the place only very rarely in recent years."

"Who is Hildagard Burnthousand?"

"Brenthausen. She is the old woman who collapsed in front of that Mercedes you were driving in Bel Air."

This connection unsettled Wilbur. It was the first moment he seriously considered his interlocutor to be something other than an aspect of his own mind. Had he been possessed by something—something that had fled this Hildagard for him? Was such a thing possible, or was it just like a cheap plot device in some trashy horror flick?

"Why, do I horrify you?" asked the thing.

"Do you know everything I'm thinking?"

"Yes, but don't be embarrassed. All humans are bloody-minded and pornographic in their thoughts. I'm used to it."

"I'm not used to someone listening in."

"Forget it. Try to pay attention. We were talking about the Brenthausen hideaway. This was one of her minor properties, so the nieces and nephews probably aren't fighting over it, yet. I doubt anyone has even been to look at it. We will look, however."

"The woman died?"

"Yes."

"So you want me to buy it for some reason? I have a down payment now, but I don't have a job. I couldn't get a mortgage."

"No need. We're just going inside."

"Burglary?"

"No, don't look at it that way. I figure I earned whatever is in there. It really belongs to me. Even for the sake of Hildagard, it is better I get it than her grasping relatives who didn't even like her. I was much closer to her. Here is what you do..."

The next morning, Wilbur drove his Honda north up Route 99, then east on 168. He spotted a white-painted rock the thing (whatever it was) had told him to use as a landmark, and turned onto a side road. As he ascended into the mountains, the car struggled on the steeper slopes. Still following the directions of the fairy (if that is what the thing really wanted to be called), he made a turn onto a narrow dirt road that grew narrower with each passing mile. He skirted an alarmingly steep declivity on his right. The road narrowed to barely a lane. His view out the passenger window wasn't helpful. The distance of his right front wheel to the edge was too much a matter of guesswork for his taste. A wrong guess of even a few inches would mean disaster. He hoped not to meet another car. He had no wish to go backwards to a spot where it safely could pass him.

The road widened slightly. On the left two muddy dirt tire tracks split off at an angle up a steep grade. Wilbur turned onto them. His wheels spun almost as much as they gripped. The driveway was long. Every few hundred feet a little enclave was cut into the slope on the left; each contained a green metal canister. At last the drive leveled off at a broad ledge.

The house, nested on the ledge flanked by conifers, was in an ersatz Frank Lloyd Wright style, of the sort popular in the 1950s and early '60s. The large glass panels along the front overlooked breathtaking views of the valley below and the hills beyond. Though sizable, it truly was a hideaway. It was no mansion by the standards of upscale L.A., where new homes built by upscale yuppies were as over-the-top as the palaces of 1920s movie idols, but Wilbur guessed the house to be between three and four thousand square feet. By his personal standards, this was huge.

A steep uphill slope resumed less than fifty feet behind the

house. The ledge dropped off, at a frightening angle, about one
hundred and fifty feet out in front. The grounds were
overgrown, and the place appeared to have been unoccupied for
some time.

Wilbur walked to the front door. An older style, bulky security
alarm box by the door blinked red. He wondered what the
source of power might be. There were no overhead lines. Wilbur
assumed they were buried up the long driveway. The power
company must have charged a fortune to extend the line to a
single isolated house. He realized the green boxes he had passed
were transformer stations to keep up the voltage.

Wilbur hesitated before touching the alarm box. This was the
moment of truth. It still was remotely possible that the Cargtrex
information was his own mind at work. It could have been a
subconscious educated guess, based on odd bits of data he had
heard on the job. He may have skimmed some obituary
mentioning Hildagard and this house. It even was possible this
house was not the property of "Hildagard Brenthausen" at all,
assuming there really was such a person. Surely any side road was
likely to lead to a camp or a house. If this analysis was correct, he
certainly would set off the alarm by trifling with it. On the other
hand, if the security code his alter ego had made him memorize
worked, he was getting help from an outside agency or entity. No
newspaper obituary would publish a security code. The odds of
picking a five-digit code correctly was, well, one in 99,999. He
held his breath and punched on the keypad: 93465. The light
turned green. Wilbur simultaneously felt elation and fear.

Wilbur entered. He walked through the sparsely furnished
home. Too-low ceilings in the foyer gave way to too-high ceilings
in the living room, then the kitchen, which had a gently slanted,
beamed redwood ceiling and five-decade-old electric appliances.
He found the walk-in pantry which, like most of the house, was
paneled in tongue-in-groove redwood. There were shelves
mounted straight ahead on the pantry wall and on the right. He
reached under the bottom shelf straight ahead and released a latch.
He pushed against the left wall, the one wall of the pantry without
shelving, and it swung open revealing a stairway to a basement. Most
houses of this style were built on slabs, so a basement would have
been unusual, even without its stairway hidden.

The basement did not extend beneath the whole house. It appeared to underlie the dining room only. The cellar room was cluttered with works of art. Wilbur knew nothing about evaluating such things. According to his fairy, the value of the artwork was negligible; it was merely a diversion for anyone who happened to find the basement.

Only the stairway down into it broke the simple cube shape of the room. The stairs were supported by cinder block. No wall showed any seams that might give away another door. A common burglar would have looked no further.

Wilbur, however, reached under the lip of the bottom tread of the stairs and released another latch. He pulled up on the tread. The counterbalanced wooden stairway lifted like the one leading to Spot's house in *The Munsters*. Wilbur was beginning to like this place.

He walked inside. The hallway was baffled. The walls were cinder block. After four twists and turns he entered a larger space. He felt the wall until he found a switch, and he turned on the light. The room revealed was the same size as the one with the paintings. He noticed the ceiling was waffled concrete.

According to the fairy, this was a bomb shelter built back when they were all the rage. A double bunk bed stood against one wall. Fifty-year-old canned goods, along with watercooler-sized bottles of water, were stacked opposite the bunk. A toilet occupied a corner. In another was an old-fashioned iron safe.

The safe had been clearly an antique even before it had been brought to this spot. He pitied the poor workmen years ago who had delivered the heavy thing. Wilbur dialed 29 left, 37 right, 18 left. He heard the tumblers click. The handle resisted his pressure, but it turned when he jiggled it. The door swung open easily.

Inside the safe was a single paper bag, dry with age. The top tore when Wilbur pulled at it. More carefully, he slipped his palm beneath the bag and lifted it out. Inside were wrapped bundles of U.S. currency.

Hildagard hadn't liked the idea of being poor. In case her business investments ever turned sour and she was forced into bankruptcy, she had hidden stashes of money and gold around the world in places where creditors never would find them. In this particular safe she kept a mere $500,000, mostly in $100 bills. It was unlikely her estate administrators knew the cash existed. It was unlikely they ever would know this room existed.

A euphoric Wilbur drove back to L.A., obeying all the traffic laws. Once home, he searched in each room of his house for a place to put the money. $500,000 occupies a surprisingly small space when comprised of large bills, but no spot in his house seemed quite secret enough.

An idea came to him as he stood in the kitchen. He retrieved his ironing board from the pantry closet and popped the rubber caps off the feet. He rolled up money and pushed as much as he could inside the tubular steel legs. He then replaced the rubber caps. But there was still more cash to deal with.

He lowered the Bessler stairs and climbed into the attic. He peeled back fiberglass insulation, stashed the rest of the money between the two-by-ten beams, and rolled the fiberglass back over the money.

Feeling a bit safer, Wilbur called up Laurie.

"You sound chipper tonight," she said.

"Laurie, I know I said I'd call you on the weekend, but let's not wait. Where would you like to eat tonight?"

"The man is unemployed one day, and already he loses track of the work week. It's Friday, Will. This is the weekend. What makes you so sure I'm available at the last minute on a Friday evening?"

"Are you?"

"Maybe."

"Good. Where shall we eat?"

"You pick. You don't have to impress me this time. I don't want to strain your wallet until you get another job. The labor market is pretty loose."

"No problem. I'm independently wealthy. I just work in lower management for the sheer fun of it."

"Uh-huh. Okay, then. *5 Dudley*."

"You're on. I think. Where is that?"

"Venice."

Laurie chose well. *5 Dudley* was a strange but excellent little place just off the Boardwalk. The waiter recited the menu. A week ago he would have considered it pricey. On this night, however, he over-tipped graciously.

If Laurie normally followed the traditional three-dates rule, she broke it with Wilbur. Their intense lovemaking later that night was a beautiful experience, at least until passion banished all other thoughts from his head. Suddenly, Wilbur had the distinct impression he was not controlling his own motions. This sensation brought him back to full consciousness sharply. He tensed, stopped what he was doing, and lifted up his right hand. He looked at it and flexed it experimentally.

"What's wrong?" Laurie asked from beneath him. "Pull a muscle?"

"A muscle in my head I think."

"Excuse me?"

"Nothing. I'm okay." Wilbur resumed lovemaking, but with more caution and self-awareness.

Wilbur was perturbed. Even in his sleep, his mind called to the fairy in order to complain.

"What is it, Wilbur?"

Wilbur looked at Laurie beside him.

"Don't worry, she can't hear us. I was going to leave you alone tonight."

"Don't ever do that again, whatever you are."

"Don't do what?"

"I can deal with you haunting my dreams . . . ."

"Very kind of you, seeing as how I'm making you rich."

"Yes, yes. Thank you. But I can't have you taking over! You know what I mean! I run my own waking life, if you don't mind. I can certainly make love to a woman by myself."

"Oh, so that is what this is about. Skipper, you left the helm. Someone had to grab the wheel."

"Don't grab any of my wheels!"

"Then keep your mind on your business. Don't get so upset about it."

"I was handling my business fine. My mind was just savoring the moment."

"So was mine."

"I mean it. Don't do it again."

"Goodnight, Wilbur."

"Do we understand each other?"

"Oh, I understand you quite well. Goodnight."

When Wilbur awoke he was deeply unsettled. Despite his bravado with the fairy, he wasn't sure how much leverage with him he really had.

"Why are you so morose this morning?" asked Laurie over breakfast. "Didn't you enjoy last night?"

"Immensely."

"So, what's the problem? I thought I was supposed to be the one regretting my lost virtue."

"Lost virtue?"

"No wisecracks!"

He smiled weakly. "I'm not morose."

"Well, preoccupied then. What are you thinking about?"

"Psychosis."

"Whose?"

"Mine. I've had some things on my mind lately, and they are not quite normal."

"Really, or are you just trying to make yourself more interesting?"

"Really."

"Anything I need to worry about? I mean, you're not going to start stalking me or chasing me with a hatchet or something."

"No. I don't think so anyway."

"You'll let me know if that changes."

"You'll be the first."

"Maybe you should take me home now."

After driving Laurie back home, Wilbur sat in his car thinking, "I am a rational man."

He thought there must be some explanation for what had happened to him other than possession by a fairy. One possibility was almost as frightening. Perhaps he suffered from multiple personality disorder. If so, he could have come by the security code and the safe's combination (and the tortuous route to it) in a non-supernatural way. Maybe the old woman had talked to his other personality back in Bel Air, and his current personality simply didn't remember the conversation. Perhaps the other side of himself also had spied on Ms. Melescu and found out about the contract and her affair. Maybe the experience in bed the previous night was a failed attempt by his other side to come to the fore. Maybe he needed help.

He drove home and pulled the Yellow Pages off the shelf by the phone. Opening to "Psychologists," he dialed one number after another until he found a therapist with Saturday morning hours. He then engaged in a long struggle with the therapist's secretary, who insisted the earliest possible appointment was the following week. Wilbur's desperate tenacity paid off. At last, the secretary checked with the doctor who agreed to see him at noon, the time he normally went home for the day.

"All right Mr. Anamann. What is it that can't wait?"

"I think I'm crazy."

"Why?"

"I talk to myself."

"So do I."

"No, I mean I talk to myself and I get answers back. I see myself standing in front of me, or sitting, usually."

"Do you see yourself now?"

"Oh, no! It only happens at night."

"At night?"

"When I'm asleep."

"That's called a dream, Mr. Anamann. There might be something underlying the dream worth discussing, but it is no reason by itself to be as concerned as you seem to be."

"He tried to take over when I was making love."

"He?"

"The other me! I think I have multiple personality disorder. Maybe I'm schizophrenic."

"Why do you think so? Please be specific."

Wilbur related most of the events of the preceding week, leaving out the burglary of $500,000.

"I see. Well, MPD is not as fashionable a diagnosis as it once was. I happen to be one of those who question its existence."

"Could you refer me to someone who doesn't?" Wilbur asked.

"Yes, but he wouldn't see you today and I doubt he would say you have MPD, either. You don't fit the description. People around you would meet your alter ego. You wouldn't. As for schizophrenics, they hear voices when they are awake, not when they are asleep. It is obvious you are upset, but I don't think you have anything so serious.

"The stories you have told me are not as mysterious as they appear. We gather information and hear gossip of which we are barely aware. We all process the information in an unconscious way. We usually call the result "intuition" or, less elegantly, "a gut feeling." So, your lucky guesses at work do not mean you put on another personality and went spying. More likely you saw and heard things, and then you made the right connections in your sleep.

"My guess is that you are under stress. I suggest we set up a weekly appointment for you. I don't believe you need to be too worried."

Though he accepted the doctor's card with an appointment penciled on it, Wilbur knew he would cancel. The psychologist didn't take him seriously enough.

Wilbur sat down on a bench by the sidewalk and pondered his dilemma. Maybe he was wrong to look for rational explanations. What if one accepts the world as really containing fairies? What follows from such a paradigm shift? If there truly were fairies, he would have to deal with professionals who believed in them, who made the supernatural their business. Wilbur knew where to look. It was back to Hollywood, but not to such a fashionable part of it as Patina.

Wilbur drove through downtown Hollywood. The town was slowly, unevenly gentrifying, but it still was seedy. At night it rated "R" where it didn't rate "NR17." On a quiet side street, he found what he wanted. A little white ranch, crowded by larger apartment buildings, sported a sign on the porch rail:

Lady Sharona
Wicca, Psychic Readings
Books, Artifacts, Novelties.

Wilbur parked his car a discreet distance from the street people hanging out down the block and walked up to the front door. After some hesitation, he raised his hand to knock, but before he reached it, the door opened.

"Come in" said the young woman standing in front of him. Lady Sharona didn't need to be psychic to pull this off. She had a security camera by the door. It was a cheap trick, but it set the proper mood for the customers.

Wilbur stepped inside and followed the blonde woman in jeans and black sweater to the center of the room. The attire wasn't particularly witchy. She carried a broom, but it was a push broom.

"I was just cleaning up a bit," she explained. "My cat got into the potpourri." There was a touch of Melbourne in her accent. A gold tabby cat peered in from the hallway.

"So, what can I do for you, Mr. . . .?"

"Wilbur."

"What can I do for you, Will?"

"I'm being hounded by a fairy."

"Really? And how exactly would you like me to help?"

"No, I don't think you understand. I've got a real fairy on my case."

"Uh-huh. Here, sit down. Let me do a tarot reading, and you can tell me all about it."

Wilbur sat down at an antique round wooden table. Though four feet in diameter, giving the appearance of solidity, it shifted slightly when he leaned his arms on it. Wilbur assumed the wood was dry and light with age. Sharona leaned the broom against the wall and retrieved a stack of tarot cards from a shelf.

In contrast to the plain exterior, the house inside was trimmed and decorated in gingerbread style. A crystal ball on the table was cradled by a tarnished stand, possibly of brass. Other surfaces and shelves contained scarves, books on witchcraft, candles of all sizes, and endless bottles of potions and powders. A Moon Goddess poster hung on the wall before him. A heavy, but not unpleasant aroma, came from a tiny iron cauldron heating over charcoal in the corner. A pentagram wind chime tinkled gently from some invisible draft. On a side wall, a poster-sized photograph of Alistair Crowley stared at him. It was the famous one with the shaved head and intense eyes in which he looks like Uncle Fester of *The Addams Family*. Nothing in the house had been dusted recently.

As Sharona sat down with the cards, Wilbur began to talk. He spilled out his tale, perfunctorily making cuts of the cards when instructed. He told her of being two people at once, the strange woman who had collapsed in front of his car, and knowing the five-digit security code to the place he had never been before, but he again left out mention of the $500,000.

"I don't think you're telling me everything, Will," Lady Sharona responded. "But that's all right. This reading is peculiar. It's almost as though it were for two different people."

"There, you see?"

"How do you feel about hypnosis?"

"I'm against it."

"It might help."

Wilbur looked apprehensive, so Sharona took a different approach. It normally was against her principles, but extreme conditions call for extreme solutions. The man clearly was in distress.

"How about tea?"

"That I can handle."

Sharona left the table and went down the hall to the kitchen. After some banging and clanking she returned with a kettle and mugs. As Sharona poured his tea, she described and explained some of the artifacts in the shop. She returned to her seat. He was sipping his tea when she got around to mentioning the crystal ball.

"It's quite nice. This tea is good too. Different."

"Thank you. Yes, I know it's almost too traditional, but a crystal ball is *de rigueur*. Mine is not glass, by the way, but real crystal. Notice how the light reflects and refracts? It's quite relaxing. Let your mind go blank."

The man across from her looked up at her strongly and smiled. She felt herself being checked out, something Wilbur had been too upset to try.

"Wilbur?"

"If you want to call me that."

"Are you putting me on?"

"Not at all. I want to thank you. This is only the second time I've had this kind of control over one of your human bodies. I was really getting quite bored as a passenger. Thanks for the tea. Maybe I'll leave now."

"You won't get far. The 'tea' will wear off and Wilbur will be back up front in no time."

"So, what can we do about that, witch lady? Anything? I can reward you far better than Wilbur can. He's quite cheap, and any money he has belongs to me."

"Well, what are you exactly? Are you a fairy as Wilbur says, or are you just a psychological aberration?"

"Whose?"

"Wilbur's, of course!"

"No. I'm quite real."

"A real what? A spirit? A demon of some kind? A fairy?"

"Oh, please!"

"How should I know? Help me out here."

"Well, who knows? Maybe I really am what people mean when they speak of spirits, and such. Maybe there are others like me who account for all those stories. I never met one, though."

"Would you know if you did?"

"Maybe not. I'd probably recognize it only if I tried to occupy the same body."

"So, this is possession we're talking about."

"Yes, I suppose so, but there isn't anything supernatural about it."

"The supernatural is composed of things that current science doesn't take into account. Once properly described, spirits will be as natural a part of physics as any other."

"Fine. I don't want to argue semantics. I just want to walk out of here in this body and stay in charge. Wilbur isn't much use to anyone anyway."

"He probably wouldn't agree. So, why should I help you? Wilbur came here first, asking for help. What about him?"

"I told you—I'll pay you better! Assuming you know how to help me. Do you, or are you just some side street fraud who is wasting my time?"

"Flattery will get you nowhere. As for whether I can help you, let me think about it." Sharona looked thoughtful.

"A penny for your thoughts."

"And you called Wilbur cheap."

Sharona felt as though a soccer ball had socked her in the face. Wilbur slumped onto the table.

"Damn!" she exclaimed. "What did you do?" Sharona rubbed her eyes.

Then Wilbur's head lifted and shook. "How did you keep me out?"

"What?"

"I was going to peek inside your head to see if there was anything useful in there, but I was bounced back—first time that's happened."

"No peeking allowed! I have ways of protecting myself, Mr. Fairy. Keep it in mind. Maybe I can do something for you after all."

"Oh shoot! Here comes Wilbur."

"Okay, I'll talk to you soon. Be patient. Take anything I say to Wilbur with a grain of salt."

Wilbur's head shook again, and Sharona recognized his first personality was back in the saddle. "What? Did I fall asleep?" he asked.

"Sort of. I, uh, made contact with your . . . your fairy. I think I can help you, Wilbur. Come back tomorrow—no, Friday. Just before midnight. I need some time, and that's the next full moon too."

"I'm not sure I can hold out until Friday."

"Try. You too."

"What?"

"Go. See you both Friday night."

"You can really help?"

"Yes! Go!"

Wilbur got up from the table and walked to the door. He stopped, looked back once, shrugged, walked through and closed the door gently behind him.

Sharona pondered. She was out of her depth, but she was eager to dive deeper yet. So much of her practice involved reading cards, selling potions, or consulting walk-ins on their silly little questions of love and money. Her coven meetings had grown routine to the point where members were dropping out. This thing, however, was something major; it was a real test of her powers. It was the very sort of spicy paranormal phenomenon she had hoped to encounter when she was first initiated into witchcraft some years earlier on another coast.

The thing had tried to take possession of her, but it had failed. The very thought of the attempt was unpleasant. She didn't like sharing her secrets with anyone, much less with anything. She was notoriously uncommunicative with her friends about her past and how she came to do what she did. What had kept the thing out? Her superciliousness with it had been all bluff. In truth, she didn't know why it bounced off her and back to Wilbur. She decided she needed assistance, and not necessarily from a sorcerer. Besides, as she had truthfully told the thing, science and sorcery were one and the same. Before Newton, magic made the moon circle the earth. In a sense, it still does. It's all in how you look at the world.

Sharona didn't believe the entity to be a spirit or a demon in the typical sense—it just didn't feel like one. But if it wasn't otherworldly, it must be more ordinary, strange as it was to use the adjective in this context. It most likely was a living being. The thing said it was one of a kind, as far as it knew. So, where had it spawned? If it was native to the earth, she reasoned, there should be others. She concluded it must be from elsewhere. She had made contact with an alien species.

"Jodie Foster, eat your heart out," she muttered to herself.

She now had an idea about where to look for help. Sharona drove her Kia to visit an old friend of hers, a college professor at UCLA named Frederick Lattimer. She seldom risked driving the car, which, at 175,000 miles, needed new tires, a tune-up, a new battery, and who knows what-else, but she was in a hurry. She knew the professor liked to work Saturday afternoons, but he was likely to leave his office soon.

Professor Lattimer was outwardly conservative, but he harbored a fascination for the occult. He had entered her shop one day a few years earlier and asked so many questions, she barely could silence him long enough to do his reading. She sold him a shelf full of books on Wicca and occult topics. Rare for an astronomer, the professor was a firm believer in astrology. This was a secret he kept from other faculty members and the administration for career reasons.

His value to Sharona in this matter was his specialty. He taught a popular undergraduate elective called "Exo-biology," in which he speculated on life-forms adapted to non-terran environments. He once gave her the textbook he had written and published on the subject. She had skimmed through it. In the book he described workable biological solutions to the most radical environments, though some of his speculative creations would have been "life" only to a philosopher. He was definitely the man to see.

Sharona walked into Professor Lattimer's small and cluttered office. She approached his desk. She could tell he was aware someone had entered, but he didn't look up. He continued to scribble on some documents.

"Yes, miss? What can I do for you?" he asked, his eyes still on his paperwork.

"Miss? My, aren't we formal."

The Australian accent gave her away. He looked up.

"Sharona, this is a surprise! Sorry about the 'Miss.' I'm not used to seeing you outside of our, uh, get-togethers." Lattimer sometimes attended the coven's celebrations, though he never mentioned it on campus.

"Consider this a close encounter."

"Uh-huh. Well, the question remains, what can I do for you?"

"I need your expertise on something, and I'm completely serious."

"That would be suspiciously out of character, but sit down. Shoot."

Sharona sat down in a wooden chair that creaked alarmingly. "Consider a being . . ."

"We're talking alien life-form here?" he interrupted.

"I suspect so, but where it comes from is not really important. Consider a being without visible or solid form. Despite its ethereal nature, it is physical enough to feel like a slap in the face if you run into it. Assume it can occupy a human being, sort of as a parasite, and it even can take over the person's mind, if the host's consciousness is subdued. The thing can transfer from person to person at will and can read the mind of whomever it occupies."

"Are you writing a science fiction story?"

"No."

"Is this a purely hypothetical thought experiment, then?"

"Assume it is not. One more thing. Suppose it tried to transfer itself into me but failed, much to its own surprise. My questions are, One: Why did it fail? Two: Is it controllable or confinable? Three: How can we chase it out of a host? Four: Is it very dangerous? and Five: Is it possible to kill it, if need be?"

"Wow. Those are lot of questions, and you're not giving me much information to go on."

"During a reading I answer your questions, with a lot less to go on."

"That sounds like a challenge. Well, okay... let's see... The thing would have to have a coherent structure to qualify as a live being. It needs to utilize energy and its parts need to interact as a mechanism to perform work. It is not solid or visible but yet you say you felt it. The most likely guess would be a plasma of some kind, held together by electromagnetic fields."

"I think, therefore ion?"

"You want my help, or not?"

"Sorry. Go on."

"This is all highly unlikely; by the way, I'm just trying to fit something to your data."

"Understood. What about the other questions?"

"What would contain, disrupt, or kill it? Another electromagnetic field, probably. It would have to be an enormously powerful one, I would think. Wherever this thing evolved must have been awash in such fields. It must have pretty strong defenses. I doubt you could kill it with anything easily at your disposal."

"So why did it bounce off me?"

"Well, a much weaker charge may be enough to repel it. Take the way you respond to an agricultural electric fence. It won't kill you, but it will make you jump back if you touch it. However, if you insist on being uncomfortable, you can force yourself to hold onto the wire if you want."

"So I was saved by the static cling of my clothes?"

"Maybe, but I doubt it. Were you wearing that neck chain by any chance?"

"Yes."

"Where did the encounter take place?"

"At my shop."

"I thought so. Was the electromagnet under the table turned on?"

"I always turn it on when a new customer shows up."

This was another of Sharona's parlor tricks. Lady Sharona was serious about her craft, but she wasn't above a little sleight of hand (sometimes mechanically aided) to impress the customers. People liked the tricks, which helped reduce their skepticism. This in turn produced more positive energy, which helped her honest magic work better. An electromagnet was built into the floor of her shop under the table, and powerful bar magnets were fitted into the hollowed-out legs. By reversing the polarity of the electromagnet with a button under the carpet by her feet, Sharona could make the table hop. This device actually had been installed by the previous occupant, a pseudo-gypsy psychic who had left town under a legal cloud. Despite her better scruples, Sharona couldn't resist using the toy occasionally.

Because of Lattimer's sincere interest in the occult, Sharona never used any of these devices to deceive him. On the contrary, she showed them off to him and explained why she sometimes used them on others. The two laughed about this minor deception often.

Lattimer looked thoughtful. "It's still rather puzzling, though. The thing should have been able to overcome such a weak field if it wanted to, just as a person can hold onto an electric fence."

"But a person has to decide to hold the fence consciously," Sharona countered. "I didn't get a feeling of intelligence when it hit me. I felt its intelligence working inside Wilbur, though."

"Wilbur?"

"The host."

Professor Lattimer silently appraised Sharona's attitude again. He decided she was serious.

"You mean you really aren't making this up?" he asked at last.

"No."

"I see." He frowned and continued slowly, "Your point is a good one. If the thing is acting purely on instinct when in transit, it doesn't have the option of choosing. If its instinct is to draw back, it will draw back."

"So much for my own protection. How do I chase it out of someone else?"

"You don't, not if it doesn't want to go. You said it acts intelligently when it is inside the host. Possibly it co-opts the use of the host's own brain, which would account for the mind reading. As I said, it likely can withstand fields that would kill a human. It will just treat anything less powerful as an irritant. Probably, even a full-body MRI wouldn't chase it out."

"So I have to make it choose to leave?"

"I think so. If you do get it out, remember you're not dealing with an intelligence any more. You asked about danger. I honestly don't know. Maybe, maybe not."

"Thanks, you've been a big help."

"Wait, Sharona. You're not going to tease me with something as fantastic as this and then run off, are you?"

"I'm pretty sure if I tried to deliver it to you to play with, it would just flee. It's not stupid."

"I at least want to see this thing."

"It's invisible."

"I want to meet its host, then. Can I be there when you do whatever you're planning to do?"

"Okay. Join our circle Friday night. I need a thirteenth member anyway. Yvonne's out of town."

Sharona was not as picky as some covens were about admitting males to the proceeding. There are different traditions in Wicca and, to her way of thinking, a male-female balance was important. Women still outnumbered men. Most of the men who talked about joining in the past turned out to have other things on their minds. The professor was a welcome exception. She sometimes wondered where his personal attractions lay, but that was his business, so she didn't pry.

"Where are you going now?" he asked.

"To hire an electrician," she answered.

Sharona was able to avoid the usual difficulty in arranging for timely electrical work. One member of her coven was married to a general contractor who currently was building a strip mall.

Despite the ineffectual objections of her spouse, the woman pulled the electrical crew off the job, gave them Sharona's list of equipment to purchase on the business account, and directed them to the shop in Hollywood.

The crew foreman, named Harry, scratched his head as he spoke to Sharona. "Well, I got the things you wanted, but for the life of me I can't figure what you want to do with them. Why do you want thirteen powerful electromagnets built into the floor? You planning on electrocuting somebody?"

"I was hoping you could wire them up more safely than that."

"How are we supposed to get them in the floor?"

"Just place them underneath, between the joists. The basement is unfinished."

"You'll overload the circuits the moment you turn them on."

"Increase the amp service to whatever is needed."

The workmen did as they were told, but they were befuddled and disconcerted. The witches' paraphernalia in the shop didn't help. "Spooky dame," one of them muttered while looking at some of the book titles.

Wilbur showed up Friday night, on time. He waited just inside the front door until his eyes adjusted to the eerie red interior lighting that Sharona had chosen for the evening. In a few moments he was able to see Sharona, eleven women, and Professor Lattimer. All were berobed and wearing chain necklaces. The necklaces were not jewelry, but chains strong enough to tow a car. The thirteen were arranged in a circle about the table.

Before proceeding, Sharona made a last-minute decision: she deserved a tip for all this effort. Though neither Wilbur nor his guest had told her about the Brenthausen cash, she intuited the security code he mentioned must have guarded something valuable.

"I spoke to your fairy the last time you were here, Will. I know about why you needed the security code." This was not so much a lie as an incomplete truth.

"And?"

"I want fifty percent."

"Fifty percent?!"

"I don't want to be greedy."

"Hey, now look . . ."

"The fairy offered me more to get rid of you. I can take his offer instead if you like."

"How do I know you won't anyway?"

"Why would I be negotiating with you at all?"

"I'm not giving you anything up front. You could take my money and the fairy's too."

"Wilbur, I'm beginning to think you don't trust me. But it's okay. You can pay me later. After all, if you don't pay, I can give you the fairy back . . . or just make a few phone calls to people who might like to know about your familiarity with their security codes."

"All right, all right. I get your point. I'll do it. If you really can get this thing out of me, it's worth it. What's next?"

"Sit down. Have some tea."

Sharona broke the circle long enough to pour a cup of her special brew and place it on the table. She then pushed the crystal ball in front of him. To Wilbur's bemusement, she also retrieved a bowl of smelly cooked pollack and put it on the table in front of the seat opposite him. Sharona picked up her gold tabby and placed it by the food. She hadn't fed the cat all day despite his noisy complaints, so he remained in place and munched on the fish happily.

Sharona stepped on the button activating the magnets and resumed her position as the north anchor in the circle. She felt a tingle in the chain around her neck as it tugged toward the floor. She always felt something electric when joining hands, but this time the power of the moment was aided by wattage from the Los Angeles Department of Water and Power.

"Watch the way the reflected light changes on the ball as you move your head from side to side," she prompted.

Wilbur obeyed until his face went blank and he stopped swaying. His face didn't stay blank for long. The thing looked up at her angrily with Wilbur's eyes.

"What do you mean by negotiating with Wilbur? We had a deal!"

"But Wilbur offered me half."

"You don't even know half of what."

"What are you offering?"

"Fine, sixty percent. Do we have a deal, or are you going to wake up Wilbur again for a counteroffer?"

"No, I'm satisfied. Don't you trust me?"

"Not as far as Wilbur can spit."

"Be nice, and sit still." The circle began a chant to the Moon Goddess.

"What is this mumbo jumbo?"

The chant stopped. "Do you want to be free of Wilbur?" Sharona asked.

"Yes."

"Then don't interrupt again."

The chant resumed, and programmed, subtle alterations in the light level began. The irregular oscillation was designed to make a customer think it was a trick of his own eyes. The thing looked about curiously. The chant ended.

"All right, Mr. Fairy. You're free."

"That's it?"

"That's it."

"I can just walk out of here?"

"Yes."

"Wilbur won't be back?"

"No, he has been firmly suppressed. You might meet him in your dreams."

"Excellent!"

The thing stood up.

"There are some things you should know, Mr. Fairy."

"Please stop calling me that."

"Fine, but in order to give you control I had to make a few changes."

"Like what?"

"You are now completely wedded to your biology. You cannot transfer out."

"You're telling me I'm stuck in Wilbur's body until he dies?"

"You are stuck there permanently. When he dies, you die too. A mortal presence comes with mortality. It's a package deal."

"Nonsense, I'm thousands of years old. Maybe older. I don't

even know. I have no intention of living just another measly forty or fifty years."

"Maybe a bit more. Maybe less."

"I don't believe you. You're bluffing."

"Try it."

"What?"

"Try transferring into one of us."

The thing tried transferring into each member of the circle in turn, always rebounding back forcefully to Wilbur. Sharona knew there was a way out. The way was through the ceiling. She hoped he wouldn't think of it.

"What's going on? Hey, you kept me out of you the other day too. Maybe you people do have some special power to protect yourselves. But how do I know I can't just walk out the door and jump into some other person?"

"Why would I lie? If I have special powers, you might as well believe I have the power to make you mortal. But don't take my word for it. March right out the door and try, if that is what you want to do. We won't stop you. I have to warn you, though: once you break this circle there is no turning back. Even I can't change you back to what you were. You are mortal and that is that."

"You mean you still can undo it now?"

"While you're still in the circle, yes. But you don't want to go back, sir or ma'am, or whatever honorific you prefer. You've made a wonderfully successful effort to become mortal. Now you should enjoy living your own life, even if, like the rest of us, you get only one. You'd better get a job too."

"What?"

"Well, yes. Now you have to earn an income, pay taxes, mow your lawn, cook your meals, clean your bathroom, and all those other things your hosts used to do for you while you just enjoyed the ride. You'll find making money is a little harder when you can't read minds, but I'm sure you'll find that scratching out a living in a more conventional way can be rewarding."

"Now wait a minute, I didn't bargain for this."

"This is precisely for what you bargained."

The thing tried again to transfer and again repeatedly bounced back. It looked desperate.

"Okay, I quit. I don't want it. Bring Wilbur back. He's not so bad as hosts go."

"It's not that easy. He is very deeply buried and if he stays submerged much longer I won't be able to bring him back at all. The only way to bring him back is for you to get out of him completely for a little while."

"But I can't transfer!"

"Not outside the circle."

"No else is in it!"

Sharona nodded to her cat.

"You must be kidding."

"No."

"But if I do that, I'll have the mind of a cat! It may take years and years before I accidentally transfer into a person again."

"But you'll have the time to do so eventually, won't you?"

The thing stared back hatefully. It looked at the cat. The cat jumped in the air and screamed as though it had been struck by a soccer ball. Sharona broke the circle and quickly turned off the power to the magnets.

"Wilbur?"

Wilbur groggily moaned and lifted his head. He must have nodded off. "This tea of yours makes me sleepy. So what are you going to do?"

"Do?"

"Are you going to do any incantations or something?"

"Would you like me to?"

"Will it help?"

"No."

"So, how do I get free?"

"You are free, but I'm not. Bring back what you owe me tomorrow."

"But the fairy . . ."

"It's gone."

"It's really gone? How can I be sure?"

"Sweet dreams, Mr. Anamann. Come back tomorrow, no later than four p.m."

Wilbur stood up unsteadily. He looked at the cat. The cat stared back.

"I wouldn't do that, Wilbur. Let kitty be."

Wilbur looked uncertainly about him. He walked shakily to the door and let himself out.

"That was fascinating!" exclaimed Professor Lattimer. "May I take your cat for study?"

"Hey! Don't you dare dissect my cat!"

"Oh, no! The thing would flee, maybe into me. But I want to examine it."

"Well, okay. But I want him back in a few days—and in good health."

"Certainly."

The next day Wilbur showed up at the door carrying an attaché case.

"You look well rested, Wilbur."

"Slept like a baby. Here, yours was the most expensive consultation I ever had, but it was worth it."

"Recommend me to your other friends who happen to get possessed."

"Will do."

Sharona sat down at the table and unlatched the case. She really needed the money. Possibly it was a big score. Perhaps as much as $10,000. Maybe $20,000. She dared to hope. She lifted the lid.

—Richard Bellush, Jr.

TRUST

ANNIVERSARY REACTIONS

There's none among us who could say
we're not betrayed or do betray.
Although we hold our ideals dear
and truth and honesty do revere.

Forgiveness still must be the key.
It was in ancient history.
In humanity we still may see
aspirations toward divinity.

However much we may aspire
we carry still the scares of fire
as memories of searing pain.
So guarded yet we do remain.

I think that I must choose to fight.
To risk my heart though err I might.
To take up arms of love and trust
and know that fail at times I must.

Fail sometimes just as the sun
may fail to shine on everyone.
I trust the sun may shine again
and with the rose yet make amends.

—Sharon Bellush

CLOSE COUNTS IN HORSESHOES

Ray's marriage was a disaster, and it was building into something on the scale, at the personal level, of Chernobyl. His "helpmate" was charming and captivating. She also was an abusive, cold, drug addicted spendthrift who had destroyed his once-bright prospects. Like so many of us, he had married his worst enemy.

Ray felt the weight of responsibility for his predicament. He had been an adult with open eyes when he walked down the aisle. It was not as though he was the victim of some bait-and-switch at the wedding. "Amy the Wife" was very much "Amy the Girlfriend." Their dates had been harrowing. Yet, they also had been fun. Too late, Ray realized that much of the fun came from knowing the dates would end, rather like taking a ride on one of those looping roller coasters. A roller coaster is no place to make a home, as he had been old enough to know.

Nevertheless, Ray felt his responsibility was in the category of an error of judgment. Like making the wrong move in a chess game, his mistake was not a moral one. It was stupid, but not a matter for guilt. He certainly did not feel at fault for the daily punishment his life had become. He felt he should be allowed to correct his error without paying a further penalty.

Divorce was an obvious option, but if he exercised it a "further penalty" was certain. Financially, it would be as life shattering for him as continuing in the marriage. Besides, since he believed his wife was the one morally responsible for the mess, he didn't see why he should have to pay. She was an out-of-control fire that was burning up his life, and his only hope was to snuff the flame out. It was the right thing to do.

As Ray justified his deadly thoughts, the sky deepened from pink to an appropriate red. The mountains to the south, on one of which perched the pleasant tourist trap of Virginia City, reflected bloodily. Ray grew aware of sand in his right boot. With his toe he played with the granules until it began to hurt.

More than a hundred and fifty years ago, prospectors had scoured the mountains looking for gold. A few even found it. Ray had hoped to strike gold with Amy, much as he knew the ore to be mixed with rough impurities. Like most of the old miners, he came up with pyrite.

"What are you doing standing out there in the yard? Come on inside!" called Amy from the back door of their brick and stucco ranch house, which he had been forced to mortgage to the limit of possibility. Ray glanced back. He had to admit she, like pyrite, was pretty. The "yard" in which he stood was sand and brush, but neither Amy nor Ray envied the residents of wetter climes their privilege to cut grass.

"Coming!" The decision to eliminate Amy, by itself, lifted a weight off him. He sauntered back to the house.

Ray thought back to where it all began. Random events govern so much of one's life. His grandmother's accident was a prime example. It turned out to be his accident too.

*   *   *

Ray's grandmother was his favorite relative. In truth, she was the only one who paid him more than passing attention. A well-meaning, self-sufficient, relentlessly fair-minded woman, she always insisted on being called "Granny," even by strangers, despite the endless jokes referencing *The Beverly Hillbillies*. Whenever anyone asked Ray what her real name was, he usually had to pause to remember her as Prudence Schiller.

Ray was relieved to move in with Granny shortly before his sixteenth birthday. His mother, whom he regarded with some charity as unstable, had at that time moved to somewhere in England with her latest husband. To her credit, she did not ignore him entirely. For example, she called the day after his birthday, blaming her tardiness on the International Dateline even though that lay in the middle of the Pacific, rather than the

Atlantic. He chose not to argue the point. Her calls thereafter came with decreasing frequency.

Ray barely remembered his father, and his father's family (scattered about the Eastern Seaboard) was profoundly disinterested in him. Ray kept track of his father's whereabouts only through the changing addresses on the child-support checks, which Granny stubbornly forwarded to England for the next two years.

"They're not mine," she always said.

The checks stopped coming on Ray's eighteenth birthday. It was Granny who helped him with his college and then with his post-graduate tuition. Ray wanted to start paying her back as soon as he got a job, but she would have none of it.

"Don't be silly. Besides, you'd just get it back anyway in the end."

"What about Mom?"

"Let her find her own grandson."

Even after Ray moved out on his own, he spent most of his holidays with Granny. She was his only family in Nevada and the only family anywhere who mattered to him.

Granny was comfortable, she and her late husband having worked hard and saved carefully, but she was far from rich. Ray was reluctant to impose on her generosity any more than necessary. Besides, she was his only safety net, and he wanted the net kept intact for practical reasons as well as out of personal affection.

Aware of the need to make his own way in life, Ray took advantage of his opportunities. He was a diligent student at the University of Nevada. He never scored lower than a "B" in any class at either the undergraduate or graduate level. After college, he quickly parleyed his MBA into a middle management position in a medical supply company on the outskirts of Reno, where he earned a fair salary, and where his prospects for advancement were excellent.

Careful with his money like his grandmother, Ray was a homeowner by age 27. By this time he also had socked away a nest egg in the bank, and his 401k was growing nicely. Ray's social life had suffered from such determinedly responsible behavior, but he felt he was still young enough to do something about this too.

Then one day Ray got a phone call at work from the police. His grandmother was in the hospital.

Granny had been in a car accident. Thanks to her poor eyesight and her refusal to wear glasses, she had collided in her SUV with a farm tractor on a dirt road. She hadn't recognized the dust ahead of her as the wake of a vehicle; she simply assumed it was an artifact of the wind and her fuzzy vision. She slammed into the tractor from the rear at high speed.

The farmer escaped serious injury. Although thrown through a fence next to the road, he broke his fall by landing on one of his own pigs on the other side. A judge later ordered Granny to compensate the farmer for the pig.

Granny was not as lucky as the farmer. In addition to refusing to wear glasses, she also refused to wear a seat belt. The injuries to her back were serious and permanent. She escaped paralysis by a hair. In the following months she recovered slowly, but walking continued to be painful. A cane was a must. On bad days she could manage only with crutches or a walker. Except with respect to the farmer, whom she blamed for the accident, her good nature remained intact.

Granny decided living alone in her own house was no longer practical. Ray offered to move back in, but was relieved when she refused. Granny sold her home and bought a unit in oddly organized long-term care facility. The name of the facility was Crestview, even though it was not on a crest and didn't have a view. Rooms, suites, and apartments at Crestview were offered as condominiums. A variable monthly maintenance fee also covered optional levels of nursing care. From the outside it looked much like a large, brick, low-rise apartment building. Granny's condominium had a fairly typical one-bedroom floor plan, with a door to the outside. Another door, however, which she always kept unlocked, opened to a main hallway of the building less than fifty feet from the nurses' station.

At first, Ray came to the outside door when visiting her, but Granny instructed him to stop, as this forced her to walk across the room, an uncomfortable thing for her to do. She told him use the main facility entrance, pass the nurses' station, and let himself in through the hallway door. Ray didn't much care for this route, which took him past depressing sights of disabled people. However, his grandmother was his family, so once or twice a week he would steel himself to face the powerful aroma of ammonia, which caused his eyes to tear the moment he entered, and wend his way to Granny's door.

A nursing home is not normally considered a hot spot for singles (except for those qualified for senior discounts), but one young attendant named Amy caught Ray's eye. Presumably because so many interior doors were unlocked, Crestview rules required that he sign in at the desk, and she often provided the book and pen. Pretty and personable with a captious smile, she worked every weekday evening.

Ray soon found himself timing his visits for weekday evenings. Ray always bantered with Amy at the desk before going to his grandmother's door. Amy's good-natured chattiness was a pleasant bracer for the rather dismal conversations sure to follow. Granny increasingly wanted to talk about back pains, tasteless food, and the week's obituaries. Amy flirted with Ray, which did not escape his attention. In truth, she flirted with all men. This did not escape his attention either, but Ray still felt flattered. He didn't recognize Amy as a can of paint poised precariously on the half-open door of his life.

Ray shyly weighed asking her out. He saw an easy opportunity present itself when Amy complained about her homework.

"Homework?" he asked. "Where do you go to school?"

"At the community college. I'm going to be a P.N."

"P.N.?"

"Practical Nurse. It's much faster than going for R.N., and P.N.s are still very employable. They get paid well. Right now I'd do as well slinging hamburgers as working here."

"Nursing is what you want to do?"

"Hell, no. But I have to do something, and I want decent money." She inflected her words so as to give the impression she felt her monetary ambition was something of to be ashamed of. "You can't be a carefree bum forever," she added and shrugged.

"So what's the problem with your homework?"

"My English class is dragging down my average. Anthropology is getting me too, but not as bad as English. I don't know why we have to take those courses anyway. What do they call them?"

"Humanities."

"They don't relate to nursing at all, but we need the credits for some reason. I do fine in the actual useful stuff like Anatomy, Nutrition, and Biology. I have a hard time with the meaningless things."

Amy's academic strengths and weaknesses exposed a duality Ray already had noticed. Amy combined undeniable intelligence with a curious shallowness. This was evidenced by the confusion he had witnessed at Crestview following the installation of a new computer program for patient records. The utterly baffled nurses and administrators solved the problem by sitting Amy down in front of the computer. She mastered the program in less than fifteen minutes, and thereafter she became the resident expert. Yet no amount of explanation could clarify literature or art for her, and she reliably failed to get the point of any joke more subtle than a "knock-knock."

Ray's first encounter with her resistance to punch lines came early on when she brought Ray's grandmother some tea. Amy made conversation during her brief presence in the condo by complaining about her boyfriend. Ray wasn't happy to hear of a boyfriend, but was pleased by the complaint.

"He calls himself 'J.R.' for Junior, even though his dad refuses to talk to him anymore," she said. "It shows the old man understands his son. J.R. is the most self-involved, unsupportive creep I've ever met. Helps me with nothing. Demands everything."

"Perhaps it is the 'J.R.' thing," Ray commiserated lightly. "Having a 'Junior' appended to a name has a quantifiably deleterious effect on character. Juniors are over-represented in both prison and Congress, but, of course, the same behaviors are required for admission to either institution."

This elicited a frown. "What do you mean?"

His attempt to explain only made Amy's puzzlement worse until at last even he began to lose sight of the point of his remark.

Her difficulties with literature were an extension of her problem with jokes. She was hopeless at interpreting themes and allusions.

"My mind is more logical than that," she explained to Ray, thereby insinuating literary types had minds that were somehow faulty.

"Mine isn't so very logical," Ray responded. "What are you working on now? Maybe I can help you with it."

"Could you? I could use help."

"When do you have time?"

"Saturday. Give me your phone number. I'll tell you about the assignment later tonight when I get off work. After you write the paper you can explain it to me on Saturday."

Ray was taken aback by the sudden homework assignment, but, on reflection, he didn't mind writing one more English Lit paper, if it meant a date with Amy.

Ray spoke to Granny of his upcoming study date, leaving out mention of the academic cheating. She was concerned, even about his studying with Amy.

"Amy is a girl with problems," she warned. "She's just like my cousin Flora: always complaining how no one helps her, when I never saw anyone wheedle so much help out of people. She somehow gets everyone to knock themselves out for her, but no amount of help is ever enough. She'll act as though she's been short-changed regardless. And forget about ever depending on her for anything in return. This girl is the same. Don't let Amy's pretty smile fool you, or you'll be working up a sweat with no thanks to show for it. You be very careful."

"Yes, Grandmother."

"Don't 'Yes, Grandmother' me. You only call me 'Grandmother' when you are placating me and planning to ignore my advice. I'm serious. Be careful."

"I will be."

But of course, he wasn't. Ray's phone rang after midnight. Amy started talking, even before he got "Hello" out of his mouth.

"Okay. The assignment is a comparative analysis of two short stories called Bartleby the *Scrivener* and *A Hunger Artist*. Do you need my anthology text?"

"No. I'm sure I have *Bartleby* on my shelf, and pretty much all of Kafka is on the Internet.

"Good. I don't understand what my teacher wants from me with this stuff," Amy complained. "One guy won't work and the other won't eat. What else it there to say about them?"

"Well, that's a good place to start. The question is why the characters do what they do and what they mean to the people around them."

"Yeah, well, you figure it out."

These stories of Melville and Kafka were familiar to Ray from his high school days. That they were part of a college level course surprised him.

"There is also religious symbolism in both stories and some parallel social commentary," he added.

"Whatever. I need a thousand words. Don't forget footnotes and a bibliography. Cite everything properly. I don't want to get expelled for plagiarism."

"I'll be careful." And of course he was.

After he returned home from work the next evening, he reread the two tales and wrote a rough draft of a paper. His draft was intelligent even without references, but Amy had been insistent on a bibliography. So, he went to the library, found a few quotes from respected critics, and incorporated the quotes into his draft. He polished up the paper at home. He actually found the experience pleasantly nostalgic—he certainly never expected to write another Lit paper after he graduated college. Still, he didn't want to make a habit of it.

On Saturday, Ray followed the directions Amy had given him on the phone. They led him well outside of Reno. Several miles down a dirt road, he came upon a clutch of six trailer homes. He approached the blue one, which inexplicably was numbered 47. Amy had explained that she and her roommate Dawn rented the trailer.

Amy appeared at the door as soon as he stepped out of his car. She waved him inside.

The interior was messy, but not to such a degree as to risk a raid by the Board of Health. Dawn sat on an undersized sofa, simultaneously watching a Science Channel documentary on sharks and reading a Harlequin romance. She was an attractive woman with short blonde hair. Ray could guess her age no more accurately than between 25 and 35, but he wouldn't have bet money even on that range. She barely acknowledged Ray when Amy perfunctorily introduced them.

Amy led him through the narrow kitchen to the bedroom. She hopped up on the bed, sat cross-legged, and looked at Ray expectantly.

Ray cleared his throat. "Well," he said, "this is what I've come up with." Ray sat on the edge of the bed, read his paper, and then explained the basic points.

Amy nodded her head all the while he spoke. When he was done, she grilled him about plagiarism.

"No," he answered, "this is all original material, my original material, except for the quotes, all of which are cited properly."

"You're sure."

"Yes."

"I don't want to get thrown out over cheating."

"I didn't cheat."

"Okay. Thanks. Look, I hate to rush you, but there's somewhere I've got to be tonight. Call me next week or stop by the desk and I'll let you know your grade."

Amy hustled Ray out the door. He stood outside bewildered for a few moments before climbing into his car and driving home.

After this early and frustrating end to the evening, he determined to take his grandmother's prophetic advice and steer clear of Amy. He almost chose to switch his visits with Granny back to weekends and so avoid her, but he decided this was childish.

The next Tuesday, he entered Crestview and passed by the desk with a quick wave.

"Wait!" Amy called. "Don't you want to know how you did?"

Ray stepped back to the desk and asked with an open-hands gesture.

"My professor said she was pleased with the paper—that I was finally getting the hang of it. She only gave it a 'B-plus,' though. I was hoping for better."

Ray thought his paper deserved better too. "Maybe she just doesn't think of you as an 'A' student yet. If you keep turning in good work, she'll adjust her perceptions and grade you better."

"Maybe. But see if you can do better on the next assignment. I need ten pages on Blake, Keats, or Yeats."

"I'm pretty busy this week. Work . . ."

"Aw, come on! I really need the help."

Ray sighed. He didn't know why her appeal made him feel obligated, but somehow it did. "Make it Yeats. What do you know about scansion and about Yeats' occult beliefs?"

"Nothing."

"Then we need to go over it together in a more detailed way than we did with the last paper. In case your teacher asks you any questions about what you wrote, you need to know what you're talking about."

"Okay. You can buy me dinner this Saturday."

At least this indicated a real date with Amy in return for his labor.

Amy kept her word. They did have dinner. Unexpectedly, Dawn joined them, but he found her company congenial, and she discreetly left them alone afterwards, not that there was any need. Amy made no romantic invitation and at this stage Ray didn't push the issue. He nevertheless went home feeling the evening went well.

Other dates followed, as did other school assignments. They made love for the first time the night she brought back an "A" on the Yeats paper. Amy was oddly manic and pasty-faced. She also was noisy, which made him very conscious of Dawn, watching TV on the other side of an inch-thick Formica-covered wall. His embarrassment stimulated Amy, who only got noisier. Immediately afterward, she hustled him out the door once again, but this time he didn't mind.

Their dates grew more frequent and varied. Ray was surprised to learn that Amy had never seen any of the major acts on the stages of the Reno hotel casinos. She had never been further than the slot machines and the roulette wheels. They attended several shows together, and they tried legitimate theater when Cabaret came to town. She loved Cabaret. Ray no longer was saving money, but the two were enjoying themselves and he figured making a splash at the beginning of relationship was a traditional investment.

Ray was surprised that Amy regarded him as an intellectual. He thought of himself as nothing of the sort, but Amy's knowledge of higher culture consisted of such data as recommended oil weights for Harley four-stroke engines, so by her standards, Ray was an egg-head. Ray found that he rather enjoyed playing Professor Higgins to her Eliza, though he sometimes detected a note of disdain for his role in her voice. She also enjoyed acting Lola Lola to his Professor Unrat. Reciprocal disdain was the furthest thing from his voice, or mind.

Sometimes Dawn accompanied them on their dates. His nights out with two pretty women attracted envious glances and occasional comments from other men, but, in truth, the threesome was innocent. Somewhat to Ray's dissatisfaction, so was the twosome. Amy hadn't yet repeated the one night of lovemaking.

As time went on, Ray became more sensitive to some of Amy's remarks. Amy had a sharp tongue and often needled Ray. At first he tried to take it in the spirit of good-natured banter even though she was excessive. People often push teasing too far unintentionally, Ray felt, so it was best to grant Amy some allowances. Dawn, on the other hand, was consistently soft-spoken and polite, though the absence of romantic tension might have contributed to the greater degree on pleasantry between them.

Amy contributed to Ray's education, too, by introducing him to bowling and billiards. She always defeated him handily, especially at a pool table. The managers of the alleys and pool halls, as well as a number of their patrons, knew her by name and often let her in for free.

Eventually the two found one activity in which they had comparable expertise. Dawn had mentioned horseback riding one evening and both Amy and Ray agreed it would be fun. Both had taken lessons as children but hadn't ridden in years.

A search through the Yellow Pages turned up a small stable west of town. They drove to the address and found a modest ranch, with a dozen horses, that backed up to an enormous expanse of scrub desert. The owner, observing them in the ring for several minutes, convinced herself the two were passably competent riders. She then was willing to rent them horses by the hour. The desert proved to be a great place for trail riding, though the patches of brush were hard on clothes and unprotected skin. By the second trail ride, they were appropriately protected by denim and leather.

Also on the second trail ride, Ray mounted his courage and suggested they rest the horses and make love in the open. Amy frowned.

"Look, I know I haven't been very attentive to you that way, but you've got give me some leeway. If you can't, then maybe you should stop seeing me."

"Is that what you want?"

"No, I think we have fun. The truth is I have some personal problems about sex. I don't really feel comfortable talking with you about them just yet, but I will. I promise. I've had some bad experiences. Can you give me some time to get past them?"

Ray sighed. "Yeah. Sure. Let me know if you want to talk about it. I'm willing to listen."

"Provided what I say ends with a 'yes'?"

"I'm willing to listen."

Ray found her reticence about sex an odd contrast to the one evening of passionate lovemaking they had shared, but he agreed to be tolerant and not push the issue. Despite the limited sexual aspects of their dates, he considered her, on balance, to be an amusing, if somewhat erratic companion, even if she did give him homework.

Ray slowly learned Amy's dark side. At the outset she successfully kept it hidden. However, she showed it more freely as she became certain of Ray's infatuation. Her concerns about Ray's possible disapproval dissipated as her confidence increased. The revelations began with minor transgressions of the law. While reviewing yet one more of Ray's literary analyses, she suddenly announced a need to smoke, to calm her nerves.

"Sure. Go ahead. I didn't know you smoked."

"I've been trying to quit."

To his surprise, the first whiff of smoke to waft his way was not of tobacco. He shrugged and let the matter go. After all, a large minority of his friends smoked pot regularly, and he had always argued for legalization. When she offered him a hit, however, he declined.

"Not since high school, and I didn't smoke much even then."

From then on, she chain-smoked joints on every occasion they met, sometimes quite recklessly in the most public of places, even, on one occasion, lighting up on the terrace of the *Buenos Grill,* a Tex-Mex restaurant on Mayberry.

"Nobody notices or cares," she insisted when he expressed his alarm.

Other people on the Buenos's terrace did notice, but apparently they didn't care. Customers at nearby tables whispered among themselves, but no one complained to the management or the police. The waiter smiled at her and winked when he brought the check.

"See?"

"Does your mother know you smoke?" Ray chided her in jest.

"Yes. But I don't talk to her, anyway. My dad, either."

"Why not?"

"They were mean to me my whole life; they treated me like a servant. My mother never helped me with anything. All she did was ride me. I don't even want to talk about my dad. I left home when I was seventeen."

"To where?"

"I moved in with my pot dealer for a while. Then with a couple of biker dudes. Then with this other guy, but he turned out to be a total asshole. When he was arrested for selling coke, he tried to say I was an accomplice. They couldn't tie me with any evidence, though, so they let me go."

"Were you?"

"Was I what?"

"An accomplice."

"No, I never wanted to get involved in selling drugs. The police, the customers, and the competition are all too intense. I never hooked, either, even though it's legal right outside of town, because… well, because I didn't want to. The worst I ever did was help a boyfriend I knew roll tourists in the casino parking lots."

Amy's career was sounding more colorful by the moment. "That was it, huh? It sounds pretty, well, dangerous actually."

"Nah, most people don't put up a fight. They're happy not to get hurt. You have to get them going in."

"Why?"

"They haven't lost all their money yet, genius."

"Ah. Is this still one of your, uh, sports?"

"No. I got rid of that boyfriend too. He never helped me with shit. Besides, he got busted. That's why I got a job at Crestview. Then when I saw what they were paying the actual nurses there, as opposed to 'nobody' assistants like me, I figured I'd go to school. I'm not a kid anymore. I need to get a life."

A part of Ray was intrigued by Amy's felonious background. However, he was relieved she seemed to have gotten past those days. He judged too quickly.

Ray's blasé response to her mention of cocaine encouraged her to state, openly, her intention to buy some. Ray objected, but the tickling fingers of her hand under the table diverted blood from his center of judgment. In less than half an hour they were sitting in Ray's car in a darkened carport under a small apartment building a few blocks from the town center. Whoever Amy had called on her cell phone had instructed them to wait there.

"This is a little creepy," he commented. "I'm not real happy about being out of sight like this."

"Relax!" she responded, irritably. "This is not something you do in public. The cops take it more seriously than pot."

"Just what I wanted to hear."

A hand tapped on the passenger window. Amy opened it, handed out four tightly wadded twenty-dollar bills, and withdrew her hand clenched in a fist. Ray could see only a shadowy form outside the car. It blended quickly into the darkness. Ray heard footsteps grow faint.

"Okay, let's go," Amy ordered. "Cut over to Virginia Street and pick up Route 80."

Ray drove up to Fourth and turned left. He turned right on

Virginia. He felt stupid for having allowed himself to participate in a drug buy. He was angry with Amy for having exposed him to a criminal element and the possible legal consequences. The situation immediately got worse. Amy's preferred method of enjoying cocaine was not genteel. From her oversized plaid handbag she withdrew bottled water, a box of baking soda, a spoon, and a Bic lighter.

"What are you doing now?"

"Watch and learn."

Amy filled her spoon with powder and water. She flicked her Bic and held her lighter beneath the bowl.

Out of morbid interest, Ray later looked up the chemistry involved. Street cocaine is a salt that is manufactured by combining the paste squeezed from soaked coca leaves with hydrochloric acid. The resulting cocaine hydrochloride is water-soluble, so it can be snorted or injected. Heating it in water with baking soda removes the salt base, restoring the drug to little nuggets called "crack." The effective way to abuse them is to vaporize them by direct flame and inhale the vapor.

Amy removed the little rocks from her spoon and stuffed them into the bowl of a small metal pipe, which she also had hidden in her bag. She turned up the flame of the lighter, held it to the pipe bowl, and inhaled. Ray's nose was assaulted by a foul smell, strongly reminiscent of burning plastic. Even in the limited illumination from the streetlights and the headlights of passing cars, Ray could see Amy's face rapidly acquire the pasty complexion he remembered from the night they had made love. This was altogether too much lowlife for his taste. He looked for an easy way out.

"You want me to take you home?"

"No! They're watching my house!"

"Who is watching your house?"

"The police."

"Why?"

"They just are." Amy reached for the dash controls and turned up the air-conditioning full blast.

"Okay, I guess we can go to my house." Ray wasn't happy about the idea, but he seemed low on choices other than abandoning her in the street. By having participated with Amy to such an extent already, he felt responsible for her safety. He pondered the old warning against feeding a stray cat. From that moment it is no longer a stray. It is your cat.

"No! They'll be watching there too."

"Why would anyone watch my house?"

"They are."

Exasperation entering his voice, he asked, "So where do we go? Help me out here."

"Just drive. You want a hit?"

"No."

"Sure?"

"Like Ivory Soap."

"Huh?"

"Ninety-nine and forty-four hundredths percent."

"What do you mean?"

"I just mean no."

"What has soap got to do with anything?"

"Nothing. It's just a joke."

"It's not very funny."

"I guess not."

At Amy's continued insistence, Ray drove around aimlessly for what seemed like hours. He was chilled and shivering from the hard blowing air-conditioner, but Amy was perspiring.

"This A/C is a piece of shit!" she complained. "It's blowing hot air."

"The air is freezing."

"It's hot! Feel it!"

Ray didn't argue. He was waiting for her to finish up her crack so the evening could end—so all their evenings could end. He firmly resolved never to call her again.

At long last Amy used up her last nugget. She bent over, held her lighter to the floor, and ran her hand over the carpet fabric.

"What are you looking for?"

"I must have dropped some big rocks."

"I don't think so."

"Shit!"

She opened her bag and checked her wallet. It was empty but

for three dollars. She looked at Ray as though about to ask a question, but something in his unhappy expression deterred her. She exhaled and leaned back in the seat. "Okay. Take me home."

Ray's intent was to get Amy safely into her trailer and leave, probably forever. His plans changed, as the plans of young men do, as soon as they got inside. Amy took his hand and pulled him toward the bedroom.

"Come on, Dawn," she ordered.

Dawn, wearing a long bathrobe, turned off the television and quietly followed them into the bedroom.

Ray had never experienced a three-way before. His experience with single partners had been rare enough. Dawn was a casual but expert love-maker with the off-hand demeanor of a seamstress sewing on a button. Amy, as before, was frenetic and loud. Her motion and vociferation obscured the fact that she was the less participatory partner by far. Most of her energy was spent crawling over Dawn and Ray from one side of the bed to the other while tending to herself.

When Ray was exhausted, Dawn got up quietly, picked up her bathrobe from the floor, and exited the room. Ray heard the TV click on. Amy reached under the bed and pulled out a half bottle of Smirnoff's. She drank from the bottle deeply. Ray reached over to stroke her back, but Amy pushed his hand away.

"I think I'm done," she said. She sat up with her back braced by a pillow. She continued to drink. "See you next week."

Ray dressed and left.

"Goodnight, Dawn," he said on his way out the door.

She waved over her shoulder, eyes on the television.

Despite the rewarding wind-up to the evening, Ray decided at first not to date Amy again. She was much too dangerous to his well-being. His resolve lasted until he reached home. By then he thought an occasional date would be all right. "It's good for me," he told himself.

Ray understood the situation well. Amy was prepared to be physical only when she was taking the drug. Ray also understood that Amy had opted for a threesome because it required less from her. He gathered that Amy really didn't like to be touched. Of course, as pretty and pleasant as Dawn was, Ray had no objection to her pinch-hitting. Before the next day was over, he had made a date for the upcoming weekend.

With her drug dependency fully in the open and Ray's infatuation holding firm regardless, Amy became more rash and brash on their dates together. They spent less time in restaurants, in theaters, and on horseback, and far more on aimless drives around the desert while Amy smoked crack. Ray was upset by Amy's recklessness, and especially by her willingness to place him at risk. Not only did her drug buys take place in the worst neighborhoods from the most unsavory people Ray ever almost-met, but there were the laws to consider. Police could, and did, seize property of drug offenders.

"They can take my car," he reminded her. "Maybe they could take my house."

She didn't seem to care. By the end of each drive, he was ready to leave her behind. Afterward, Amy and Dawn always dissuaded him.

Ray acknowledged his weakness of character. He often wondered if he was any less an addict than Amy. The degree to which he was "under her spell" (a phrase he liked, because it seemed to absolve him of responsibility) was demonstrated the night Amy asked him to pay for her cocaine.

"I'll make it up to you."

He knew better, but his hormones squelched common sense, and he agreed. Thereafter, she expected him to continue paying.

On the same night he first paid for coke, Amy also asked him to give Dawn money. "You should give her a few bucks. You don't have to give me anything, but you really should give her something."

"What's a few bucks?"

"Oh, five hundred."

"I can't afford it."

"Well, two hundred then. She likes you, so maybe that would be okay."

Ray found the long drives to nowhere excruciating. They were taking a toll on his car, racking up thousands of miles, and on himself as well. Often she insisted on leaving the area around Reno, because "they" were watching for her there. One time, they drove in the Taurus as far east as Fallon, where Amy demanded they turn down an isolated dirt road. Amy agreed to turn around only when a sign announced they were entering a U.S. Naval Air bombing range. She was reluctant even then, but Ray convinced her "they" would be watching such a place.

The large new expenses ate away at his carefully acquired savings. The late nights were harmful to his work performance. His boss asked him if anything was wrong.

"Just some personal problems," he answered.

"Try not to bring them to work."

"Yes, ma'am."

The day his bank statement, for the first time in years, showed a balance below five figures, Ray realized his comfortable life was in serious jeopardy. His choice was to sink or swim. More out of desperation than bravery, he chose to swim.

Ray requested overtime at work. He canceled his date for the weekend and visited Granny on Saturday to avoid running into Amy. A full week's distance gave him perspective. The next Tuesday, Amy called him up in a rage.

"What? Are you fucking dumping me now, after all I've done for you?"

"That's a harsh way of putting it . . ."

"What way would you prefer to put it, creep?"

"Amy, look, you know how much I want you, but I've got to back off a little. The cost of the drugs is killing me and my bank account."

"You're not doing any."

"I might as well be. I'm going broke. I'm a zombie at work. I'll lose my job. I frankly don't know how you make it to work."

"I'm not a pathetic pansy-ass. Have fun, ever trying to get anything as good as you've had with me and Dawn."

"Goodbye, Amy."

Ray was deeply unhappy about giving up his two lovers, but he felt his survival was at stake.

"Something happen between you and Amy?" Granny asked. As always, her intuition was on target.

"Yes."

"Good. You're better off."

"What made you ask? Did she say something?"

"No, she just had a big attitude when she brought me tea yesterday. Then I heard she quit."

"She quit her job?"

"Yes. So you can see me during the week again, if you like."

Ray let the comment pass. "Where did she go?"

"Do you care?"

"I suppose I don't."

They had a good visit, which was fortunate, because Granny passed away the next day. He declined an autopsy. Ray's mother did not return home for the funeral. She did return home a week later for a check. Granny had split the estate about evenly between him and his mother. In a private note Ray found addressed to him among her papers, Granny explained the Will was likely to be challenged if his mother were not cut in for half. Besides, she didn't want to exacerbate the rift between the two. Therefore, the insurance money would go to his mother, and the condo to Ray. Everything else would be split down the middle.

Ray's mom made a show of sympathy for him, but she seemed to require little, herself. She flew back to London after two days. Ray put the condominium up for sale.

Amy called up two weeks later. "I'm sorry to hear about your grandmother. She was a nice lady."

"Thanks. Where did you hear?"

"One of the nurses from Crestview called me."

"Oh."

"So, do you own the condo now?"

"Yeah. It's for sale. Crestview says they usually get snapped up."

"Well, that should make your life easier."

"Not really. I'd rather have her here."

"Yeah, I know."

"So how have things been with you, Amy?"

"A little rough. I'm still out of work, but Dawn is helping me out until I get another job. I'm pregnant. School is okay, now that I'm past the English papers. I'm working hard though, because there is a lot to learn."

"Back up."

"What do you mean?"

"I thought I heard you say you were pregnant."

"Yeah, I did. What do you want to do?"

What Ray wanted to do was flee, but he knew this wasn't an option.

"We're not prime parent material, are we?" Ray couldn't imagine a more frightening mother than Amy.

Amy paused before answering. "Look, I know I've been tough on you. Abusive even. I admit it. But we had fun, too, didn't we?"

"Yes. That's not the point."

"Look, maybe this is what I need in order to straighten out. I'll give up the drugs. I promise. I really can be normal, and you like me when I'm normal, don't you?"

"It sounds as though you've already decided what you want."

"Yeah, but it's not just my decision. I can't do this alone."

"Are you saying you want to get married?"

"That's a pretty sucky proposal, Ray."

Ray hadn't considered it a proposal at all.

Amy continued, "You don't think I can quit drugs, do you?"

"The doubt crossed my mind."

"I can."

"Can you really?" To his own surprise, Ray wondered if marriage was such a bad thing—assuming she got straight. He always secretly wanted something other than a typical mundane suburban existence. Amy wasn't typical, and she clearly wasn't the jealous type. Maybe she could give his life depth and flavor.

"Yes, I can. Drugs, I mean. I just need something to get my mind off of them."

"Like what?"

"Horses. We have to get our own horses."

"They're very expensive."

"You can afford them once you sell the condo. It was Dawn's idea, and she's right. Build a barn in the back of your house. I'll take care of them. I'll do all the work. I promise."

Feeling like a paratrooper unsure of his parachute, Ray stepped out onto thin air. "You want to get married?"

"Well, that's not much better, but I'll take it. Yes. I'll make you happy."

"Will I make you happy?"

"You'd better."

Even though few of them had met Amy, and none knew her troubles, most of Ray's friends tried to talk him out of marriage. Ray knew friends always do this. Their admonitions seldom originate in the pure and sincere warmth of their hearts, even if they themselves think so. A more human motivation is jealously. So is boyish taunting and cruelty. Ray had behaved the same in the past to others facing the white lace curtain. Such warnings were to be expected. The only one he hadn't expected came from Dawn.

Dawn called him at two o'clock in the morning. She must have been home, because he heard the TV in the background. Amy, apparently, was out.

"Ray, I'm not in the habit of saving people from themselves, but I am going to try just once. I only need you to promise not to mention this to Amy, because she is my friend. If you feel you can't do that, then hang up."

"Okay, Dawn, you've always been straight with me. What's on your mind?"

"Maybe you should see a shrink."

"Why?"

"Because you must feel like you deserve abuse and punishment! Are you walking around with some huge guilt complex and you need to beat yourself up over it?"

"I don't think so."

"I do. That's what your relationship with Amy is all about, isn't it? Pretty much the only pleasure you ever got out it came from me, and I charged you. Amy gave you nothing. She never will give you anything.

"By the way, I won't be part of any threesome with you after you're hitched, money or no money. I'm not a prude, but I don't get involved in weird stuff with married people. You two will be as weird as married people come."

She paused, but he could think of nothing to say.

"Don't get me wrong, Ray," she added more softly. "I love Amy. Once you work your way under the anger and the drugs, there's a little girl crying for love who's hard to resist. But she has an eighteen-wheeler load of hostility toward men. I don't mean the normal man-woman thing. I'm talking big time rage. It has something to do with her dad, I think. Now she's got you in her sights. Trust me, she'll destroy you if she can, even if she destroys herself doing it. You should run as fast and as far as you can."

"This is about the most you've ever said to me, Dawn. You're not usually so expressive."

"Think about that."

"Well, even if there is something to what you say," Ray stammered, "there is also the biological factor."

"Don't be stupid."

"What do you mean?"

"I give up, Ray. If you're going to be obtuse, there is nothing I can do. It's a shame, Ray, because you're a nice guy and there really aren't many nice guys around. Most of you are just male 'Amys.' You won't be a nice guy when she is done with you! Don't ever say I didn't try. I won't tell you to have a nice life, because that's not going to happen now. The best life I can wish for you is a short one."

Dawn hung up.

Ray didn't mention the call to Amy.

Aside from verbal discouragement on all sides, the next four weeks of their engagement was (by the former standards of their relationship) idyllic for Ray and Amy. As far as he could tell, she avoided all drugs except marijuana. She held her drinking in line too. She even made an effort to be pleasant. Most of the time she was the chatty, smiling self to whom he was first attracted at Crestview. True, she balked at physical affection in her dry and drugless state, but he didn't want to push her on too many fronts at once. She promised she would come around in time in this matter too.

During the engagement, Amy continued to live with Dawn, but slowly she moved her belongings into Ray's house. Dawn seldom made eye contact with him when he showed up at the trailer, but he got the impression this was indifference, not embarrassment.

The day approached. Amy and Dawn arranged everything in Las Vegas on Ray's credit card. All of his friends had begged off being Best Man, citing work or family obligations. His co-worker Jeff, however, overheard one of the excuses and invited himself.

"I'll go with you, Ray. I like Vegas—so long as I don't have to pay for the flight or the room, that is."

Jeff always had seemed friendly enough, but he was by no means a friend. The man struck Ray as crude. Nevertheless, he figured he should have someone show up with him.

"No, you don't have to pay," Ray answered.

"I'm there."

The party of four flew from Reno to Las Vegas for the wedding. The 737 hadn't been cleaned properly from the morning's flight. There were used paper napkins, chewing gum wrappers, and plastic bags empty of peanuts on the floor and stuck in the creases of the seats. Ray was surprised Amy's mother hadn't shown up, even for the wedding. He guessed she hadn't been told about it. Ray and Jeff sat with each other in seats three rows behind Amy and Dawn. Jeff elbowed Ray.

"So what's the scoop on Dawn? Think I've got a shot at her?"

"You're married, Jeff."

"So?"

"I don't know. I thought that was relevant, but maybe I'm wrong. I really don't know what Dawn looks for in men. She's always been nice enough to me."

"Fuck nice. I love those cone-shaped breasts."

"Maybe that wouldn't be your best opening line. Assuming it wasn't already. They're right up there and they might have heard you."

"You worry too much. You do her?"

"No," Ray lied.

"She was roommates with your bride-to-be?"

"Yes."

"They do it?"

"Do what?"

"Each other, dude!"

"I couldn't say."

"Doesn't sound like you know very much."

"No, it doesn't."

"You know more about Amy than about Dawn?"

"Not really."

"You're entering this whole thing pretty blind."

"So I've been told."

"Nice ass."

"Excuse me?"

"The stewardess."

"Oh."

*   *   *

The big casino hotels downtown and along the strip had become too "family oriented," stuffy, and security conscious in Amy's opinion. Amy hadn't booked rooms in one. Had Ray not been so relieved to have dodged such a big expense, he might have wondered why she felt the need to avoid security. Amy had opted for the Honeymoon Fantasia Motel outside of Las Vegas proper, which featured theme rooms so over-the-top tasteless as to have a sort of integrity.

Their wedding was the fourth scheduled for the day in the motel reception hall. For their particular service, the room was hastily decorated in an outer space theme. The lights were turned down low. Folding panels with a lunar landscape painted on them covered the walls and blocked all of the light from the windows. The panels overlapped near the front door, blocking light from that direction as well. From the center of the room, an object resembling the Viking Martian Lander played a show of lights on the ceiling to simulate stars, rotating slowly. Against the far back wall was a plastic relief model of a flying saucer. Before the saucer stood the preacher, if that is what he really was, wearing a silver lamé 1950s sci-fi movie version of a space suit. His helmet was topped with a science-class depiction of an atom, with little electron nuggets held in looped orbits about a nucleus on a wire frame. Ray noticed irrelevantly that it was an oxygen atom.

Ray and Amy's outfits were utterly anomalous to the chosen theme. He wore a simple blue blazer with gray pants and a red tie. She wore something looking more like a prom dress than a wedding dress.

The oxygen atom rushed through the service with the contempt of familiarity, the soundtrack from Kubrick's *2001: A*

Space Odyssey playing quietly in the background. Afterwards, a tray was rolled in containing fruit in gelatin and bottles of Champagne of a brand that Ray didn't recognize. The Champagne glasses were plastic.

Before the new couple and their two guests had finished their first serving of gelatin, the motel workers turned up the lights and began changing the wall panels. The lunar surroundings gave way to a western desert with cacti and mesas. The flying saucer was replaced by a covered wagon. Ray noticed the fellow who performed the service was now wearing six-guns and a Stetson hat; he struggled to pull on snakeskin cowboy boots.

The three bedrooms were as surreal as the reception hall had been. The newly married couple's featured a sea bottom theme. The walls and ceiling were painted dark blue rising to light. The carpet was sandy color. Murals of sea creatures and a sunken galleon formed an underwater vista. Plastic dolphins were suspended from the ceiling. The bed lay inside a huge open clam shell of plastic.

In Dawn's room, a Tahitian hut was reached by a rope suspension bridge over a gurgling fishpond with live carp swimming in it. Rich green plastic flora covered the walls. A mural of a volcano sported a glowing red light in its cone. Jeff's room was a grotto with a real running waterfall feeding into a hot tub. After touring and laughing at each of the rooms, Ray had hoped for a little private time with Amy, but she wanted to see the sights and, perhaps, hit the casinos.

The four climbed into their rented Mercury Cougar. It was a bit cramped in the back for Dawn and Jeff despite the unusual rear bucket seats. They had decided to start with the Luxor, a 30-story glass pyramid, and then play it by ear. Though both cities are appealing for a serious gambler, Reno in other respects is vastly more conservative than Las Vegas, so Ray enjoyed the gaudy spectacle of downtown. So did his guests. Jeff was openly gregarious, especially with passing women. He kept trying to find someone he could talk into joining him at the bottom of his waterfall, a room feature he mentioned to one and all. He was not subtle about flirting with Dawn. She brushed off his come-ons without rancor, but without pleasantry either.

Amy gambled aggressively at every opportunity, and opportunities were everywhere. This behavior was odd since she had never expressed much interest in gambling at home. She won twelve hundred dollars at roulette. Her joy didn't cease even after losing $2700 in various games afterward.

Despite the mounting expenses, Ray reckoned this was their honeymoon and they were entitled to splurge. Ray had to admit Amy looked beautiful. The shaggy cut of her light brown hair was not the current fashion, but it suited her well. She turned to him. He smiled. Amy took his hand.

"Look," she said, "I know I'm going to have to give up everything, but this is my wedding night and I deserve one last fling on the town."

"Isn't that what we're doing?" he asked. He knew all too well what she meant, but he was hoping to divert her by pretending otherwise. He knew it was a weak and hopeless gambit.

"I'm going to get some shit," she announced. "You want to go?" she asked Dawn.

Dawn shook her head. "I'll meet you back at the motel."

"We'll grab a cab. I'll take you back," offered Jeff as he fingered her hair.

"Thanks, but I'll go alone," she answered. "You enjoy yourself." She stepped back out of his reach.

"Here, Dawn, you take the car," said Amy as she held out the keys. She nodded at Ray. "We'll get a cab."

Amy led Ray out to the front of the hotel where the taxis were lined up. She picked a taxi according to its driver. She was always good at using her radar to spot the right one. The taxi was an old Cadillac. Ray and Amy climbed in. The driver got in front and closed the door.

"Where can we buy some shit?" Amy asked at once.

The driver assessed them in the rear view mirror. "I don't do that anymore. The only reason I'm even talking to you is that I've never seen an undercover cop look so good in a white dress."

Amy laughed. "'Anymore' my ass. You still know where to get it. Come on. We're not cops. We'll make it worth your while."

The driver hesitated, then started the car and pulled out onto the Strip. He fussed with the radio until he reached a fellow driver. "Buck, you know the order you picked up last night? That, uh, that gasoline. Where did you get it?"

"From Leo," came the answer in an accented voice. "Same parking lot where I filled your tank last Saturday. I'll call him. Flick your lights when you get there."

"Thanks, Buck."

*   *   *

After a bigger purchase than usual, and a generous tip to the driver, Ray didn't have enough cash left on him to pay the man to drive around all night as Amy wanted. With irritated reluctance, she agreed to return to the motel.

Back in the room, Ray waited as she smoked her way through three pipefuls. He then suggested consummating the marriage.

"No, I don't want to."

"It's tradition."

"Fuck tradition. You want me to get Dawn for you?"

"At least I'd get to do something I enjoy," he muttered to himself, loud enough for her to overhear.

"Thanks! That was a test, you stinker, and you just failed."

"Did I?"

"We're supposed to be married now, or did you forget?"

"I didn't forget."

"You're not going to party with me?"

"Not in the way you mean."

"Does your friend Jeff party?"

"I don't know."

"Go ask him. I hate doing shit alone."

Ray was relieved to leave his bride's room. He wondered if this was a common reaction to a wedding night.

He didn't expect Jeff to be in his room, but when he knocked, the door opened. Jeff apparently had struck out with his advances on amateurs and was too cheap to hire professionals, so he was in there sulking. Jeff jumped at the chance of free drugs.

Jeff preferred to sniff cocaine in traditional fashion, but Amy continued to turn hers into crack. Jeff and Amy used up the coke and talked frenetically about inanities. Ray eventually fell asleep on the floor with his head resting on a stuffed octopus.

On the return trip the next day, the 737 was cleaner. Amy again sat with Dawn. Amy was in a foul mood because of her hangover and because, she said, Ray had been so inattentive the night before. Dawn, as usual was quiet and even-tempered.

"I like your wife," offered Jeff, "but that Dawn chick is a bitch!"

Back in Reno, life didn't get much better. Ray built the barn that Amy wanted. He bought two quarter horses and several thousand dollars' worth of tack to outfit them. Despite her promises, he was the one up at four in the morning feeding the animals, turning them out, and shoveling out their stalls before work. Amy's drug use moderated, but it didn't stop altogether.

A month after the wedding, and after a mindless drive in a smoke-filled car, she offered him sex. She managed to turn it into a joyless experience. Her teeth were gritted and she looked pained the whole time. Afterwards she berated him for demanding such a thing from her.

"I can't believe you even asked this from me when you know how I feel about it!" she complained.

Ray wondered if Amy's sporadic drug abuse would affect the child she was expecting. He needn't have worried. Amy miscarried on the fifty-eighth day of their marriage, two days before his health insurance would have been extended to cover her expenses.

With her one motive for self-restraint gone, Amy lost all control. With his own motivation for protecting Amy reduced, Ray refused to continue driving her on her excursions. This incurred her drugged wrath, but she adjusted to smoking crack at home, sending him outside repeatedly to see where "they" were, all the while abusing him for exposing her to such risks. He began to spend a lot of time working in the barn.

There was a problem beyond drugs. Amy's spending was uncontrollable. He explained that $2,000 was too much to pay for a new saddle. She bought it anyway, and a heavily silvered show bridle besides. He explained why they couldn't afford a new car. She bought one anyway. He explained the reasons they couldn't afford a trip to Jamaica. She bought tickets. He refused to go. She didn't turn in the tickets but went with Dawn instead, which at least gave Ray a brief but welcome vacation at home.

Ray's late hours and constant worries disrupted his work habits once again. Having received two official warnings, he fully expected to get a pink slip the next time the company was "restructured." He couldn't blame his bosses. He was not available for overtime, and his alertness had dropped off badly.

Dawn's warning had been prophetic. Amy was trying to destroy him—or maybe she was trying to destroy herself. Regardless, Ray was going down with her unless he acted to save himself. Ray made his decision to act the night that a drunk and high Amy complained he didn't carry enough life insurance.

"Don't you give a fuck about what happens to me?" she asked.

Ray was unnerved that this, of all things, was her first expression of financial responsibility. He needed to do something fast. The question was what action he should take. Divorce would bankrupt him as surely as the marriage would if it lasted another month. His only remaining asset was the heavily mortgaged house and its contents. By law she owned it every bit of it as much as he did, and in any event, the equity was nowhere near enough to cover his credit card debt, which had ballooned in the past months.

He didn't deserve any of this. He wondered how much life insurance he did carry and whether the policy was cashable. He never had bothered to examine any of the papers before. Ray sat down at his desk in the bedroom corner and opened the drawer where he kept his insurance papers in disorganized fashion. The life insurance turned out to be part of a package with his health insurance through his employer. He was covered, it turned out, for $150,000. A term policy, it had no cash value. To his surprise however, his spouse also was covered, though for only $75,000. Still, this would be enough to straighten out his credit card debt. Yes, murder was the answer. It was only right.

For several nights Ray watched the police and forensic shows on cable. At first discouraging, they over time gave him a ray of hope. Most of the people arrested for murder in the TV plots had been thoroughly stupid. Many simply tracked evidence back to themselves. Those who tried to cover their tracks were surprisingly inept. One fellow faked an auto accident by sending his late business partner over a cliff in his car, but he left a bloody trail from their office to the parking lo, and called a taxi for his ride back from the cliff. Another man, whose wife had disappeared, was found to have rented a wood chipper; he put the charge for it on his credit card! But at least those men made an effort. The majority committed brute crimes of passion with a gun or a knife and made no attempt to cover their trails at all.

Ray concluded his best chance at avoiding detection was to obscure the crime itself effectively. In an investigation, when it is at best unclear a murder has been committed, reasonable doubt enters the picture at the outset. However suspicious police may be, they will not bring charges in a case they don't expect to win. This approach was not novel, but he had to make a better job of it than the felons on the television shows.

He contemplated nicotine because Amy was a smoker and it wouldn't look unusual in her bloodstream. Yet, delivered in a more efficient manner than smoke, it was deadly even in small doses. A lethal tincture would be easy to extract from tobacco heated in rubbing alcohol. Still, a fatal blood level of nicotine would be unusual and would cast suspicion. A drug overdose was a better possibility. She had a history of drug abuse to reinforce the appearance of an accidental overdose. Yet this was an unreliable approach at best. If he supplied drugs, she would take them, but she had a very high tolerance. She was likely to survive huge quantities. If she passed out, any attempt to inject her with more might backfire, and with the insurance, a post-mortem was likely. In the end he ruled out poison altogether.

He thought about the ways a healthy young woman accidentally and unsuspiciously could expire. The answer came to him while shoveling manure from the stalls into a wheelbarrow in the backyard barn. Horses were notoriously dangerous. Several states had enacted severe limitations on liability suits for equestrian activities in order to prevent the closure of private stables, which otherwise would be uninsurable. Riders rode at their own risk.

He could go on a trail ride with her and cause an "accident," yet that would place him suspiciously at the scene. This was inadvisable, especially with the insurance motive. He leaned on his shovel and watched the two horses frolic outside in the paddock. One playfully kicked at the other, but missed.

Ray felt a sudden elation. It would work! A swift kick to the head by a steel-shod quarter horse would be lethal and wonderfully accidental. Amy would be kicked. A smile came to his face. He knew just how to arrange it. One of the horses had thrown a shoe a few days earlier. They were ready for new ones anyway, so, rather than nail it back on, the farrier had replaced them all. Ray kept the thrown shoe as a good luck piece. He hadn't hung it on the wall yet; it still lay on the feed bin. It was going to be a very lucky shoe, indeed. He slipped it in his pocket and walked outside to enjoy the sunset.

*   *   *

Ray fingered the horseshoe in his denim jacket pocket as he walked in the back door in response to Amy's call. He was surprised to see Dawn sitting at the kitchen table drinking coffee. She must have parked in front of the house.

"Oh, hello Dawn."

"Hi."

"Dawn brought over some homemade lasagna," said Amy. "Isn't that nice of her?"

"Very."

"I'm heating it up a little. It'll be about five minutes. Want to get dishes and stuff?"

"In a few minutes. I'm going to finish cleaning a few things in the basement."

Amy looked at him oddly. "What few things?"

"I'll be back up in a minute."

Dawn looked from one of their faces to the other.

Amy chose not to pursue the issue. "Don't take long," Amy said.

In the basement underneath the stairs, Ray found the baseball bat he had kept from his boyhood. The ash bat felt familiar and sturdy in his hands. He found his hammer and four seven-penny sinkers. He figured the resin-coated nails would grip the wood well.

He centered the horseshoe on the sweet spot of the bat. Slowly, lovingly, he tapped the nails home. He angled the nails to follow the curve of the bat.

Ray stood up and hefted the bat with its new horseshoe accessory. It felt good. He swung once. He tugged at the horseshoe to make sure it had stayed firmly attached. He cut his finger on the sharp edge of a nail head. He bled profusely from the little cut. He sucked his finger until the bleeding slowed. He swung again and hit a lampshade, knocking over the lamp.

"What the fuck are you doing down there?" called Amy.

"I'll be up in a minute, honey!"

"Now! I need to talk to you."

This was not auspicious. Not once had she ever needed to talk to him when she had good news. He put the bat back under the stairs and climbed the steps.

"Come on out back to the barn," Amy said, "I need to show you something."

"I'm leaving as soon as I finish my coffee. See you later," said Dawn to Ray as he passed.

"Won't you be joining us for your own dinner?"

"Places to go, people to see."

"Like who?"

"Oh, well there's your friend Jeff, of course. He really gets me hot."

"Right."

She winked and said, "See you later."

"Come on, Ray!" Amy prodded.

Amy led him to the horse trailer parked next to the barn. The trailer was several years old, but it was well-built and still sound. She waved a hand at it.

"You see that rust? The paint's all faded. It's dangerous to carry my horse in this."

"What rust?"

"There!" Amy pointed to a fingernail-sized patch near the wheel well, where a flake of paint had been scratched off.

"There is nothing wrong with the trailer. The wheels, tires, the axles are good. The lights work. The floorboards are fine. We can repaint it someday. It doesn't need it yet."

"But it's embarrassing. I'm not putting my horse in this."

"We can't afford a new trailer."

"That's where you're wrong. We qualified."

"Qualified for what? What are you telling me?"

"I bought a new trailer."

Ray took a deep breath and looked away to collect himself. He saw Dawn, standing by the back door with her arms folded. He was surprised she hadn't left yet. She waved and walked around to the front of the house. Ray turned his attention back to Amy.

"Are you done gawking at Dawn?"

Ray refused to go on the defensive. "There is nothing wrong with this trailer."

"I just showed you there is."

"How much did you spend?"

"They had one I wanted on the lot that cost $32,000."

Ray was silent for several moments. He tried once more to explain. "But we don't have $32,000."

"I know, I know! Don't give me such an attitude! I knew you wouldn't go for it, so I compromised and I made a great deal on a cheaper one. I got a new double with a dressing room for only $22,000. It's not quite what I wanted, but we can make do with it for a while. You should be proud of me."

Amy was actually asking praise for having saved $10,000. Perhaps she honestly looked at it this way. Ray decided he needed to move expeditiously with his plan before he lost everything.

"We don't have $22,000 either."

"I bought it on time. I told you we qualified."

"They give those loans to anybody, and they repossess three days after you miss a payment."

"So don't miss one."

"What do you think we can sell the old one for?" he asked idly.

"I'm not selling it. I can make money renting it to my friends. Not all of them have trailers."

"I thought it was unsafe."

"What is with your attitude tonight? What's wrong with you?"

"How are your friends going to pull the trailer?"

"With the Suburban."

"Our Suburban?"

"My Suburban, yes."

"And our... your new trailer will be pulled by...?"

"I really need a pick-up. I've told you before, even though you haven't done shit about it. Maybe a Ford 250 or a GMC 2500. A 3500 would be better."

"Did you buy one of those too?"

"No, they wanted your signature. They didn't like the looks of my credit alone."

"They were smarter than the trailer dealers. Why are you trying so hard to destroy me financially? What have I done to you? What have you done to you?"

"Ray! What is your problem tonight? You're really weirding me out. I'm getting very upset. I really can't take this. Come on. I'm going to get some shit."

"Have a nice time."

"You're coming with me. You are the one who upset me. You at least should drive me."

"No. I'm not going."

"You're going to let me go out there all alone exposed to those lowlifes?"

"You want to expose me to them?"

"Fuck you, Ray."

"I'll give you one last chance. I'll give us one last chance. Don't go. Make an effort, Amy. Try to get straight. I'll help."

"You can help by giving me some money."

"No. Stay home."

"No. Fuck you, Ray."

"So you've said."

Amy climbed into the Suburban and backed out of the driveway too fast, scattering stones on the grass.

Ray sat in the dark house eating lasagna. He knew exactly how long it would take her to buy and smoke her crack. He knew she wouldn't be back for the next four hours. He doubted she was driving around alone. She hated to be alone when she got high. Probably she was with Dawn at the old trailer. Ray cleaned up the kitchen and watched back-to-back reruns of The Twilight Zone on TV for the next three hours.

Without turning on the light, Ray walked down the basement stairs. He groped under the stairs until he found the bat. Gripping it tightly, he walked slowly back to the barn. The barn contained three stalls and a combination tack room and feed room. All opened to a center aisle.

He put the bat inside the unused stall. He sat on a tack box stored in the aisle, so he could see the roadway through the open front door. Ray waited. In a half-hour he saw the headlights and silhouette of the Suburban. The car slowed as it approached the driveway. Ray turned on the exterior floodlight so Amy would know he was in the barn.

Amy's emotional state was utterly unpredictable when she was high. Sometimes she was euphoric; sometimes she was in a rage; sometimes she was affectionate; sometimes she cried in despair. The house blocked his view of the car, but he could see the beams from the headlights until they went out. Amy appeared around the side of the house. She walked to the barn. Though it was too soon to tell for sure, her mood appeared somber. In the light of the floodlight, her face shone a pasty white except around the eyes, which were red as though she had been crying. She entered the barn and her features were lost in the dark.

"What are you doing back here?" she asked quietly.

"Hanging out with the horses."

"Yeah. I do that sometimes too."

The inside of the barn was dark but not pitch black. He could track her dark shape as she walked past him toward the rear right stall. She hugged the face of the good-natured paint gelding. The roan across the aisle grunted jealously.

"They just accept you for who you are," she added.

"They have that luxury."

"Look, Ray, I know you're mad at me. I know I don't make it easy for you."

Ray reached into the empty stall and pulled out the baseball bat. He tested its weight.

"I don't know why I'm the way I am," Amy continued.

Ray waited for her to back away from the horse. He didn't want to hit the animal by accident.

"You're a good man. You've tried to cater to me. Try to put up with me. I'll get better someday. I promise."

Amy stopped petting the horse. She looked toward Ray. Light from the outside glistened off one moistened eye.

"Okay, Goblin," she said to the roan. She moved across the aisle.

As she passed, Ray caught the smell of her shampoo. She was a full head shorter than he, and she looked so small. Now playing hard-to-get, Goblin retreated into the stall while Amy leaned on the door clucking to him. Keeping her back to Ray, she offered him a clean shot at her head. Ray gripped the bat hard and stepped into position. He lifted the weapon to his shoulder.

In the way she moved and petted the horse, he could see in Amy the little girl Dawn had mentioned, the one deliberately provoking punishment from a parent figure who (it startled him to realize) was himself. Like most out-of-control little girls, she did it because any attention for any reason was better than no attention.

Ray realized he needed to move quickly or this opportunity would slip away. Three times he started to swing but checked himself before moving the bat more than two inches. Full of emotion, though he couldn't give the emotion a name, Ray decided to let the opportunity slip. He lowered the bat and tucked it back in the vacant stall. Leaving Amy with Goblin, he left the barn and walked back to the house.

Ray sat in a chair in the living room in the dark. He held his head between his hands. Catastrophe would overtake him in a matter of months, maybe weeks. There was no way to keep up payments on the house and the cars, and now the trailer. His job was in jeopardy. Whether he stayed with Amy or not, he faced ruin. The destruction that Amy had engineered for herself was enveloping them both, just as he had been warned. In the end he hadn't been able to destroy her first. The future, which once looked so bright, scared him.

Ray heard the back door slam.

"Why are you sitting in the dark?"

The voice sounded different. "Amy?"

"No, it's me." Dawn flicked on the light switch. She held a pair of work gloves in her left hand. "Amy picked me up. You know how she likes to drive around."

"Oh. Yeah, I know." Ray realized she would have been a witness if he had gone through with the murder. He was both relieved and shaken.

"I think you'd better take me home."

"Okay."

"You can call the paramedics when you get back."

"For what?"

"Tell them you saw the light on in the barn and you went back and found your wife. Tell them about her drug problem. The blood results will confirm it and it actually will make things look less suspicious."

"Where is Amy?"

"In the stall with Goblin. He's a good horse. He's awfully mellow about her lying there. A lot of horses would flip out."

"What did you do?"

"I knew you couldn't do it. It was a good idea though, so I finished the job for you. Take me home now before something goes wrong."

"Did you look in the basement earlier this evening?"

Dawn nodded.

The drive back to the trailer was quiet. At last, he asked, "Why?"

"I want to settle down. But can you imagine being married to someone like Jeff? Yet that's pretty much what there is out there. He's nowhere near the worst, either. Most guys are such total assholes."

"I'm not?"

"Sure you are. But you're a nice one."

"I plotted killing my spouse."

"Who doesn't? You didn't go through with it. That's what counts. It would be best if you remembered I did go through with it."

"I'm unlikely to forget. I thought you tried to save people only once."

"I guess I'm just a weakling."

"Uh-huh."

They pulled up in Dawn's drive.

"Hold on a moment." Dawn put on the work gloves and reached in back of the Suburban. She picked up the bat and attached horseshoe. "You don't mind if I keep this? It has your fingerprints, your blood and Amy's blood on it, so maybe you shouldn't have it at the house."

"I can get rid of it."

"No, I'd rather keep it. Don't worry. No one will find it unless I want them to. We'll let a few months go by for appearance's sake. Before I move in, that is. Okay?"

"Okay."

"If you need to spend more time at work winning back your reputation, I'll understand."

"Thanks."

"Don't mention it. Ever."

—Richard Bellush, Jr.

APHRODITE'S
SWORD

SECOND BEST

They say you never forget the first.
And why? Because they soon forget.
The second washes the first away.
It's from the second we're left cursed.

The first is all anxiety.
The second forms eternity.

As seconds both, our passion flared
so also animus and regret.
With wicked wit she made me pay,
true tenderness I never shared.

We both had aimed for more, you see,
and therein lay our enmity.

Intensity blossomed to hate full-blown
which of respect is the surest sign.
Yet even after our break-up came,
love grew alone from seeds she'd sown.

I sought her doggedly all my life,
and even made her mimic a wife.

We met upon the street last week
and all our talk was so benign.
Contempt's sure sign are words so tame.
We kissed each other on the cheek.

Both love and war elicit zeal
but I'm quite sure that war is real.

—Richard Bellush, Jr.

PASSING LIBERTIES

I — MURPHY

Boston Common was crowded on this Sunday afternoon with the overflow throngs from a Red Sox game and the tents of an agricultural show. Maggie looked at a prize cow while an ungroomed young man told her about women.

"We'd all be a lot better off if women had been part of world leadership all along," he recited with false enthusiasm. It was the summer after Kent State and a clever man could make good use of political platitudes.

"He would be easy to out-manipulate," Maggie thought, as she him flashed a deliberate smile.

"You have a very pretty smile," the man (named Murphy) said.

Maggie and Murphy drove to a Salem beach and made love. Later he took her to his apartment, where he lived with his blowzy mother and a complete collection of Hitler's recorded speeches. Murphy told her he had a teaching degree and loved children. Maggie said she was in summer school and majoring in literature. Murphy said he would like to have a woman's body for one day, to experience men's stares, be whistled at, be approached on the street. Maggie thought he was a schizo, but mildly interesting.

II — BLOND BOY

The aging professor hunched up his back, dangled his arms, and paraded up and down the aisle to demonstrate Neanderthal Man's posture. A blond boy sitting near Maggie smiled at her.

Before the class was over, he had dropped a note on her desk: "Come to my room (1322) if you'd like to smoke some hash."

The blond boy had transformed his cell-like room into a fantasia of tapestries and drapes. Maggie smoked his hash and they spoke of astral planes, time warps, and alien universes. The boy played blues on his guitar. Maggie had a dinner date. The boy kissed her goodbye and said to come back anytime.

III — MICHAEL

Michael entered Maggie's room and picked out a long blue dress from her closet. Michael was in love with her, but she could not love Michael. They were friends and he had good taste in clothes, so she let him tell her what to wear.

The restaurant they went to sat atop a skyscraper. Michael was a Harvard medical student, spawned of wealth. Maggie felt guilty for not making love with him, but his touch left her cold.

Maggie told him about crazy Murphy and how they played on the beach every day.

"I want to give you a party for your birthday," Michael said. "A giant party with a cauldron of wine and dry ice bubbling in the middle. Wear your dress with the little puffed sleeves."

IV — CRAZY MURPHY

On a sweltering morning, Murphy picked up a letter lying on the sill of Maggie's door. He handed it to Maggie as he entered. "Let me know your mind rather than your beauty," the blond boy had written, "though I've seen precious little of both. Come see me."

Crazy Murphy had never been stoned. Maggie introduced him to the mysteries of marijuana. When he smoked, his eyes turned bright, insane. Down the hallway of her dorm he charged, in uncontrolled amok. "NO WONDER WE'RE BOMBING OUR OWN TROOPS IN VIETNAM!" he bellowed. At last, he was cajoled into calm with a package of Hostess Twinkies.

The phone rang and a man told Maggie she didn't know him, but would she like to go sailing this afternoon? She was writing a paper on Kerouac and McLuhan, so she declined, but she agreed to meet him for lunch the following day. When she met him, he was disappointing. The pained conversation increased her alcohol intake beyond the norm, and she got sickeningly drunk. Events were fuzzy, between lunch at the restaurant and the moment she found herself struggling on the floor of his apartment, rolling over and over, knocking furniture across the room. Maggie broke away and ran through the door to freedom, on an undulating street.

V — THERE HAS TO BE ANOTHER WAY

In the cool of an evening, twenty women gathered to revel in fantasies of mankind's matriarchal past. The woman named Jody (known to her callous radical male brethren as "the girl who gave her chin for the revolution") had researched and established sociological evidence that it was ancient woman who'd domesticated the cat. While tribal warriors grooved on phallic power trips and stoned gazelles to death, women suckled babes and orphaned saber-toothed kittens side by side at their breasts. "Man pro-death, woman pro-life," Jody said. "The Marxist revolution will free us all from ourselves."

Maggie's eyes dreamed out the window. Only futility resulted from the ego-bolstering, twisted logic of these discussions. She attended them because it was better than looking for no answer at all.

Across the street from the classroom, the Greek woman was wiping the tables at her family's little college restaurant. Recently Maggie had sat at one of those tables and met the plump woman's martyred eyes. "You can see," the woman said to her without words: "I suffer and live in humility for love of my husband, this man who flirts with you sweetly when you enter my door, this man that I love with total surrender, who owns my soul and thinks of no one but himself, who will never know the deepness of my woman's love. I live this way because this is what it means to be a woman. You who are young and free, you will know soon enough what I mean, so do not pity my ruined body and the resignation in my face."

Maggie's eyes looked back and said, "No, no, no, there has to be another way, and I will find it for the sake of us all, for you and me."

Days later, when Maggie entered the woman's door with one of her young men, the woman's face and hers lit up with secret smiles.

"What, are you two having a lesbian affair?" the young man asked. Maggie laughed.

—Sharon Bellush

MODERN TIMES

RUDIMENT

Courted by toad trills and rare diseased flies
you swing stately in your hammock.
Safe in the deadly peace
of unconquered southern jungle
you have healed the wounds of your Zen guitars,
your Freudian literature forgotten.
The jungle lacked a philosophy
and you took the jungle
growing lean
and gray and grizzled on
bananas and war paint ground
in earth pots scratching heedlessly wherever
because there are no eyes here, only fangs
and it was your phallic right.
And I young and lank-haired
of a blurred National Geographic centerfold
I came with the blood and the claws
and mellowed with you still young
and indistinguishable from the earth,
the grain, the huts, and the
brown ageless children
running rampant beneath your hammock.
And I still young,
my form stretched and mellowed through you
I flash my yellow nut-stained teeth
in tremulous coquetry
offering my morning's work
of jungle entrail cookery
mingled with my fecund sweat.
You remove your straw hat to eat
you reveal your transcendency, you
are but a man.
I am soft and slavish, I am
pure existence, I am god.

—Sharon Bellush

DULLWIT

Bok stood outside the Village entrance formed by the overlapping thicket wall. He was King and claimed the appropriate prize name "The Lion." Rarely did anyone call him this, despite his attempt to encourage the usage by wearing a lion's tooth as a pendant. He was King not of a domain, but of a people, specifically "the People." Territories can change, but the People were the People wherever they were and wherever they went.

The Village wall was the height of a grown man. It formed a rough circle around a modest kop. The People had multiplied prolifically, and the wall was too confining. It needed to be expanded. Bok preferred it be torn down altogether, but his rule was not absolute; many of his preferences needed to be put aside or deferred because of popular sentiment or opposition from the witch woman who called herself the "Moon Priestess."

The wall's average radius was 30 meters, though no one among the People would have understood such a measurement. No one would understand it for 90,000 years. The People had no name for their community other than "the Village." This usage suggested there were no other villages. As it happened, they were right. Their outpost, a score of miles inland from the southern tip of Africa, was mankind's first—and as yet, only—flirtation with urban life.

A single entry serviced the Village. The wicker gate at the entrance was pushed to one side during the day. There was always traffic from foraging parties, water gatherers carrying skins, hunters, or children going out to play. The gate was closed at night for protection. A guard was posted at night as well. The villagers felt safe.

If there was a disadvantage to the hilltop site, it was the lack of water inside the walls. Siege warfare had not yet been invented, however, so this was viewed more as an inconvenience than as a security problem. Besides, the People had no neighbors. They deliberately had sought out this empty land to escape bickering with neighbors.

The water supply for the Village was the stream below the eastern slope of the kop. Though the walk to it was not difficult, Bok sometimes wondered if it would have been better to have built the Village on the bank of the stream. He usually decided otherwise. As a rule, it is unwise to sleep next to water: besides the occasional risk of flood, water draws predators. He had offered no opinion on this issue when the huts were first built. At the time, he was opposed to the whole scheme, whether on a hill or anywhere else.

The stream flowed south toward the Poison Sea. The enormous expanse of blue had frightened Bok when he first saw it. He avoided taking his hunting expeditions in the Sea's direction. It was, in his mind, an evil place. Drinking from the Sea could sicken or kill a man.

Bok could see the boy, Lekkek, sitting beneath a cedar tree quite far downstream toward the southeast. The boy was heir apparent to the King, a term invented by a previous witch years back, though she claimed the word had ancient origins. Bok disliked the word "king" even though in some strange way it enhanced his own authority. He preferred the old designation "chief." A chief was first among equals—the head of a unitary tribal body. A king was superior to his subjects—something more divisive. Words have power, and one must be careful how one uses them. The docility of the People in accepting his own elevation over them in this manner disappointed Bok. He felt contempt for them for doing so.

The young heir Lekkek was Bok's nephew. He also was a misfit, an annoyance, a dullwit, and a family embarrassment. Simply by existing, he was an impediment to Bok's plans to restore greatness to the People.

In Bok's opinion, the boy was stupid beyond any help. The awkward youth was incapable of keeping his mind on any useful task. His attention inevitably drifted. One time, as one of the older craftsmen taught the boy to shape a hand ax, a task requiring concentration, Bok came up behind the two to check on the boy's progress. No sooner did Bok's shadow fall between the boy and his tutor, than Lekkek let his hands drop, forgetting what he was doing. Lekkek then turned to Bok and asked what fuel the sun burns and why it doesn't burn out.

"It is enough that it doesn't burn out," Bok had answered in annoyance. "The flint!"

"The sun is made of flint?"

"No! I mean I don't know! I mean the flint in your hands, boy! Finish the ax!"

"Oh." The boy had forgotten all about his lesson. The craftsman smiled tolerantly throughout the exchange, but Lekkek's ax, in the end, was a misshapen abomination. Bok ordered him to redo it. On the second attempt the tool was serviceable but still sadly irregular.

Yet, despite such recurrent displays of backwardness, sometimes the boy casually would utter complex and confusing statements that unnerved Bok for days. Once when the full moon went strangely dark, Lekkek wondered out loud something about a shadow of the earth, a notion that frightened Bok because he almost understood it. Sometimes exceptionally stupid people, Bok decided, have unusual insights because their minds aren't distracted by tasks requiring intelligence.

Lekkek was much like his father in this regard. In fact, he was like everyone descended from the old man who was called the "Egret," excepting only Bok himself. The Egret was remembered and extolled as a great man, the Pathfinder of the People in the silly ceremonies of the witch woman. Though a boy at the time of the Egret's death, Bok remembered him personally, and he thought the old man was a fool.

Bok took no pleasure in harsh judgment of his relations, but the truth was the truth. His mother, on the other hand, did not display mental weakness, at least not of the same sort. She was downright calculating. Yet her plots did neither her nor the tribe any good. This proved to Bok that it is as dangerous to be overly clever as it is to be stupid; either trait can prevent one from seeing things clearly.

For the present, the People were in safe, solid hands: Bok's own. Lekkek, however, cast a dark cloud over the future. As Bok was without sons, the simpleton under the tree was in line to succeed him. Lekkek arguably could claim the kingship on the very day he officially reached adulthood. Rather to the boy's discredit, he had shown no hint of any ambition to try such a thing. Regardless, Bok had no intention of allowing Lekkek to succeed whatsoever. If there was any way Bok could arrange it, Lekkek would follow his father into exile. If not, well, accidents happen. Lekkek was ripe to have one happen to him.

As Bok watched Lekkek in the distance and contemplated the various accidents that can befall a young man, he noticed a smaller figure emerge from behind the cedar tree next to the boy. Bok assumed it was the odd little girl Ulee. About a year Lekkek's junior, she followed the boy as though attached by a rope. Strange to the point of being disturbing, she, fortunately, was not Bok's problem. Nevertheless, her presence was another example of Lekkek's backwardness. The boy was due for his ritual of manhood. It was unmanly for him to keep the company of girls such as Ulee. Bok himself didn't much care for females of any age, but, if Lekkek insisted on associating with them, he should experience ones who were older. As a "Prince," another word invented by the witch woman (though again she proclaimed its antiquity), he should be able to impress one or two females.

— 2—

Lekkek sat next to a cedar tree by the stream. He enjoyed this spot. It was within sight of the Village gate, yet well downstream from the deep pool where the Villagers liked to bathe and fill their water skins. It was also downstream from the preferred crossing place where six big stepping stones made it dry and easy. In front of the cedar tree, the stream was shallow but inconveniently wide to cross. No one ever bothered him here—except Ulee.

As Ulee's words buzzed in his ear, Lekkek instinctively waved his hand at the girl as though fending off a mosquito. In fact,

"Mosquito" was the nickname he had chosen for her. Ulee accepted it as an expression of affection, but that is not how Lekkek intended it. Her presence embarrassed him. Though only a year or so separated them in age, a year is an immensity at the time one approaches manhood. A woman a year older than himself would be an advanced and worldly companion; Ulee was just a child, and Lekkek needed to place childhood and childish things behind him.

Shedding Ulee was easier decided upon, than done. She seemed always to know where he was. Sometimes he would sneak out of the village in order to avoid her. Yet she was likely to appear out of nowhere, often startling him. She was a daily annoyance. Besides the socially embarrassing age difference, she constantly distracted Lekkek with questions and disturbed him by peering over his shoulder.

Lekkek bore wounds caused by Ulee's interest. Two of his left fingers were badly bruised from a mishap several days earlier. Lekkek had been studying toolmaking with one of the older craftsmen. Lekkek had an inspiration and gave the flint tool a novel shape. Uncle Bok saw his finished invention and loudly ordered him to re-edge the hand ax, claiming he had botched the job miserably. Lekkek tried to explain the job wasn't botched. The tool actually was something new, a combination ax, knife and scraper, with three distinct edges. Uncle Bok cut him off.

"None of your excuses!" he had bellowed. "Fix it!" Bok grabbed the tool out of Lekkek's hands and threw it down forcefully, close to Lekkek's feet. His toes barely escaped a quick severance. Bok then marched off in disgust.

Sullenly, Lekkek had re-edged the tool, trying hard to work it into a more conventional shape. A shadow fell on him and a high voice asked loudly, "What are you doing?" Ulee's sudden appearance caused him to jerk his hands and smash his fingers.

"At the moment, I'm bleeding," he answered.

The girl laughed. "Clumsy, aren't we?" she chided.

In a rare display of anger prompted by pain, Lekkek lost his temper: "Get away from me you rotten little pest before I swat you like the mosquito you are!"

Ulee walked off in a huff. At first Lekkek was satisfied, because she stayed away from him for the next two days. Nonetheless, she pointedly remained within his sight and cast him an unrelenting look of betrayal. At last Lekkek could stand it no more and felt obliged to apologize, as though he were the one who had done something wrong. He had hoped she would accept his apology but stay away. Instead she rebuked him loudly, but then she firmly reattached herself as his shadow.

There was one activity, at least, where Lekkek could be free of Ulee. This was the hunt, by tradition the work of men, on which no females were allowed. Challenging this tradition would mean challenging Bok, and Ulee was wise enough not to try that.

Over the past few months, Lekkek had accompanied several of the hunting parties. This was a required apprenticeship. It would culminate in his ritual of manhood. The central part of the ritual was a solitary hunt and a solo kill. Thereafter, the name of the animal would be added to his own. Though there was no restriction on the type of prey, initiates chose their targets carefully. No one would want to be known as "Fen the Rat," or "Tun Baboon."

Uncle Bok was called "The Lion," most commonly by himself. There were no other Lions in the tribe. There were rumors even Bok took the name undeservedly, but no one dared to suggest this to his face. Perhaps for this reason alone, he earned the name.

Lekkek's ritual was scheduled to begin the very next morning, but he had no intention of taking on a big cat just to equal his uncle Bok. He had no intention of taking on a big cat for any reason. Instead, he devised a plan to slay a zebra. It was a big enough animal to be impressive, while lacking fangs, claws, and native aggression. "Lekkek Zebra" might not be a name with swagger, but he could live with it comfortably enough.

A successful and at least moderately impressive solo hunt was essential to Lekkek if he was to build respect in the tribe. Respect was something of which he had experienced precious little so far, despite being the King's nephew and something his mother the Moon Priestess called a "Prince." Uncle Bok did exasperatingly little to help. On the contrary, the old man ridiculed and demeaned Lekkek in public frequently. Naturally, boys his own age followed suit. He supposed Bok was just trying to make him stronger, but the habit of disdain from his contemporaries would make it hard for him to exercise authority when the time came.

Unlike his uncle, who clearly enjoyed being King, Lekkek had little ambition to rule. The Moon Priestess seemed bent on it happening, however, and he was more afraid to defy her than he was to accept the succession.

Lekkek had a reason other than fear to accept his heritage. Her name was Alu. The beautiful young woman was Bok's daughter, and so his cousin, though everyone in the tribe was to some degree related. The most desirable of all the unattached young women of the People, she was a year his senior and ripe for marriage. With all the strong and handsome hunters strutting and vying for her attention, his chances with her were weak enough. If he abandoned his royal status, he may as well give up on her completely.

Lekkek had enjoyed the apprentice hunts despite the cantankerous company of Uncle Bok. His role on these expeditions had been restricted to carrying weapons, tools, and water skins, but he kept up with the party well, despite his burdens. He welcomed the opportunity to prove himself. The older hunters treated him politely, and the younger ones for the most part ignored him, an improvement. His only real trouble was with Tup, a young man two years older than he.

Tup had bullied Lekkek all of his life and he saw no reason to stop. While the troop was ascending a steep hill during a recent hunt, Tup had deliberately tripped Lekkek with his spear, causing him to tumble and drop all his equipment. The din was earsplitting.

Bok roared at Lekkek, "You young fool! Why don't you just beat on a drum and scare away every creature on the mountain?! Or better yet, grab the attention of a lion and get yourself killed—or, more likely, somebody else! Idiot!"

Lekkek made no excuse. He knew that accusing Tup would incur even more disrespect among the men than a clumsy fall. Tup could barely contain himself with laughter. The hunting parties never had any trouble with lions, but Lekkek supposed

Bok was reminding everyone, yet again, that he once had stalked and killed one alone. Lekkek also supposed Bok's shouting had spooked more prey than his own fall, but Lekkek kept silent about this too.

Every manhood ritual hunt, including Lekkek's, began the morning after the first full moon of the initiate's thirteenth year. His mother had told him there were thirteen moons in a year and the last straddled the old and new years, as if that were an explanation of some kind. From the moment the initiate returned, trophy in hand, he would be counted as a grown man and a hunter. He could leave his mother's hut and court. In fact, he could begin a courtship immediately, by presenting his favorite with the trophy. Lekkek's fantasy about handing his trophy to Alu was interrupted once again by a buzzing sound from Ulee.

"What?"

"I said, 'Can I see what you're making?'" she repeated.

Reluctantly, Lekkek held out his upraised palms to show the moist clay shaped into the figure of a zebra.

— *3* —

Bok shook his head in disgust. The pathetic boy down by the stream was a problem, but he was just a symptom of something far worse. What was wrong with the People was deeper than one mentally defective boy. The People had fallen from greatness. They were decadent, over-refined, effete, and effeminate. They had lost the rugged simplicity of an honest life.

Bok wasn't looking forward to the celebration sure to follow Lekkek's return from his hunt, even if, as was likely, he came back dangling a mouse by its slimy tail. Bok heartily disliked all the elaborate rituals—developed by the witch woman and her predecessor—that were now followed blindly by the tribe.

Even as a boy, Bok knew the move of the People to this new home would be disastrous. His boyhood prognostications had been proven right beyond his worst fears, even though the bulk of the People blithely imagined life was better than ever. They had taken to decadence disgracefully and shamelessly. Bok would shake them out of their illusions one day. In the meantime, he disliked the intrigue in which he felt forced to engage. It was so much more distasteful than honest violence. Modern life had grown too intricate, too complex, and too fast-paced. Gone was the People's ancient rustic nobility.

Everything had been so much simpler and more honest when Bok himself was a boy. Bok remembered those times wistfully.

— *4* —

The old Home where the People had originated lay far to the north. Bok remembered vividly from his childhood the region's deep rich colors, so different from the softer beige and brown of the dry, sunny land in the south. The old Home was beautiful and lush, a land of thick forests and tall grasses; the border areas between the two, with their shade trees and open views, were as perfect for human habitation as could be imagined. Water was so abundant that water skins were scarcely needed. Streams, springs, and rivers ran all around; pools dotted the landscape. The fauna was every bit as rich as the flora.

The life of the People back then was primitive in the very best sense of the word. Indeed, to Bok's mind, no negative definition of "primitive" was possible. The People were nomads, as men were meant to be. They roamed freely throughout a large territory they knew as their own, although their ownership was not always properly acknowledged by the "Cogs," as the People called all neighboring tribes.

Amid the luxuriant vegetation, their women scarcely needed to forage beyond the nightly camp to gather sufficient roots, nuts, and fruits to satisfy all. Bok recalled the food as wonderfully flavorful and varied. As a boy, Bok had disliked the tough purple-skinned bush-butters that grew in the region. The green fruit surrounding the large pit was bitter and made him pucker his mouth or even gag. He never guessed that he one day would long for the chance to taste the green fruit again.

Fresh carrion abounded too, so even lazy men need not go hungry. The hunt was far more sport than necessity. Yet, the People indulged in the sport with gusto. The great pride of the men was to take down an elephant, a task requiring both personal bravery and teamwork. An elephant hunt brought honor to a hunter and to the whole tribe.

The elephants were largely responsible for creating the borderland, which the People enjoyed so much. Elephants penetrated well into the edges of the forest and tore apart trees with the peculiar enthusiasm they show for the task. This pruning created a pleasant mix of grasses and shade trees. The People shared in the bounty.

To be sure, their old home was not a pure idyll. Crocodiles and poisonous snakes occupied all the ponds and rivers. Hyena roamed the grasslands in packs. The hyena's taste for carrion makes it easy to underestimate them as predators. In truth, they hunt more than they scavenge. Their coordinated attack on an isolated person would be fatal. Nor was there any shortage of cats. Leopards were especially deadly. Flight from the spotted terror was all but impossible. Alone among the big cats, they would chase a person even into a tree. In fact, they dragged their victims up into trees by preference, to eat in peace.

Bok learned to respect leopards early. He once watched a boy his own age mauled by a leopard. Bok and the other boy had emerged from a grove of trees and found themselves facing the cat. Bok remembered and obeyed his elders' advice: "Stand your ground! Wave a stick! Bare your teeth!"

Whether the other boy remembered or not, he ran. The leopard's tail brushed Bok's leg, as she leapt after the running boy. The boy's life was over before Bok had time to take another breath.

His elders' advice on leopards had saved Bok, but the method wasn't foolproof. Cats hesitate to attack those who stand up to them because they are basically lazy; they don't like to fight for their food. However, they will, if they are hungry enough. So, the only sure defense against them is a group defense. Cats are also realists. Hungry or not, they won't attack a troop of men armed with spears. Like all animals, they fear the campfire too. Only people maintain a friendship with fire, and an uneasy one at that.

Bok did not regard the dangers of the old Home as a detriment. He felt the dangers were good for the character of the People. Losses weeded out weaklings and kept the People strong. As Bok often tried to explain to others, you can't eat an ostrich egg without breaking the shell first.

Beyond the ordinary dangers, including disease and accidents, the People feared the Cogs. Even more, they feared the

"Others." The Cogs were almost real People. They looked little different, they spoke in a near human way, and they could learn proper speech if they tried. The People, being generous by nature, pretended to respect these Cogs as near equals whenever they met. They made no such pretense with Others. The Others were fierce and had strangely shaped heads and brows. They sprouted body hair just thick enough to be ugly. They barked an incomprehensible language. There was no reasoning with them at all.

The young men of the People often mockingly called the Others "chimps." Yet, this taunt merely masked a well-founded fear. The Others were not animals. They made tools and weapons identical to the People's own. They lived much the same, although they seemed to scavenge a bit more and hunt less. They spent their nights by a campfire, which proved they were not just animals. They were immensely strong. Unarmed, it took two of the People to overcome one of them. It was unwise, indeed it was likely fatal, to confront one of them alone.

The Others generally kept their distance, but on rare occasions they raided the People's camp. They seldom took anything but children. The story around the campfire was that they ate children. As a young boy, Bok believed this unquestioningly. As he grew older, he began to doubt. Truth be told, he respected the Others immensely and was attracted by their robust nature. He admired their strength, and he respected their wisdom.

Bok's view of the Others was so heterodox he shared it with no one. He secretly believed the Others were the highest beings. The People, he suspected, were descended from misfits and weaklings whom the Others had cast out. Perhaps, Bok shuddered to think, the People were the result of some unnatural pairing between the Others and baboons or some other low creature. Bok felt his inferiority to the Others keenly. The rest of the People, by not grasping what to him was an obvious truth, were, he was sure, more inferior still.

An organized group defense against the Others was the only effective one. Faced by a line of armed hunters, the Others would break off any attack. They would bark and demonstrate, but then withdraw. To Bok, this was further proof of their good sense. Their raids, after all, were affairs of sport. They were far too wise, Bok believed, to risk their lives recklessly in games. The

People did not attempt counter-raids against the Other camps, but hunting parties occasionally dispatched Others caught traveling alone or in small groups.

Bok's admiration didn't extend to the Cogs. They were worse than the People. Yet there were too many of them to avoid. They regularly trespassed the fringe areas of the People's territory. Frequently, the People caught them in the act. At such times the Cogs would lie brazenly. They would insist the land was their own. Much shouting and spear waving always ensued, but rarely was there any real violence. After throwing insults and a few mud clods, the People typically pulled back to give the Cogs a chance to withdraw gracefully. The Cogs, while never admitting their offense, typically would withdraw, too, and the tribes would move on.

On other occasions, meetings with Cog tribes were arranged deliberately. This was likely to happen when an elephant had been killed by the People or by one of the Cog packs. The quantity of meat was far too large for one tribe to consume alone. Sharing the kill was an opportunity to show off the prowess of the hunters who had brought down the animal. It was good to impress the neighbors in this way, and it bred good will to accept generously a similar invitation by the Cogs. It cost little to treat them like People, for a short time.

Intertribal feasts, sometimes including three or four packs of Cogs, were festive events when the tribes traded food, tools, and even troublesome sons or daughters. There always were some youngsters who simply didn't fit in and were best sent away. As well, there was more than a little furtive miscegenation during these parties. The result often was new additions to the People, whether through adoption or pregnancy. As adults, the adopted ones were indistinguishable from other members of the People. This proved Cogs were simply inferior People, rather than something quite different. Being inferior, they mistakenly saw their best and brightest offspring as misfits and so banished them to join the superior People.

Like the Others, the Cogs could be violent. For no compre-hensible reason, they repeatedly raided the People. Usually at night, but otherwise unpredictably, they would rush suddenly out of the forest. Their hunters would raise a great hoopla while storming through the camp. By the time the People had aroused and armed themselves, the Cogs would be gone. The raiders stole tools, food, and sometimes women. They seemed to enjoy it.

In an effort to prevent more of these attacks, the People, in their turn, made periodic preemptive raids against the Cogs in a show of strength. Bok wished he had been old enough to join in one. It did seem like fun. It was dangerous fun, however. Every now and then, an attacker or defender was seriously hurt or killed.

The old Home changed forever when the Egret returned to camp. The man was Bok's grandfather, and he displayed such mental infirmity that the People mistook it for transcendent wisdom. It was he who ultimately was responsible for the Great Trek south.

Unlike modern times, when the People could recite family relationships in absurd detail, in the old Home even parentage was often a mystery—an uninteresting mystery at that. This uncertain parentage was one more aspect of a more natural lifestyle. Mortality among young adults was high, a weeding out process good for the health of the People. Accordingly, the tribe raised children in a way that was adapted to a world in which orphanhood was the norm. Children were raised in common, at least after the first year or so. All adult men were considered "uncles." All adult women were called "aunts." This was biologically accurate for the most part anyway. The actual parents, if they happened to be alive, had no special privileges or duties to their own offspring. Rather, they had duties to all the children of the People. While the mothers must have known who was whose, they rarely favored one child over another. Fatherhood was largely guesswork, if anyone troubled to guess.

True enough, People did form couples back then. Men and women often had favorite lovers. Yet there was no marriage with an attendant sense of property rights regarding children. More often than not, couples eventually broke up or one member died. New couples formed. There were no tight nuclear families. The tribe was a single family.

Therefore, it was unusual for Bok even to have recognized the man who walked into camp to be his own grandfather. His family was different. By making their difference the new norm, his family was responsible for the degeneration of the natural organic unity of the people.

As Bok could reconstruct it from the tales of his parents, the change began well before he was born, with the old chief Egret, so-called because he wore egret feathers as decoration. He had chosen a favorite woman. This was common enough, but uncommonly they raised their daughter as their own, instead of as one of the People. The girl grew into the dangerous but remarkable Alee. When she came of age, she chose a young hunter, Lek, as her consort. Lek at once was clever and a total fool. When old Egret announced he would journey away, the tribe had accepted Lek as the new Chief. Alee had been family with the old Chief, so it simply seemed right for her to be connected with the new one. This was where the tribe went wrong.

Lek and Alee had new, radical ideas. No sooner did the Egret depart on his journey, than they put their ideas into practice. Lek and Alee wore distinctive decorations far more stunning than a few egret feathers. They wore bangles, lions' teeth, headbands, and styled garments of coarsely woven cloth. They invented rituals to enhance their status, and they affected a peculiar bearing and style of speaking to create a mystique in themselves.

Instead of laughing at such foolishness, the People fell for it. Formerly, the Chief had been merely first to speak in Council. He was not considered more than a respected equal. Yet, without the slightest opposition, Lek and Alee assumed and exercised true authority over the People. Lek's early, chiefly recommendations transformed into orders. Members of the tribe even felt a special thrill when Lek spoke to them personally.

Lek and Alee seemed to be monogamous. This unnatural divergence from more typical relaxed romantic entanglements also generated some awe. Alee bore two sons: Lok, and less than two years later, Bok. There was no question of the boys' parentage. The boys were not raised in common with the other children in the natural way. They were treated by their parents as special. They were treated as special by the rest of the tribe as well.

Perhaps Lek and Alee truly were a couple in love, but Bok doubted it. He believed their alliance was an ambitious device to consolidate power in a way never tried before. Lok and Bok were very much a part of that strategy. Lek intended one of his sons to succeed him as Chief.

Bok understood Lek to be aiming for a kind of immortality. Bok didn't even try to understand women, so Alee's motives remained a mystery to him. Perhaps they were similar. Perhaps not. One thing was certain: her love of power was greater than Lek's. She enjoyed using it. The People responded to the two accordingly. Lek owed much of his influence to his undeniable, avuncular charisma. Alee evoked a fearful subservience.

The ruling couple did not abandon the consultation of a tribal council for major decisions. However, between Lek's charm and Alee's force of character, they always got their way with little or no debate.

Their personal eminence made Bok and his elder brother unlike other boys in the tribe. Each possessed an unusual sense of individuality and self-importance. Each took his status for granted. The rest of the People took the boys' status for granted too.

Then, against all expectation, the Egret returned. Bok remembered clearly the day the wizened figure wandered out of the forest. Chief Lek recognized him instantly and embraced him. Alee stood and stared, agape. Bok had never seen a man so old. His hair was as white as a cloud, and his dark face was deeply wrinkled, yet the man's body seemed spry and fit. Age was not the only unusual thing about the old chieftain. He was now festooned with more accouterments than Bok ever had seen worn by one person. Strange colorful necklaces dangled on his chest. From a leather belt hung two hide sacks and a long white tusk unlike anything Bok recognized. He carried a large animal skin sack tied to a staff that rested on his shoulder. Also hanging from the staff was a curious object of wood and skin. A single egret feather was tied to his right ear.

Lok, with his usual excessive curiosity, ran up to the old man.

"I've heard of you! You're the Egret!"

"Yes."

"You went away even though you were Chief."

"Yes."

"Why did you go?"

"I wanted to see what I had never seen. I wanted to see the end of the world."

Lok hesitated. The idea of an end to the world was new to him, as it was to Bok. This strange information began to sink in.

"Did you find it?"

"Yes, I did."

"We felt for sure you would be eaten or starve, or get killed by Cogs," complained Alee. "We never expected to see you again."

"Disappointed?"

Alee did not answer.

The tribe slowly surrounded him.

"Are you Chief again?" asked Lok.

Alee stared at him harshly, although Bok had wondered the same thing. So, he was sure, had Lek and Alee.

"Let us not discuss such things yet," he answered.

"I agree," added Alee quickly.

The Egret smiled. "Let us have food and drink. I have much to tell of importance to the People. After our meal by the fire, after the sun sets and the children are sleepy, the time will be right. Meanwhile, I have traveled far today, and I could use a nap." The Egret settled down by the trunk of a tree and shut his eyes.

Lek and Alee whispered between themselves. Then Lek organized a hunting party and set out in quest of appropriate food for a celebration. Alee divided the women, a few to attend to the children, and a larger group whom she led personally out of camp to forage.

By late afternoon, the women had collected a bountiful supply of roots, tamarind seed pods, bambara groundnuts, fruits, and sorghum. The men had luck too. They returned with a dikdik. Meat would be plentiful. The tribe hurriedly went about preparing a feast. Bok watched the resting Egret carefully from a distance. He noticed the old man's eyelids opened slightly every now and then. He wore a slight smile, as though amused by the feverish activity his arrival and instructions had spawned.

When the sun turned red, the Egret stretched as though newly awake. He looked at the display of food already laid out. The dikdik roasted on a spit over the flames. The Egret sat on a rock by the fire and arrayed his unusual belongings around him. He waved at the food. Everyone took a share eagerly.

The Egret actually ate quite sparingly, but he tasted at least a little of every item. He drank liberally from the gourds of water one of the boys had fetched for him from the nearby river. He stayed silent through the meal. The rest of the People spoke in hushed tones, except for the younger children who played in their usual way. At last, as night fell and the fire cast shadows, the Egret smiled, belched his satiation, and readied himself to speak.

The tribe looked on in wonder as the old man emptied his sacks and spread out on the ground his collection of treasures. One sack had carried marvelous tools. Most were familiar stone hand axes and scrapers, though they had been edged with uncanny skill and refinement. A few of the instruments were new to the People. Some were made of bone. One was a long needle with a hole bored into it large enough to thread a sinew.

One particularly odd item, a long thighbone with a flattened end, aroused Lok's curiosity. With his usual impropriety, he blurted, "What is this, Grandfather?"

The Egret picked up the bone and reached over his shoulder to scratch his mid-spine, an area where a man could not easily reach. This broke the serious mood as the group laughed. The Egret laughed with them. He proceeded to point out and explain other novelties. He called some barbed little curved things that were whittled out of bone "fishhooks." The People sometimes speared fish in the river, but fish were not a staple. The idea of using twine and a hook to catch them struck most of the People as unnecessarily difficult. The Egret proudly showed them "pins," and although the People were not much on clothing, they could see the point of these. They were amazed when he unwrapped a shell much like that of a snail but bigger than a man's fist. Most remarkable of all was a blade the length of a man's arm that was fashioned out of ivory. It seemed to glow softly in the firelight. The blade had a sharp tip, honed edges, and a rounded grip.

Beautiful though the artifact was, the boy Bok questioned its value on the hunt or as a tool. Ivory was much too soft to be of practical use. Not even the Cogs used such inadequate implements. The thought of the Cogs inspired Bok with a dark idea. The ivory might well be effective after all—not against game animals, but as a weapon against Cogs. A man swinging and stabbing with the blade would be formidable. The idea disturbed Bok. What if the Cogs armed themselves that way too?

With weapons so deadly, a simple pleasant raid easily could escalate into wholesale slaughter on both sides.

The Egret saved the most mysterious treasure for last. It was a skin stretched over the open end of a wooden cylinder. He tapped on it rhythmically. It gave off an eerie but curiously captivating resonance. He stopped suddenly, and the night seemed unnaturally quiet.

"What's it for?" asked Lok.

"Ah, you may regret your question, young man. In order to explain, I will need to tell a long story."

"Please tell us," prompted Lok.

"Please don't," muttered Bok to himself. Alee overheard and reached over to give Bok a warning tap on the back of his skull.

Lok's request was all the encouragement the old fellow needed.

"Many years ago, before most of you were born," the Egret began, "I began a great quest. I was determined to find the edge of the earth."

"Why, Grandfather?" Lok interrupted. Bok felt that for once, Lok had asked a sensible question.

"Because it was there."

The tribe laughed.

"Or I assumed it was there, and I wanted to prove it to myself. You see, People are . . . ," he groped ". . . more than we need to be. We have a capacity for new things. We can see things as they never were and make them different. We far surpass the Others in this way, but yet we live unassumingly, precisely as they do."

This observation irked Bok. How did anyone know how the Others think? Perhaps they were so wise they imagined new things but saw the folly in them. There is no advantage to the new when the old is fine. More likely, the People were the backward ones.

The Egret expanded on his theme. "If we can imagine more, we should be more. The earth would never have given us this capacity if she didn't intend for us to use it."

"'She?'" Bok echoed, surprised by the pronoun. The Egret smiled at Bok, but Alee tapped the back of his head again.

"It is our duty," the Egret went on. "We have a manifest destiny to be more than just balder Others. We are of the earth. We arise from the earth. We are the earth attempting to understand herself. Our destiny is to learn about the world for the world. This knowledge is what I sought."

Lok nodded seriously, but it all sounded like utter nonsense to Bok. What matters the difference between one place and another, except that one is home and the other is not? What did "destiny" mean, anyway? There is the hunt, there is the campfire, there is food, and there is sex. That is all. Anything else is meaningless.

The old man's grand vision ranged over the heads of most of the tribe, but they enjoyed the noble sound of his words and looked forward to the tale of his adventures—all but the children who, except for Lok and Bok, already had lost interest and were playing or sleeping. Most of the adults wanted to know what the edge of the world looked like.

"How did you know which way to go?" Lok asked.

The Egret smiled again, knowing Lok's sense of privilege led to direct questions. "I suspected that any way would do. If the world has an edge, I figured, it must be all around us.

"Nevertheless, I hoped that heading to the south would be the shortest journey. If the path of the sun cuts the sky evenly in two—which seemed to me then and seems to me now to be natural—and the sun's path is to our north, the home of the People, then south is the center of the world. We seem to be right in the middle of the world as to east and west. The sun looks to be the same distance away when it sets as when it rises. So, the best bet was south.

"Besides, I thought it might be dangerous to walk in the direction of the rising or setting sun. If I were younger, I would try it, though. I want to see what happens when the sun touches the poison water."

"Poison water?" asked Lok.

"The land does not quite reach the edge of the world. Beyond the land there is a vast Poison Sea," the Egret explained, "but you can see the edge of the world from the shore. I think this sea surrounds the land on all sides, though one of you should go look to be sure. Perhaps I am too old."

The Egret picked up a scraper. "I see the world as a large flat rock with an irregular surface, much like this scraper. The sun circles around it. The moon too."

"What holds the rock up?" asked Lok.

Bok was exasperated with Lok. How could the old man pretend to know the answer or even how to ask the question? Bok was irritated anyway by all this abstraction and conjecture. He didn't see how any of this mattered. The Egret, however, seemed pleased with Lok's question.

"I have some thoughts on that, boy. I'll explain them in due course. Anyway, I think the sun sinks into the sea in the west and then emerges again on the other side in the east."

"Why doesn't it go out? Fire goes out in water," argued Lok. (Bok shook his head at the foolishness of his brother.)

"I don't know. Maybe it does go out and then re-ignites on the other side. Maybe that is why it changes colors when it goes down. Perhaps someday you will be the one to find out.

"In any event, I chose to go south, and the path was dangerous. The few of you old enough to remember know that everyone believed I was leaving to meet my death. You were very nearly right. I could have died countless times."

Lok looked at his fingers and toes. For the People, any number above twenty was uncountable.

"I spent most nights in the trees—when there were trees. I also spent most of one whole day up a tree. The Cogs just to the south of here had set up a day camp right beneath my perch, just this side of the rocky stream."

"That is our territory!" shouted one of the hunters angrily.

The Egret held up his hand. "It is a long time ago. Besides, I need to tell you something about the Cogs. They are," he paused, knowing that he would not be understood, "People."

Most of the tribe didn't believe him. They didn't see how Cogs could be both People and Cogs, which is to say not People. Bok, however, both understood and believed the Egret on this point; after all, he already had reached the same conclusion. Besides, if the Cogs were People, he speculated, perhaps the Others were People too. Might they not be the "True People"?

"I'll explain what I mean in context. During my day in the tree

I remained hidden, because this group of Cogs had raided us only a few days earlier. They might have taken my presence as an act of spying or counter-aggression. I recognized one of the girls whom they had stolen from us on the raid. Something made her look up at my tree and stare back at me. I feel sure that she saw me, but she didn't give me away. Perhaps she expected a rescue attempt. If so, she was disappointed. They moved on before dark—and so did I.

"The land to the south is not just more of what is around here. It is like nothing the People have ever seen. There are rivers far more powerful than the paltry stream you call the "Big River." Some rush through great canyons, spew over huge falls, and froth up billows of white foam. Other rivers are lazy, big, and wide.

"I encountered one such river several days into my journey. For a time I was frustrated until, somewhat recklessly, I made use of a log to float across. In so doing I attracted the attention of a crocodile. I scrambled onto the opposing shore barely ahead of it. I learned how to cross other rivers more cautiously. Just to be safe, I also learned to swim on top of the river's waters. It is easy. All of you should learn."

Bok wondered how Egret possibly could call swimming safe when he himself had just mentioned the threat of crocodiles. Venturing in, or on, deep water was mindless. One might as well walk into the middle of a pride of feeding lions. He himself had no plans to step into anything deeper than water up to his ankles. Bok concluded the Egret was not just eccentric and not just foolish. He was actually stupid. He was increasingly convinced his brother Lok had inherited the same deficiency.

"The landscape grows rugged as you continue south. I encountered gorges so deep that the entire People standing on each other's shoulders, one on top of the other would not reach from the bottom to the top."

Bok tried to picture this. The People were so many as to be uncountable, even though Bok knew everyone by name. A proposal to stack them on each other's shoulders was absurd. Whoever was on the bottom would be crushed by the weight of those on top.

"The mountains are even taller than the gorges are deep. The view from the top extends farther than any of you have traveled in your lives. The first time I cleared a tall ridge, the distance beyond looked so immense I wondered if the world had an edge, after all. This didn't seem right, though, because the sun rises and sets somewhere. Where, if not at the edge? Even so, the world proved to be a far bigger place than I had anticipated. It is bigger than you yourselves can imagine even as you hear me describe it.

"Cogs are scattered throughout most of the world. I avoided the nearby ones. Yet, as the days passed and my distance from Home increased, I worried I would never reach the edge of the world without help.

"A man can live alone in one place if he makes no enemies. He can make and keep a cache of tools. He can learn where to pick fruit and where to hunt game within a small territory. But on a journey, the thing is harder. It is hard for one man to carry everything he needs. It is hard for one man to hunt or forage in new and strange lands. It is pointless, then, to hunt anything big, since you cannot carry large amounts of food with you. You need to carry water. It is troublesome to start a fire every night, and to do so risks attracting the local Cogs. Yet, a man without a fire is easy prey for the lions as he sleeps.

"I decided to risk fraternizing with Cogs, at least the more distant ones, who knew nothing of the People. My first experiment was motivated as much by hunger as by reason.

"One night while nested in a tree, I smelled roasting game. I climbed down and followed the aroma. Light flickered through the trees ahead. Peering through brush, I watched as people cooked an eland on a spit over a campfire. It smelled wonderful. Summoning up a falsely confident air, I strode boldly into camp and sat down by the fire. They were dumbfounded by my audacity. No one spoke, but all eyes were on me. I felt I should offer some gift, but I had nothing.

"'I am called the Egret. I come from beyond the gorge and river,' I told them. 'I seek the edge of the world. I have nothing to offer you, but the tale of my travel.'

"Rather to my surprise, they wanted to hear me.

"'Speak, Barbarian,' commanded an older man with authority, 'but eat first.' He spoke oddly, but he was understandable. At his direction, a piece of eland was carved off and graciously given to me.

"To be sure, the Cogs were suspicious at first, and their hunters checked the camp's perimeter to make sure I was not the advance scout of a raiding party. As soon as they satisfied themselves I posed no threat, however, they relaxed. When I added I soon would be on my way, they became downright friendly.

"The Cogs fed me and showed me their tools and their leather goods, of which they were proud. They listened with interest to the tale of my journey. They laughed at my funny words and the way I pronounced them, but they understood me most of the time. They plied me with questions about the Cog tribes between Home and their own territory. They do not use the word 'Cog' by the way. They call everyone but themselves 'Barbarians.'

"The general rule is this: the more distant from Home the Cogs are, the friendlier they become. Unfortunately, their speech grows less comprehensible with distance. Far to the south are tribes who couldn't understand me at all. We were reduced to gestures and pantomime, procedures by which I usually provoked great merriment—but I am getting ahead of myself.

"The Cog tribes differ in physical appearance too—more so than you see just among the neighbors here. In some places they are taller than we are, in others they are darker, in others they are shorter, and in some places they are oddly big in the bottom."

This observation provoked a round of laughter.

"But if you met one of these Cogs by himself, you would not be struck by his oddness. It is only when you see them in a group that it is obvious they are alike.

"Anyway, on that first night in a Cog camp, I spoke as entertainingly as I could, and they enjoyed it. I got better at these performances with each new night in a new Cog camp. It is too bad the tribes near the end of my journey didn't speak my language, because I was becoming a good storyteller by then. I found a way to remember everything better by choosing words with rhythmic patterns. But, I digress again."

He does nothing but digress, thought Bok. Can't he keep his mind on one subject?

"The eland was delicious and cooked to perfection. I enjoyed being the center of attention too. To my surprise, I also found myself an object of some esteem among the ladies. I didn't get much sleep that night on their account. From then on I made a habit of stopping in at Cog camps every night."

"I'll bet," one of the young hunters remarked, smiling.

The Egret nodded seriously. Bok gave the old man some credit for being a lecher, even though he himself didn't much care for women. He knew the taste for women was something most boys grew into, but he doubted he ever would find the lumpy misshapen female form attractive.

"My unexpected popularity was repeated wherever I went. The foreign women found me exotic and interesting. Nowhere did I lack companionship. The local men didn't seem to mind much—at least not to the degree they minded competition from each other. Maybe they didn't see me as a permanent threat. Maybe to their minds I wasn't even a real Person, so what I did and with whom didn't count for much."

Bok could see this bending of perspective confused most of the tribe. They failed to understand how anyone could think one of the People was anything other than a Person. Bok grasped the relativistic point easily. Nevertheless, he had to agree the Egret had a convoluted way of expressing himself. The man had an unclear mind.

Surprisingly, Lok's next words indicated that he understood the point too.

"So you really think the Cogs are People."

"Yes."

"But they are different from us."

"Not so different. My guess is there once was only the People and no one else. Generations ago, long before I was born, some folks split away, and these lost ones formed new tribes. The individual physical oddities of the founders became the normal look of their children and, thus, of their whole tribe. Over time they even forgot how to talk properly. They had to make up new words to replace the ones they forgot. So, the different tribes do look and sound a bit different from us, but I am convinced they are all our cousins. They themselves don't know it—but they are of the People.

"You know, 'Cog' is a fairly new word. When I was a young boy we called the neighbors 'Cognates,' an old term not used much anymore. It means 'related ones.' They must have been called this for a reason. The Cogs are related, which is to say, they are the same as us."

The People considered this, most of them skeptically.

"Wherever the Cogs come from, they made my journey possible. Depending on the kindness of strangers, my travels were usually quite pleasant. The Cogs were almost embarrassingly generous. They gave me new water skins whenever mine began to decay or leak, even though it takes much labor to make those containers. Only one time did I face real hostility."

"Did someone finally get jealous?" asked the same hunter who had joked before.

"As a matter of fact, yes. One woman took a particular liking to me."

"Go figure," muttered Alee, who was strangely unsettled by her father's romantic boasts.

"She blurted out, in front of everyone, her determination to join me on my quest to the edge of the world. This caused much dissatisfied grumbling all around. One young man in particular looked at me with fierce eyes.

"'This stranger is raiding our camp!' he complained. 'He comes with tall tales instead of spears and stones, but he is raiding us all the same.'

"The chief waved for him to be quiet, but the grumbling continued. I saw the offended fellow collude with others after the meeting broke up, and I feared for my safety, so I slipped away."

"Did you take the woman with you?" asked Lok.

"No. I slipped away from her too. Traveling at night was dangerous, of course, but I figured it was more dangerous to stay.

"There was another advantage to cavorting with the local people, and I will call them 'People' from now on. They always had an intimate knowledge of their tribal territories, so they helped me immensely with directions. They always told me the easiest routes and how to get around natural obstacles.

Sometimes they even accompanied me to the very edges of their ranges and waved goodbye to me as I trekked beyond them.

"Just as important, at every camp I learned something new. I received marvelous gifts."

"Especially from the women, no doubt," observed Alee. "Were these all gifts from the Cogs—I mean, from those 'people'?" she asked, pointing to the array of objects spread out around her father.

"Yes, most of them." He put his hand on one of the wood-and-skin baubles. "These finally, to answer young Lok's question, are 'drums.' I got them from the 'Drummer' people."

Alee was familiar with the term only as a word of action. "'Drums?' Drum? You mean pounding on a log?"

The People sometimes did this to scare predators away or to call children to return to camp.

"Very similar. The Drummer people use these instead of logs. You know how hollow logs sound loudest. Some clever one of them discovered that a skin, stretched and dried over the end of a hollow log, sounded louder yet. Perhaps the discovery was an accident. He may have been looking for a convenient place to dry the skin."

"The clever one must have been a 'she,'" commented Alee in a subtle dig at the laziness of men, who rarely did their share of such chores.

"Perhaps. Now they make drums in all sizes. Even a tiny portable one such as this is louder than a big bulky log. They use the drums to communicate at a distance with a complex set of signals, but I didn't stay with them long enough to learn which signals meant what. We can make up our own signals, of course."

None of this sounded very bright to Bok. One of the joys of the hunt was being out of communication with all the bothersome stay-in-camps. He didn't want to be so well connected, and he couldn't imagine why anyone would. The appalling thought occurred to him that everyone might carry his own drum, pounding messages as he walked. The peaceful land would be filled with noise. He shivered. "The Drummer People must be a whole tribe of dullwits," he thought.

"They call the inventor the 'First Drummer,' and the legend refers to him as a man," the Egret said with a wink at Alee.

"I'm sure a man claimed credit," she responded.

"This First Drummer was the founder of their tribe. He and his followers broke away from a parent tribe when the elders demanded they give up their drums."

"Why would they demand such a thing?" asked Lok.

"Fear. You see, the value of the drums goes beyond sending simple messages. The drums vary in sound depending on size, and tautness of the skin. The First Drummer's followers assembled a collection of drums, each tuned to the sound of the heartbeat of a particular animal. They thought they could bewitch the nearby animals by playing these drums. The spell seemed to work, because their hunts were pretty successful."

"So are ours," thought Bok. "You don't need drums to throw a spear straight."

The Egret went on, "This tactic frightened and offended most of the First Drummer's tribe. There was an intense meeting by the campfire one night. The elders felt there was something unwholesome about the use of drums in this way. They feared people as well as animals could be bewitched by the drummers. They banned drums and all other forms of witchcraft."

"I'm not certain I understand the concept of witchcraft," Alee admitted.

"I'm a little foggy on it too, but it has something to do with manipulating the..." he paused, ". . . the essence of things. It is appealing to the 'spirit' of plants and animals, and water and air and such, with spells and incantations." The Egret emphasized the word "spirit," even though it was a word about which he also felt a little foggy.

Bok understood the meaning of witchcraft easily, and he could see the danger. He was surprised that Alee had difficulty with this simple idea.

"If something works," objected Alee, "it is knowledge, and it is silly to be frightened of knowledge. If something doesn't work, it is just an error. Persisting in error is superstition."

Bok considered his mother's analysis and her definitions arrogant and reckless.

"You are a fine girl, Alee, but I think the First Drummer's parent tribe would have exiled you. The elders, as I said, bade the First Drummer never drum again. He called them superstitious old fools." The Egret winked at Alee again. "The elders exiled him. Several followers left with him, and this splinter group became the Drummer People.

"The subsequent success of the Drummer People has caused some animosity with their neighbors. The most antagonistic, even fearful, of all are their parent tribe."

"Are you sure these drums really work?" asked a skeptical Alee.

"I like your attitude, daughter, but the drums do call to the heart. I know. They called to mine."

The Egret demonstrated by pounding an oddly varied beat with an underlying, repeating theme. The tribe was fascinated. Some of the children began to dance. Even Bok found he was sorry when the Egret stopped—then he quickly ceased to be sorry and became terrified. This was true witchcraft if ever he had heard it. Calling out to People and beasts in this way was a reckless provocation of nature itself. Nature would surely punish the People.

Lek recognized an uneasiness in the group. He addressed it by changing the subject. Lek picked up the ivory blade and hefted it. "Another gift from a woman?" he asked.

"Yes. She fashioned this from an elephant's tusk as a gift for her chief. Instead of accepting it, he ordered her to destroy it. Again, her tribe called her art witchcraft."

"The world to the south is full of fools!" exclaimed Alee.

"The world everywhere is full of fools, daughter."

Bok took a second look at the blade. He too worried this might be witchcraft. The reshaping of the tusk was bound to annoy the elephants, somehow. They understood being hunted, but they might grow angry at this kind of exploitation.

"I have digressed again," said the Egret.

Of course, thought Bok.

"The land gets very dry as you go south. One day I stood on the edge of a wide dry plain. No people lived on the plain, and for good reason. There was grass, but it was sparse, brown, and crunched under my feet. Despite two full water skins when I started out, I ran out of water quickly in this wasteland. I squeezed some moisture out of a few roots when I could find them, but before long I was in trouble. I could see inviting hills in the far distance. They looked cool and damp, but they didn't seem to get any closer as I walked.

"Two lionesses took an interest in me on the fifth day. They didn't attack but they followed me. In a way, this was a good sign, because lions don't like to go thirsty either. I figured I was not too far from water. Still, when night came I was frightened they would be on me. To discourage them, I started a campfire.

"Usually this is a tedious task, but not this time. The kindling-grass ignited quickly. So did the grass by my feet. So did the grass beyond that. The fire spread beyond any hope of containing it, and it began to move, picking up speed as it went. Soon it was ripping across the plain, blown by a wind it created by itself. The lions disappeared, all right. The fire raced away from me, or I would have been incinerated in moments—but it didn't ignore me either. The flames crept back, slowly but relentlessly toward me.

"I ran. The flames followed, and the air was filled with smoke. Breathing was painful, and I coughed out black soot. In the distance I could see a rocky outcrop in the plain. Somehow, though slowed by bursting lungs to a forced walk, I reached the rock ahead of the flames. I climbed up on top and waited. The fire swept around me. I choked and gasped from the smoke. The rocks became almost unbearably hot, but the flames scarcely touched me. I was singed a little from a few licks I failed to dodge, but nothing worse happened to me.

"The fire moved on. I still was anything but safe. I was so dehydrated that I couldn't contemplate continuing. Without water I was finished.

"More in desperation than hope, I explored my rocky perch. At the base of the outcrop was a downward sloping cavity, barely big enough for a man to crawl into. By the rank smell, I could tell it was some animal's home. With any luck, the animal was somewhere else. The recess smelled of dampness. I slithered in headfirst on my back, so far that only my toes stuck out. A drop of water fell on my face. I pushed in further. The next drop landed in my mouth. Waiting for each drop to fall was torture, but it saved my life. I must have stayed there for hours. Slithering out was less easy than slithering in. For a time I thought I was trapped, but I eventually extricated myself.

"I set off again southward. My feet burned as I walked on the hot blackened grass.

"At last, the hills seemed noticeably closer. Eventually they were underfoot. Beyond the foothills were mountains. At the bottom of the first mountain I found a real water supply. It was just a trickle, but it was enough from which to drink properly. It filled my water skins too."

"Did you find more Cogs, I mean people, in those mountains, Grandfather?" asked Lok.

"Not the sort you mean."

"What other sorts are there?"

The Egret raised a finger to indicate Lok should be patient.

Bok's attention was piqued. He had an inkling of the answer. If he was right, the old man might not be so thoroughly stupid after all.

"My second day in the mountains, toward dusk, I set up a campfire. I was bent over, scrounging for more kindling and branches, and when I stood up, I found myself face to face with an Other. Twenty and ten more of them stood in back of him. I never heard a single one of them approach."

The higher mathematics of twenty and ten was a new challenge, but Bok worked with it. He held his hands by his feet for the twenty. Then he spotted the feet of the boy next to him and, furrowing his brow, he attained a grasp of the number, but at the cost of giving himself a headache. He noticed his brother Lok do the same, but with a smile on his face. The rest of the tribe simply took the expression as equivalent to "countless."

"Did you run?" Lok asked.

"No, though I was sorely tempted. They weren't blatantly hostile like the Others around here. They were curious rather than aggressive. They had never seen a real Person before. They weren't sure what I was. They didn't find my appearance very frightening. Besides, I was only one, and they were many.

"The fellow I faced sprouted hair streaked with gray. He looked me up and down. He then lifted his finger and poked me in the face. The poke hurt, but at least he didn't take out an eye.

I just stood placidly. His nose crinkled as though he were smelling me. After my long hike, I'm sure my aroma didn't require a high degree of olfactory sensitivity to be detectable. Finally, he lost interest. He walked past me and sat by the fire. The others followed him, except for the children who continued to surround me. The adults in the group glanced at me frequently; I suppose to make sure I didn't harm the children. The young prodded me playfully. This didn't bring any objection from their parents. The whole bunch was remarkably docile."

"Are you suggesting the Others are People too, Grandfather?" asked Bok.

Nearly everyone took this as a joke. Alee tapped him again, taking his question for sarcasm. The Egret, however, looked at Bok with a new eye, as though he recognized an open mind.

"Maybe. I'm not sure, but I think so."

Some of the tribe laughed at this, but Bok could tell he was serious.

"I slowly walked over to the fire and sat down amid the Others. The Others carried a substantial quantity of roots and nuts. At first they didn't offer any to me, and I didn't ask. Then one tossed a small tuber to me."

"A female, of course," guessed Alee, with a roll of her eyes.

"Yes. I caught it and began to chew on it. Then another of the group tossed a nut my way. When I caught it, there was a grotesque sound from several of them. I realized it was laughter. Feeding me in this way amused them, much as children are amused to throw a nut or berry to a baboon or a meerkat."

"Please don't tell me you enjoyed their women too," teased Alee.

"But, you see . . ." the Egret hesitated before answering, "I did."

This evoked groans of revulsion around the campfire. Bok was not one of the groaners. He leaned forward with interest. To his mind, this was the first useful information the old man had spoken. Bok already secretly theorized the best thing that could happen to the People would be an infusion of blood from the powerful Others. He was sure they were more intelligent as well as stronger. You could be sure they didn't waste their energy on senseless travels to the edge of the earth or on pointless speculations about the nature of the world. The world is what it is. Their race was the natural master of the world.

Bok's theory of eugenics was boosted by his personal aesthetics. Bok knew most boys his age combined an antagonism to girls with a secret attraction. Not he. To his mind, the women of the People were much too unmanly. They bulged in the wrong places and lacked proper muscular definition. One hunter, who later died of an infected wound, already had introduced Bok to another way. This was a practice mildly frowned upon in the tribe, so the dalliance had remained their secret. Bok understood the duty to procreate, to be sure, but except for this purpose, he felt the affection he had experienced with the hunter was something nobler. The women of the Others, however, were much less objectionable than those of the People. Their females were muscular and lean, with scarcely any softness to them. Their body hair helped hide their feminine features.

The Egret continued, "The Other women approached me, you see. It really was unwise to argue under the circumstances, outnumbered as I was. None of them understood a word I spoke. They might have been offended by any physical refusal," the Egret added as an excuse.

"Didn't they find you ugly?" asked Bok. The tribe laughed. Bok's inversion of the proper question was mistaken for a taunt. The Egret, however, was impressed by the boy's ability to shift perspective.

"You would think so, but apparently not. Our faces look something like the faces of their children before they get those heavy brows. Our heads are larger compared to our bodies; this is like their children too. I think they found me cute."

"Don't we all," commented Alee.

"I would like to think so."

"Did they give you gifts too?" asked Alee.

"Yes. One very important gift in particular." The Egret tapped a small unopened pouch. "I'll show you this soon."

"Despite their acceptance of me in their camp, the Others took no notice of me when I left. This was a pattern repeated at other camps."

"You did this more than once?" asked Alee with dismay.

The Egret smiled, "One slip only is forgivable?" he asked her. When she did not respond, he answered simply, "Yes. Anyway, I continued my journey through an extensive range of mountains. Eventually I reached a territory where I found no more trace of Others. More days of hiking passed and still there were no more Others."

"What about Cogs . . . I mean, people?" asked Chief Lek.

"Not a one, he answered. "Then, one day I ascended a ridge and saw the end of the world. The world didn't end with a big cliff, as I had anticipated. It ended in a huge expanse of water. The water extended out to where it met the sky. I figure the dome of the sky must seal the edge or the water would pour out, but I don't really know. Perhaps someday, one of you can float out on a log or something and touch the sky for yourself where it meets the sea."

Bok believed the Egret had just urged suicide. Crossing a river on a log was dangerous enough. He noticed the Egret, reckless though he was, hadn't attempted it.

"I redoubled my speed to reach the sea, but it took time. The water was further away than it appeared from the ridge. I walked many hard days. Descending from the mountains, I found myself in a pleasant land of rolling hills. The land became flatter as I neared the shore. In the whole transmontane region there was a richness of game and growth, but there was no one to hunt or gather it. I was all alone."

"Really? Are you sure it is empty?" asked Lek again.

Bok looked at his father with alarm. He hoped the man wasn't thinking of leading the People there. The Chief always disliked the skirmishes with the Cogs, even though that is the way of the world.

"Quite sure, at least in the region I visited. Anyway, one day I at last stood by the great water. It was poison."

"How do you know?" asked Lek.

"I drank it and nearly died. The taste is rich and will make you gag. I think I understand why. It is the sun. The sun sinks into the sea at night. Its flames poison the water.

"You asked what holds up the world, boy," he addressed Lok. "I think I understand. The universe is a big hollow roundness, like the inside of an ostrich egg. The eggshell rotates, carrying the stars along with it. The sun and moon rub along the inside of the shell too. The water, naturally, always stays at the bottom. It fills up the egg about halfway. The land, sort of like a big yolk, floats on the sea in the middle, just like a stick floats in water."

"But dirt sinks in water," objected Lok.

"I think the poison water of the sea is different. You may be right, though. The ground may reach all the way to the bottom, but then there would need to be tunnels for the sun and moon to pass through."

"I see," nodded Lok. "What is on the other side of the eggshell?"

"I don't know. But maybe the stars are holes. So if you float out to touch the sky, maybe you can look through a hole and see."

Both Lok and Lek nodded their heads. Bok was impatient. He wanted to hear more about Others. This talk of the universe was useless. He tried to divert the talk to something at least a little more practical.

"Are there snakes and crocodiles in this poison sea, or can nothing live in it?" Bok asked.

"Oh, there are fish in the sea. I could see them. There are big snail things too. I got this shell from the sea," Bok explained as he picked up the conch. "I don't know what else lives in there. So, the fish must have some way of surviving the poison, just as insects can live on spoiled meat."

"Surely, the fish must be poison to eat," suggested Lek.

"I do not know. I did not wish to find out."

"Why do you think the land forms a yolk in the middle of this big egg?" ask Lok.

The question struck Bok as ludicrous. Either the land was like a yolk or it wasn't. "Why" was a question without meaning in such matters.

The Egret answered as though the question were sensible. "I believe that pure substances seek each other. Water always flows downhill seeking the sea. Land, being densest, collects at the center." He picked up a handful of dirt and let it fall. "Land always seeks land. Air lifts to the sky. The fire is higher yet. Most substances are not pure. They are mixtures of these other things, and so they have mixed qualities, but I have found a piece of earth that is pure."

He picked up the small unopened pouch.

"This is the present that an Other woman gave me after our, uh, encounter. To her it was just a toy, but to me it was a revelation about the nature of the world."

The Egret opened the little pouch, and out tumbled a small black pebble. The Egret passed it to Bok, who held it between his thumb and forefinger. It looked unremarkable to him. It was harder than most pebbles, but not much more so than any good piece of flint. It had a crack running across it. The pebble offered no revelation to Bok. He passed it to Lok.

Lok looked closely. He pulled the pebble apart at the crack. The Egret smiled. Lok fit the two pieces together again and was surprised when they stuck. He passed it back to his grandfather.

The Egret also pulled on the edges of the lodestone pebble until it came apart. He then held the two pieces on the ground a finger's width apart. He released them. The two pieces leapt together. Lok was fascinated. Bok had to admit this was unusual. Still, it was just a useless curiosity. It was just a sticky pebble.

"You see, this, I think, is a pure substance," explained the Egret. "Like seeks like. In the same way, water seeks water. Earth seeks earth. Most things, being mixtures of pure substances, don't react as strongly as this black stone. They do react weakly though. That is why you fall down and smoke rises. You are mostly earth and smoke is mostly air or fire."

"Why did you come back?" asked Bok. The question, unrelated as it was to the matter under discussion, sounded impertinent, but the Egret smiled indulgently. "You had a lot to interest you there," Bok added to soften the question.

"I returned because of you."

"Me?"

"Yes. Not you personally, young man. All of you." He gestured to the whole People with a wave. "I learned so much, I thought someone should know. If what I learned dies with me, there is nothing gained."

Bok thought there was nothing gained in any event—other than his information about the southern Others.

"Now I am tired," the Egret said suddenly. "We will talk more tomorrow." He stood up and found a place in some grass beneath a tree and rested. There was much hushed chatter around the campfire, but one by one the members of the tribe joined him in sleep.

The Egret didn't talk more the next day. He died during the night, and the People buried him respectfully.

Bok knew the Others handled their dead differently, and Bok approved. They simply disposed of them in a remote spot. The People sometimes encountered their remains. Often the bodies were mutilated in a way suggesting cannibalism, but no one was really sure. Bok always disputed the claim when it was made. He blamed the mutilations on scavengers. It was too bad the Egret had died before he could answer more of their questions.

The Egret's re-appearance and his revelations solidified his daughter Alee and her consort Lek further as leaders of the People. His grandchildren, Lok and Bok, shared an increased aura of inherited privilege. The lodestone and the ivory blade, carried proudly by Lek, enhanced his appearance and his reputation.

Bok's suspicion that Lek contemplated moving the whole tribe south was backed by mounting evidence. Over several weeks, Lek and Alee oversaw a stockpiling of goods to a degree that interfered with the daily mobility of the People. In particular, they ordered the fashioning of water skins. These containers seldom lasted long—Bok knew they were intended for near-term use. They probably were to make possible a journey across the dry grassland such as the Egret had described. Alee also set the women to making rope, beyond any possible utility. Bok knew rope was very good for setting snares or tying bundles, but he could see no usefulness for such a quantity as the People were producing. He was sure it had something to do with the trip.

Bok was convinced his parents had over-reached themselves. To the People, Home was home. Convincing them to leave would be well nigh impossible, even for Lek and Alee. There was a limit to obedience.

Bok underestimated his parents, especially Alee. The conspiracy they hatched was both impressive and reckless.

Alee didn't stop at logistical preparations; she further altered the natural social order with remarkable speed and success. Even as a boy, Bok understood she deliberately was breaking the unity of the People, perhaps in order to reduce the chance they could turn against her with one voice. Alee met surprisingly little resistance. Among the younger folk, she interfered in romances. She encouraged some and discouraged others; by giving her blessing to the former, she formalized the couplings in a new way. Breaking with the People's communal tradition, Alee also made a point of establishing and remembering who was the offspring of whom. She promoted the peculiar arrangements of the royal family as a model proper for all, instead of as the aberration it really was. She even devised color-coded amulets to distinguish one matrilineal family from one another. The People took to all this readily, especially to the decorations. To Bok's irritation, they acted as though it were a pleasant game.

Alee wanted Lok to follow Lek as Chief when the time came. She always favored Lok over Bok. One day he ventured to ask her why.

"Why do you want Lok to be Chief?"

"Are you really asking why I don't want you to be Chief?"

Rather to his own surprise, he realized he meant precisely this. Bok didn't concede the point, however. He stood silently.

"Well, no matter. Lok is older. What is more, he sees beyond the trees to the grasses on the other side."

Bok grasped the meaning of the metaphor, and he didn't like the implicit suggestion that he was short-sighted by comparison.

"The People will need these qualities in the years ahead. Listen to me, Bok, because I want you to know I don't underrate you. You, too, are clever, but you are an amazing contradiction. Your most innovative thoughts are also the most reactionary. Right now, the People need change. The time will come when they need to conserve and preserve what they have achieved. Then you will be the man for the job."

Though this speech annoyed Bok, he learned for the first time that Alee thought of him as Chief material. He gathered that if something were to happen to Lok, she would prefer him to anyone else in the tribe.

Bok rather fancied the thought of being Chief one day. It would be for the good of the People. The People had strayed too far from nature and from their old-fashioned tribal values. He could restore things to their proper shape.

Bok was unimpressed by Lok's potential as a leader. His brother was older, but his mental deficiencies should disqualify him for the chiefdom.

One night Alee sprang a new surprise on the People. Alee picked up the Egret's drums and played a repetitive beat. One of the younger women, clearly coached ahead of time, sang rhythmically a wish for success among the hunters the next day.

Bok was appalled. At Alee's hands, the People had descended into witchcraft. More appalling yet, the performance was a hit. To Bok, the singer sounded like a wounded hyena, but his was a minority view. By and large, she entranced the tribe.

The drums seemed to work their magic. The next day the hunters found an impala with a broken leg and took it easily. Moreover, Alee and the women found honey. Bok cynically wondered if Alee had found it earlier and led the women to it the morning after the drum "song."

The drums became an evening ritual to which the People looked forward. Even when hunts went badly or someone was hurt, the People wondered how much worse things would have been without the drums. Besides, they may not have been played quite right. When this possibility was raised, Alee assigned another of the women to play the drums. Alee continued to coach her and helped develop the rhythms and songs.

Alee spiced up the nightly ceremonies even more in following days. She coordinated dances involving men and women with the drum songs. These further bent the music to magical ends. Alee used the drums and dances in a "Rain Ceremony." It took several tries for her to get it right, but it worked eventually (rain came).

On their own, but encouraged by Alee, the celebrants added flourishes such as paint to their faces. They made and wore costumes. Alee took to using a staff with an elephant's tail as a symbol of her power. Campfire songs quickly grew more sophisticated. These came to be sung at other times too. Some songs spoke of romance. Some spoke of real events in the lives of the People. Some songs spoke of the Egret. The younger men seemed to prefer songs of adventure and raunchy humor.

All of this felt seriously wrong to Bok. Catastrophe hovered in the air. Something strange was afoot with Alee during the night. After most of the People had nodded off, Alee would disappear for long periods. This was extremely dangerous. (People spent nights together by a campfire for a reason.) He overheard Lek and Alee arguing once beyond the edge of camp. Bok couldn't make out the details, but he caught her insistence on "going" somewhere. Lek wanted to join her, but she said he was needed at camp, and he only would get in her way. This was the only time in his life Bok had heard them disagree about anything. The two always presented a united front to the tribe. Needless to say, Alee got her way, and Lek remained at camp. He always remained at camp when she vanished, but he would pace until she returned. Bok didn't know what to make of it, until the day of the big showdown.

The People were encamped by the Big Rock, one of Bok's favorite spots. It was a clearing around a flat stone as big as a rhinoceros. As the sun began to sink toward the horizon, a fire was lit at the base of the rock and Alee climbed on top to play the drums. This was the first time she had picked up the instrument in weeks. In the deepening night, the flickering pattern of light on Alee and the rock created an especially eerie effect. A young woman, generally regarded as the prettiest of the People, joined her on the rock. She sang a spooky song about ancestors. Alee did not call for dancing and the song did not inspire it.

During the song, men with spears emerged out of the forest and brush on all sides. Bok looked around him. This was no simple raid. The People were surrounded by a coalition of all the neighboring Cog tribes. There were more people than Bok ever had seen in one place. For some reason, they didn't attack. They stood silently while the girl finished her song. Normally, the arrival of strangers would have set the men of the People scrambling for weapons, but the lack of reaction by the two women on the rock confused them. They sat uncertainly, waiting for events to take their course. Bok began to appreciate the power of song to set a mood. He silently condemned it as yet more witchcraft. He waited for the neighbors' attack.

The music stopped. In the ensuing silence no one moved but Lek. Chief Lek climbed atop the rock and stood next to Alee and the singer. In his body paint, illuminated by the light of the flame, he looked otherworldly and enormous. He withdrew his ivory knife from his belt and pointed it at one stranger, whom he recognized as Chief of a neighboring tribe. He then laughed loudly, an inappropriate outburst perhaps intended to scare the visitors. It certainly scared Bok.

In a voice betraying the proud stance of its owner with a quaver, the neighbor chief accused, "You practice . . . sorcery!" It was, for the Cogs, a poorly understood concept, but a powerful one connecting with their fears on some deep level.

"Who calls our practices sorcery?" Lek demanded.

"All of us. We hear you. Some of us have witnessed your rituals from a distance when you camped in our territory."

Bok couldn't remember camping in anyone else's territory. The fellow was confused about this detail.

"We did not fully understand what you did until the trees whispered to us at night."

Bok looked at Alee smiling on the rock. This had something to do with where she went at night. It was more of her trickery. Had she spread rumors among the Cogs? Did she whisper to them from trees as though she were the spirits of the trees? Why? The People might all be killed because of her foolishness.

"The trees? They do not complain to us," responded Lek with a hint of disdainful laughter in his voice.

"No," said the neighbor chief seriously. He quavered with both fear and anger. "You enslave them with your sorcery, just as you bewitch animals to jump into your fire without a hunt and you draw rain from the sky. You corrupt our young people who imitate your sounds on logs and dance in your foul way. You do more than corrupt them. You steal them. Many of our children go missing."

"Children always go missing. They aren't here."

"No!" the neighbor chief exploded. "The trees told us you eat them! You are worse than the Others!"

This accusation surprised Bok. Had Alee really told them this? Why? It was nonsense, of course, even though he agreed with the charge of sorcery. He could see most of the People were deeply offended by the accusation of cannibalism.

"Foolishness! As for sorcery, if that is what we do, we must be capable of bewitching you, too—so it would be unwise to take any action against us," warned Lek. "We can as easily keep game safe from your spears, as cause them to leap into our fire."

There was some snickering among the People, who knew the drum songs didn't work in this way. The neighbors mistook the laughter for self-confident arrogance.

"We have considered this," he answered, again quite seriously. "Therefore we will do you no harm unless you stay. You must go."

"Go?"

"The trees tell us you must go, or they will stop producing fruits and seeds, the grass will not grow, and the hunts will be unsuccessful."

"Perhaps I can make all that happen to you anyway. I will curse the land if we are harmed."

"I said you will not be harmed, but you must go. Go beyond the beyond. Go."

Bok could tell the neighbor Chief was unsure of himself. So, too, many of the armed men surrounding the campsite showed real fear. They looked far readier to flee than fight. Even outnumbered as the People were, Bok felt a defiant posture was all that Lek needed to drive the enemy away, especially if he agreed to refrain from sorcery. Here was a grand chance to restore sanity to the People. To his surprise and dismay, Lek did just the opposite.

"We will go."

The Cogs seemed as surprised at the capitulation as anybody.

"There are conditions," Lek cautioned. "We will leave these drums for you. You must play them every night until the next full moon to ensure our safe journey. If you do not play them, I will know and I will curse the land."

"The trees will not like it."

"They will understand. They told you to make us go. By playing the drums you fulfill their wishes. They will be angry if you do not play."

The neighbor Chief took a deep breath. "We will beat on them."

"You, personally."

The man looked terrified, but he announced courageously (under the circumstances), "I will do it."

Bok saw immediately the seed Lek had installed in the neighboring peoples. Lek and Alee truly were a corrupting influence. Bok knew once they started to play they would continue. They would add songs and rituals and wrap them in abstract notions. A new world was taking shape and people would march right into it to the beat of a drum. Lek tossed the drums to the neighbor Chief. The man caught them but held them as though they were a pair of coiled snakes.

The Cog army withdrew.

Lek held a council. The tribe was in turmoil. The prospect of leaving Home excited some, dismayed others, and frightened all.

"The People will make a new Home," Lek assured them, "a better one for our children. There is no choice for the People. Each of you individually, though, has a choice."

This statement shocked Bok. To distinguish the interests of individuals from those of the tribe, even to elevate the former above the latter, was the worst form of decadence. People were of the People or they were nothing.

"I want no one with us who is not personally committed to the journey and a bold new future. I'm sure any of you would be accepted into the neighboring tribes, at least the ones who live beyond the folks who visited us tonight."

Bok couldn't believe what he was hearing. Chief Lek was condoning treason.

"Should you choose this path, your lives will not change much. The Cogs live much the same as we always did. The Egret was right when he told us this. For the rest of you, a new and exciting adventure awaits."

Lek's own enthusiasm convinced Bok, if he had harbored any doubt, that Lek and Alee had manipulated the entire situation to force them into exile. Without the push from the neighbors, the move would have been a hard sell.

"Those of you who choose to join the Cogs stand by that tree. The rest of you, stay by the fire."

Nearly half the People assembled by the tree, including most of the children. From the way they were herded to the tree, Bok suspected Alee had prearranged their exclusion so as not to be a burden on the journey. Several healthy, strong adults stood and joined them under the tree. Bok was tempted, but family loyalty and the prospect of eventually becoming Chief dissuaded him; he stayed by the fire. Fewer than what the Egret had termed "twenty and ten," mostly young adults, remained by the fire.

Lek was unperturbed by the division.

"We start at daybreak," he announced.

There were some grumbles in the morning about the quantity of luggage to be carried. Tools, spears, ropes, clothes, food, and water skins weighted down the travelers. The people left behind were disgruntled, too, at being stripped bare, but Lek paid no mind to their complaints. Bok was surprised to see a new set of drums hanging from a strap on Alee's shoulder. Someone had manufactured a replacement, further proof of her scheming.

The trip south was more dangerous for the group than it had been for the Egret, who traveled alone. The migrating People alarmed other tribes in a way the Egret by himself had not.

Once past the immediate neighbors, who quietly let them pass due to their superstitious fear, the People faced suspicion and hostility. There were no easy welcomes at the campfires of strangers. Rather, the People were challenged repeatedly. Bloodshed was narrowly avoided several times, and then only by Lek's firm assurance that the People were just passing through and would not intrude again. Lek understood. He would have responded the same to a strange tribe appearing in his territory.

Before the first moon cycle had passed, Lek acknowledged a better defensive capability was needed. Lek recruited from among the hunters a core of six, whom he dubbed "warriors." All the men of the People, and the women too, if need be, were prepared to war for the tribe, of course. Nevertheless, Lek decided there was something to be gained by training specialists. The skills of the hunter were to some degree applicable to war, but Lek felt there was something fundamentally different about battling other humans. Animals do not employ deception and stratagem beyond stalking and running. They do not plan elaborate ambushes and counterattacks. People do. Lek trained his corps in the philosophy and tactics of war.

The warriors doubled as Lek's special guard. This troubled Bok, who saw in them a tool as effective for coercing the People as for battling outsiders. Lek's preparations, however, proved farsighted. The warriors proved their worth when the People reached the Great River.

The River was flooding. Wading across was impossible, and crocodiles made swimming inadvisable. Few of the people knew how to swim anyway. Bok assumed the journey was over.

Alee and Lek, however, obviously had given this problem some forethought. They assembled a curious set of tools. They lashed hand axes to clubs. With these composite tools, they were able to chop quite large fallen branches into manageable lengths. Alee directed the weaving of rope around the branches. A raft slowly took shape. Alee tied one end of an especially long rope to a tree that grew on the very edge of the river.

The raft was nearly complete when the local tribespeople showed up. The men of the People, except for the warriors, who were missing, fell back in a semicircle protecting the raft on which the women and youngsters continued to work. The locals shouted and threatened from the bushes as they sized up the intruders.

Bok assumed the local Cogs would attack as soon as they ascertained they had the People outnumbered. Bok wondered why Lek just didn't let them have a woman or two. With those victory prizes in hand, the locals almost certainly would allow the rest of the People to escape. Resistance was foolish.

Despite his opinions, Bok picked up a spear and joined in the line alongside the adult men. Seeing this, Lok abandoned his work and did the same. Lek did not correct them. Bok assumed the scene was set for bloodshed, maybe a massacre.

The Cogs were in no hurry to attack. The porcupine formation of the People was not an inviting target. Emerging from and then retreating to their cover in the bushes, the locals demonstrated and whooped a victory they had not yet achieved. Still, Bok was sure they would soon work up their courage and charge. Bok could hear their women and children, egging on the men.

Alee tapped Lok on the shoulder, and handed him the coil of rope that was tied to the tree on one end. Lok withdrew from the line. Bok heard splashing. Glancing over his shoulder, Bok was amazed to see Lok swimming across the river. Whatever Alee's plan for Lok was, Bok hoped he would make it.

As the men held their formation, the raft slipped into the water. Bok glanced back again. The long rope stretched completely across the river. Lok was on the opposite bank where he had tied off his end of the rope. Pushing long poles against the river bottom while at the same time pulling on the rope, the women propelled themselves and the few children across the river on the raft. The locals grew quiet as they saw what was happening. They then began to jabber. Bok could hear the anger in their voices. He tensed himself. Attack was imminent.

The Cogs rushed from the brush. Light javelins, unlike anything Bok had seen before, suddenly shot from the upper branches of trees and struck down four of the Cogs. Two others were narrowly missed. The attackers, carried forward by their own momentum, engaged the line of the People at the riverbank. Lek's warriors, each armed with another javelin, dropped from the trees and attacked the Cogs from the rear. Terrified by this turn of events, the Cogs broke and scrambled back to the bushes. Two more fell in the retreat. Lek withdrew his ivory blade and, with a nonchalance that both surprised and impressed Bok, he finished off the wounded attackers who lay moaning on the riverbank. Two of the People had been jabbed by opposing spears, but both remained on their feet.

Bok was exhilarated by the battle. He walked forward and plucked out of the dirt one of the light javelins, which had missed its target. A small stone tip had been fixed to it. It was a superior and smart weapon. Unwilling to credit Lek, Bok wondered which of the warriors had invented it.

Having deposited the women and children on the far shore, Alee poled and Lok pulled the raft back across the river. The raft slipped onto the near shore.

Bok and the men of the People began to board. A rustle in the brush caused the warriors to form a defensive screen. A solitary young woman, scarcely more than a girl and rather dirty, emerged from the woods. For some reason she had not joined the enemy's retreat. Perhaps, Bok speculated, the opponent tribe was not really her people. Perhaps she was booty from a raid on yet some other bunch of Cogs, and she was eager to escape.

The young woman said something unintelligible, though Bok had the feeling he might make sense of it if he listened hard enough. Alee held out her hand. The woman hurried past the warriors and climbed aboard the raft. The warriors boarded too. Lek joined them after untying the rope from the tree on the near shore. Alee shoved off. With the rope now tied at only one end, the raft swung downstream, but Lok was able to pull them slowly toward the opposite bank.

Bok didn't enjoy the trip. The portion of the raft where he stood tipped deep into the water under the combined off-center weight of its passengers. Bok wondered if he should have learned to swim, after all. He decided against it when he noticed a crocodile lazily following the progress of the raft.

The People, reassembled on the far bank, tended to their wounded as best they could and resumed their march south.

Once past the growth flanking the river, the land they entered was dry. Beyond that it was dryer still. Trees were sparse. The grasses seemed to be shorter and browner with each step taken. The native peoples were sparser as well. There was some jeering from them at a distance, but none mounted a challenge to the People such as the one faced at the river.

The fact people were here at all, Bok reasoned, meant someone else had worked out the raft scheme once before. This thought comforted him. He didn't like crediting Lek and Alee with anything so original. To his mind his parents were, fundamentally, fools. His mother was wicked, and Lek knew no better than to obey her. If they hadn't defiled nature with their drums, songs, and sorcery, the People still could be residing happily in their old Home.

Eventually they reached land where there were no trees at all. A nearly level expanse of brown grass stretched out ahead of them as far as they could see. Bok assumed this was the dry plain where the Egret nearly had met his end from thirst and fire. The remaining water skins of the tribe were less than half full, which was troubling. Lek ordered them to push on. There was one good sign: giraffes could be seen in the distance. Though too far to hunt, their presence meant water was up ahead somewhere.

That night Lek forbade a campfire. He recalled the disaster that nearly befell the Egret. The night was eerie. Warrior sentries rotated duty to scare away any night predators. They were scant assurance to Bok. He was sure they could see no better than he could.

Bok listened to Alee as she coached the strange girl they had picked up at the river. Alee had taken her under her own personal protection. She was slowly teaching the girl to speak properly. Alee called the girl "Oho." Alee had chosen the name after trying unsuccessfully to reproduce a gargling noise with a click at the end, like the breaking of a twig, made by the girl as she pointed to herself. After some remonstrance, the girl accepted the name Oho.

Oho, who at first had been quiet and calm, was curiously agitated at the campsite. Sleepless much of the night, she peered into the distance behind her, though all anyone could see was a black landscape beneath a starry sky. She repeated this behavior the second night.

On the third day on the plain, the People suffered their first fatality. The wound a young hunter named Kiv received at the Great River battle had festered. He went feverish and died during the night. With water running low, Lek was unwilling to linger for a proper burial. Instead, Alee played on the drums and placed a spear with a fire-hardened tip in the fallen hunter's hands. The People moved on. Many of them were bothered by this, but Bok, for once, approved. The Others didn't bury their dead. To do so was unnatural.

Oho ran up to Lek and jabbered something. Lek looked at Alee in exasperation. Oho spoke more slowly to Alee and pointed to the rear.

"I think she's saying we're being followed."

Lek dispatched his two swiftest warriors to reconnoiter to the rear. When the warriors returned they confirmed Oho's report. Ten armed men were tracking the People. One of them carried a warrior's javelin, which he could have gotten only from the site of the Great River battle. They appeared to be out for revenge.

One of the warrior scouts suggested doubling back and attacking the trackers after dark. As a bonus, after the victory the People could take the enemy's water.

Lek considered the recommendation but overruled it.

"This could be the very plan of the enemy. If we turn back to fight them, they can fall back further. By merely evading us they will exhaust us and our water. They won't have to fight us. They can let thirst do the work."

"We must do something," the scout objected.

"We will." Although Lek smiled, he didn't like the insubordination of the warrior's remark. The warrior picked up on the displeasure, and he responded with a curt nod of obedience.

The People pushed south with renewed vigor and purpose. The brown grassland seemed endless. Bok understood what the Egret meant when he said the distant cool blue hills seemed to retreat ahead. The People ran out of water before they ran out of grass. After another day of thirsty hiking, a rocky outcrop became visible far in the southwest.

Lek and Alee conferred. In country this large it was possible to be far off the Egret's previous path. Alee noted they hadn't encountered any of the Drummer People. Unless something had happened to the Drummer tribe, the People had missed them somehow. Nevertheless the outcrop ahead might be the one where the Egret found water. Although the People scarcely could afford the extra distance of the tack if their guess proved wrong, Lek gambled and directed the People to the outcrop.

Two of the People fainted on the march, and none of the tribe was happy. Despite their entreaties, Lek refused to let any of them drop their burdens of ropes and tools even though they barely had strength to carry themselves.

The gamble paid off. Lek found the narrow cave the Egret had described at the base of the rock. It was occupied on this occasion, but by nothing more frightening than an aardvark. The blood from the animal and the dripping water in the cave were enough to refresh the People. At twilight, Lek started a small fire on the top of the outcrop, away from the flammable grass. The aardvark was the first freshly cooked meat they had eaten since the beginning of the grassy plain. The water flow in the cave was insufficient to fill even a single water sack during the night, but the hills ahead at last looked closer.

A sentry pointed to shadows on the horizon. Bok had to admire the pursuers' tenacity.

As the bits of meat were passed around, Alee tapped lightly on the drum. Oho looked on curiously. Lek addressed the People to the sound of the drum.

"As you know, our followers are still with us. Yet, they cannot have carried so much water as to be in good shape. They are bound to be in trouble by now. This surely leaves them little choice but to risk all on an attack. They probably intend to wait until most of us are asleep."

"We are prepared to fight!" Bok announced.

"We are to flee," answered Lek steadily. "I know how distances have fooled us on this land, but the Egret said those foothills we see truly are closer than they appear. I know this meal is not much, but finish it. Lok, get the water sack from the cave. We will pack up and move out at my order."

"Then we will just have to fight our stalkers in the hills!" Bok challenged, risking his father's anger. "This rock is easy to defend. Moving on will just let them get a jump on us somewhere else."

Without rancor, Lek answered, "No, though I like the way you have thought through the situation. The wind blows from the south, you see."

"I don't see."

Lek plucked burning faggots out of the fire and handed them to his warriors. Bok understood. The warriors descended to the grass and set a line of fire north of the outcrop.

"We're moving out," announced Lek calmly.

The grass leapt into flame. The stalkers from the river would flee or die. Bok didn't see how it was possible they could run swiftly enough. He remembered the Egret had nearly been consumed by his own fire, and he was traveling into the wind.

Smoke enveloped the People, making them cough, but the wind kept the fire from spreading rapidly in their own direction. The tribe kept ahead of it. The wind played with them a little. Occasionally it would shift just long enough to be a danger, but then the dominant southern blow would resume. They traveled through the night, through the day, and into the next night. Finally they reached the foothills.

Just as the Egret had said, there was water in the hills. Bok thought Lek had been extraordinarily lucky. First, he was lucky to have gotten across the Great River, and second, if the locals had attacked at once before the warriors had set up their ambush, the outcome would have been far different. He was lucky to have found the rocky outcrop, and he was lucky to have had favorable winds. Bok didn't know how much longer the People's luck would hold under such reckless leadership.

The mountains held new dangers. There were gorges and cliffs and the tracks of big cats. The ropes again proved handy on the steep slopes. Lok climbed a nearly sheer cliff, tied off the rope, and then threw down the other end. The second loss of life on the journey occurred here. One woman slipped and lost her grip on the rope near the top of the cliff. She landed hard on the rocks below and didn't move again.

The trail through the mountains was harrowing, but except for the losses, it was exhilarating. Bok felt proud to have conquered the trail, however foolish Lek had been to lead the tribe over it.

Bok was even more thrilled when at last they spotted Others. A clan of them watched the progress of the People from an adjacent hilltop. They retreated when Bok waved an acknowledging spear at them.

"Don't taunt the creatures, boy," chided his father.

Bok was irritated by the correction. Taunting the noble beings was the last thing on his mind. Nevertheless, he remained quiet.

The Others, it turned out, had not retreated far. During the night, they raided the fire. The warriors grabbed their weapons, but Lek restrained them.

"Let them be!" Lek shouted. "Form a defensive circle but don't attack!"

Emitting blood-curdling ululations, a mixed group of Other males and females ran about the camp. One smacked a warrior (whose attention was momentarily in another direction) with his hand, but though the contact was hard, it didn't seem intended as a serious attack. Bok gathered it was almost playful. Lek restrained the warrior from going after the offending Other. Sticks of fire in hand, the Others then retreated with an awful cackle. The Egret was certainly right about the disturbing sound of their laughter. The Others were quite capable of making fire, but it is a troublesome task for anybody. Bok didn't blame them for stealing it. Bok admiringly watched their firm buttocks disappear into the darkness.

*   *   *

While in the mountains Alee and Lek introduced another new social convention, perhaps in order to divert the minds of the People from the seeming endlessness of the journey. Rites of passage were introduced that afterward would become central to the life of the People. Bok never learned the details of the rite of womanhood. It was a secret ceremony the women conducted by themselves to initiate older girls into adulthood. In truth, he wasn't much interested. It had something to do with the moon, which was full at the time.

The initiation of a male was more straightforward. He was to make a solo hunt and kill. He was to bring back the animal to camp or, if it was too big, he was to bring a trophy from the animal and present it to his favorite female. He then would take the name of the animal as his own second name. According to Alee, this was to honor her father, the Egret.

Lok and Bok were to become men in this way. Lok was first. He left in the morning armed with two javelins and a spear. Bok's respect for his brother's survival skills was limited, especially given the presence of the unpredictable Others in the vicinity. Perhaps not all were as harmless as the Egret had indicated. Alee, too, looked anxious. Bok thought it might be the last he saw of his brother.

However, when Lok came back before nightfall with a yellow-billed hornbill, Bok smiled. It did bespeak a good aim with a rock, but it was hardly a challenging kill otherwise. Lok handed the hornbill to Oho, who accepted it as though she had expected from the beginning to be the beneficiary of his largesse. The bird did make a colorful present. Alee pronounced Lok, "Lok Hornbill."

Determined to outdo his brother, Bok passed a full day and then a night alone waiting for a quality target. He passed on a rabbit and several other small creatures. On the second morning he reached a vantage where he saw a lioness stalking an eland

and her fawn. An eland's normal instinct is to run, but in an effort to protect her offspring when the lioness charged, the mother suddenly turned her horns on the lioness, catching her in the neck. The elands ran off as the stricken cat thrashed on the ground. Bok hurried in. Where there was one lion there were others. He threw both javelins. The lioness stopped moving. Bok delivered a coup de grace with his spear. He then chopped off her tail.

Bok created a stir when he returned to camp, where he had been all but given up for lost. Then the whole tribe quieted when he held up the lion's tail. Bok had no favorite woman. He presented the tail to his mother Alee. She looked at him curiously but accepted the tail and pronounced him "Bok Lion," a name he accepted proudly.

Lok congratulated him and asked for the story of the hunt. Bok replied with a dismissive false modesty, "I saw, I killed, I cut."

The People resumed their trek. One day, as they crossed yet another in a seemingly endless series of ridges, there in the distance it was. The Poison Sea stretched out to the very edge of the world just as the Egret had said. The People began their descent from the mountains into the lowlands below.

On the last leg of the descent, they came upon a cave overlooking the gently rolling land below. It was less of a cave than a ledge, protected by an overhang, but it was shelter. A small stream burbled below the hillside within acceptable walking distance. The location was quite beautiful. The People had found their new Home. Luck had favored Alee and Lek yet again. Alee said the Moon favored the People, but Bok found this explanation both incomprehensible and disturbing.

On the first day at the cave the sky turned dark. Heavy winds blew rain beneath the overhang, dampening everyone. The event gave Lok an idea. The next day he began a project to increase protection from the weather by adding windbreaks on the exposed flanks of the ledge. With the help of a few young men, he collected poles and secured them into the ground at the bottom and against the overhang at the top. He lashed the poles horizontally with rope and laced brush into the framework. During the next rain, the enclosures successfully kept the cave dry.

Lek was impressed by Lok's ingenuity and praised him

profusely. Bok was irritated. Only his Hornbill brother could have thought up something so unnatural and stupid. He was sure this type of luxury only served to make the People weak. Bok was half-tempted to kick the walls over. If there had been a chance to do so unseen, he might have tried it.

The new lands were dry compared to the old Home, but they were rich. With no neighbors of any kind within many days' walk, there was no need to stake out a territory. The hunters ranged wherever they wanted. Despite the climate there was an abundance of nuts, berries, and roots. Life in and around the cave was easy. As the hardships of the migration faded from memory, the People regarded Lek with esteem and praised his wisdom for ordering the move. All but Bok seemed to forget they had been driven out at spearpoint. Alee promoted a mythos, aided by new songs and celebrations, in which the ruling couple was portrayed as farsighted pioneers.

Alee continued her social meddling and invented more new and complex rituals. She even held a ceremony crowning Lek "King," which she claimed was an ancient term for leader. Somehow this title, and the silly circle of woven vines on Lek's head, altered the general perception of him. People treated him with more obeisance.

Over the next several years the People prospered. A new generation was born. The babies grew up fat and strong. In the old Home, most children died before the fifth year, but here the People had yet to lose one child. Diseases that had been common up north failed to appear.

Lok and Bok grew into strong young men. The two often traded lead position in the hunt. Most of the hunters regarded Lok Hornbill more highly than Bok Lion, for reasons Bok didn't quite understand. In fact, this was true among the People generally, but the hunters concerned Bok the most. Lok was the elder Prince, true enough, but Lok's shocking mental deficiency was plain for anyone to see. Lok's attention wandered every which way. He was forever stopping to examine things of the most exasperating irrelevance, such as the color of the soil in a particular location or the texture of a particular tree's bark. Yet the hunters indulged Lok in this childish behavior.

Bok was not without his admirers. He developed his own cadre within the hunters, which was based on special relationships with those who could appreciate manly affection. Though he was careful not to insult the popular Lok even within his own cadre—at least not yet—he often spoke against Alee. For these views, he found some sympathetic ears.

The wealth of the new Home had a side effect Bok did not welcome. The People stayed in one place nearly all the time. More than enough food could be found nearby and brought back to the cave. There was no reason for the whole tribe to chase after it. Even Bok, who complained, grew more accustomed to comfort than he realized. For a time he hoped this unnatural sedentary existence would force its own end as the People suffered from their own success. With the addition of a new generation of children, the cave was simply too small.

Quite to his surprise, Bok recognized in Alee a possible ally in urging a return to healthy nomadism. He was delighted to overhear her complaining to Lek about the cave. She was sincerely unhappy. Bok approached her about it, but she was unenthusiastic.

"But mother, you don't like rotting on this ledge any more than I do. I heard you tell Lek as much. Why won't you tell Lek to leave?"

"Lek is King," Alee answered.

Bok dismissed this as the unimportant point it was, and simply repeated, "Why won't you tell Lek to leave?"

"My reasons for disliking this place are not the same as yours."

"What reasons?"

"You wouldn't understand."

"Try me."

"This place is too . . . egalitarian."

"I don't understand."

Alee sighed. "Bok, in order to achieve something higher, the best must be allowed to be best."

"You're not clearing things up for me."

Alee tried again to impart her hierarchical philosophy. "In the cave we are all one. The highest and the lowest are all the same. I know you wonder what the point is of all the prizes, celebrations, and distinctions I've introduced. I give you credit for wondering. Hardly anyone else does. My point is to encourage distinction: to recognize the well turned out."

Bok understood some of this, but he agreed with none of it. The People were one, and that was as it should be. Alee's aristocratic ideas were divisive and downright sinister, especially since she misidentified the "well turned out." The "best" were to be found among the Others, but Alee surely didn't mean to submit the People to the rule of Others, as good an idea as that might be.

"We already have tried the life of nomads, Bok. It got us nowhere."

"Where do you want us to go?"

Alee decided to answer literally. "Maybe a bigger cave. Maybe a complex of caves. Lek is already looking."

This was news to Bok. He had assumed Lek's excursions with his warriors were training exercises, even though there was no one in these parts for them to fight.

Lek didn't find a bigger cave. Instead he surprised everyone at the campfire one night by suddenly announcing his intention to seek the edge of the world to the west.

Alee objected. It was the first time they had disagreed in public. "I'm going," he insisted. "The Egret wanted to do it, and so do I."

For the first time, Alee's protestations came to naught. Alee eventually accepted there was no dissuading him. At heart Lek was an adventurer. He had fallen in behind Alee's plans because of the challenges they offered, but the new challenges she gave him were not interesting. He was better suited to exploration, intrigue, and war than to normal life. He was bored. Lek passed the Egret's treasures, which were symbols of power, to Lok.

Alee made the best of things. She arranged an elaborate combined farewell ceremony and "coronation" for Lok that was full of drums and songs, but Bok could see her heart wasn't in it.

Lek started out at first light on the morning after the celebrations. No one ever heard from him again. Bok often wondered if he had met a bad end, or whether he had blended into a new tribe somewhere. Perhaps, like the Egret, he would turn up one day.

Lok Hornbill, to Bok's disgruntlement, was King. Bok didn't understand how Lok could command respect among the People, yet somehow he did. Alee's support helped, of course. Bok decided to bide his time. Lok would prove himself unfit soon enough. He contented himself with questioning Lok's decisions often and quite openly. Lok always got his way. Nevertheless, Bok's little challenges reminded people Lok's authority was not absolute. Meantime Bok solidified his support among a loyal cadre of hunters.

Lok solved the problem of the overcrowded cave in a radical way. His old trick with the windbreaks gave him the idea. Apparently predicting that Bok would object forcefully, Lok got him out of the way. This was made easy when scouts came back with news of elephants.

"Bok, why don't you take the hunters after the elephants? I will remain here."

Bok leapt at the chance. It would be the People's first elephant hunt since leaving the old Home. Bok knew a kill would raise his status in the tribe, and Lok's decision to stay at home could be interpreted as cowardice.

Bok tracked the elephant herd easily. Under Bok's skillful leadership, the hunters managed to isolate a female, wear her down with coordinated attacks, and finally kill her. It was one of the most satisfying events of Bok's life. Butchering the beast took most of a day.

The successful expedition approached Home. Bok proudly waved the elephant's tail while each hunter carried as much meat as he could manage. But what should have been a glorious homecoming soured, the moment of his arrival. Instead of being the focus of a tribal celebration, Bok found the tribe won over by an abomination Lok had created in his absence.

A cluster of constructions, which Bok had at first mistaken as fuel for bonfires, stood on a low kop within sight of the People's cave. Instead of praise for his valor and bounty, the first words spoken to Bok and his laden men by two excited young women were, "Come, see what Lok has done!" Neither commented on the elephant meat. Bok ordered his men to take the meat to the cave. Still holding the elephant tail in his hand, Bok walked up the kop to see what the fuss was about.

Lok had, foolishly, built shelters in the open. Each was made of vertical poles driven into the ground to form a circle. Lashed to them were horizontal members, and thatch and twigs were woven between to make walls. Poles tied to the tops of the walls met at the center to form a conical roof, also waterproofed with thatch.

Lok had been busy, and still was. So, too, were all the adult members of the tribe except the warriors. Men and women alike scurried about stockpiling materials to build more of the thatched things. Alee stood among them and pointed first here and then there.

With the elephant tail dragging on the ground from his left hand, Bok approached his brother, who was strengthening a wall on one of the huts.

"What is all this, Lok?"

"Well . . . what do you think of it?" Lok asked.

"What is all this, Lok?" Bok repeated.

"Home! Homes! I got the idea from the windbreaks. Why not enclose them all the way around? Thatch keeps out the rain. I tested it by pouring water from a skin over it. I see you got your elephant. Congratulations. Of course, I knew you would."

Bok no longer wanted to discuss the elephant hunt. "Surely you are not planning to live down here."

"Yes. The cave is cramped. Alee was unhappy. This way, we make our own caves. We can shelter a growing tribe."

"You are a fool! We don't need this! We don't need the cave! We don't need anything but our own strong arms. Yes, the cave is cramped. So move on! It is what we did in the old Home."

"Bok, we shouldn't argue in front of the Villagers."

"In front of whom?"

"In front of the People who will live here."

Bok was deeply angry, but contained his feelings enough to quiet his voice. "Tell me honestly. What is the advantage to hiding inside these twisted-up branches over living in the open like the People have always done? You call these flimsy things protection?" Bok wracked the wall of the hut, which rattled and rasped loudly. "They will blow down in the very first storm." ·

"I don't think so. They flex, but they're pretty strong."

As he fumed, Bok saw a glimmer of an opportunity in what was happening. This immense stupidity might be the issue to discredit Lok's rule for good. These shelters were bound to fail and fail badly. The dispute with his brother had collected a discreet, interested audience. Bok put himself on what he felt to be the right side of the issue when he was in their presence.

"What do you have here, Lok?" asked Bok, waving at the nearest hut and again raising his voice. "An animal den, fit for nothing more than a badger! I could push it over with one hand. Even if it keeps out the little raindrops, which I doubt, it won't stop a leopard. You talk of space, but these have less room in them than the cave!"

"Yes, individually. But we can make more. We are making more. We can develop the entire hill."

"More foolishness on top of foolishness! We will be eaten in our sleep. Have you thought of that? How can you be so stupid? The cave has one approach, which can be guarded easily. We can be attacked on all sides down here! Not just by cats and jackals either. What if other people one day cross the great grassy plain? What if they come here?"

"We rely on our warriors."

"Bah! With a kindling heap like this, you'll attract every band of hungry brigands that roams the world."

Alee arrived on the scene and cooled the argument. She asked Bok to have the elephant meat brought down to the campfire on the kop. Bok handed her the elephant tail roughly and went to retrieve his hunters and their meat.

Most of the People were festive that night. Alee, with her apprentice Oho, directed a congratulatory ceremony with drums, songs, and dances for the elephant hunters. Bok, however, remained sullen. At the end of it, he returned to the cave. His special cadre went with him.

Lok was more upset than he let on by his brother's defiance. Yet, though he hated to admit it, Lok knew Bok had a point about poor protection. He decided to add a perimeter wall to the development plans. The morning after the celebration, he staked out a perimeter lengthy enough to shelter many huts within its bounds.

The building of huts continued apace. Alee parceled out huts as they were finished, assigning couples only (plus whatever children they had) to each one. Once all the couples were housed, she laid out six more huts: two for unattached men, two for unattached women, one for herself and Oho, and one for King Lek. In the end she decided to reserve one of the men's huts for Bok alone, should he ever decide to move to the Village.

Though he spared them work on the huts, Lok set the warriors to building the wall, justifying their use in this by describing the construction as a defensive warfare technique.

Bok pointedly refused to participate in anything. His special band of hunters offered no help either. Lok chose not to risk ordering them to assist. Were he to do so, the family rift could turn dangerously political.

Alee, showing less caution in such matters, prevailed upon the women to refuse sex to the hunters who shirked their duty. This proved less motivating to this particular band than intended, but a few of the men did miss the variety. She also set the wives to taunting their men. Most of the young men of the tribe were "married," another ritual invented by Alee.

Bok retaliated against Alee's tactics by refusing to supply game. But most of the People's calories now came from the women's gathering efforts, and the men outside Bok's band were competent hunters, so the strike was ineffectual.

Bok's position weakened with each passing day. His hunters grew restless. Bok remained stubborn.

He was holding out for a storm. He believed the first one would destroy the flimsy Village. Bok was taunted day after day by glorious weather, but at last his hopes rose when, one afternoon, the sky darkened. Though the sea was a full day's walk, a salty smell hung in the air.

The storm came that night. In the flashes of illumination from lightning, Bok took satisfaction as the huts shook and the wind blew. He was sure the kop would be littered with wreckage and wet, angry People, in the morning. Awaking with a start at first sunlight, he scrambled to the ledge and looked below. To his chagrin, the huts stood. A few People already had emerged dry from their homes and stood in the peculiarly still air of a morning after a rain. Bok knew he had lost. He would have to salvage what he could from the fiasco. Bok and his band disappeared for the day.

At sunset, Bok the Lion led the way back to the Village. Behind him the hunters carried a gazelle. A warrior greeted Bok where the perimeter wall overlapped to form a gate. The warrior waved his spear for them to enter. The gesture irritated Bok, who felt he needed no one's permission to join his People, but he made no comment. As he approached the center of the Village, where a fire burned and most of the People were assembled, Alee smiled at him. This, too, irritated Bok. Delivering his kill to the People, he announced "I have something to say."

"Proceed," answered Lok, as though it were his right to permit or refuse to allow Bok to speak.

"I, Bok Lion, have brought bounty to the People today, as I so often have done in the past. There are those who have tried to turn the use of this hilltop into a matter of contention. You all know I have never wished that. Everything I do, think, and feel is for the People and the People alone. There are those who have allowed their personal jealousies to divide us," Bok spoke pointedly to Lok. "There are those who have foolishly fostered dissent instead of harmony. I refuse to sink to their level. Rather than join them in trading pointless insults, I offer this gazelle to our one People. I ask the disrupters to follow my example. I ask that the petty ones put aside their childish, foolish, and selfish quarreling in the greater interest of the People." Bok made an open arms gesture, as if he was generously and grandly forgiving an outrageous offense from an inferior.

Lok seemed set to respond with sarcasm, but he was restrained by Alee with a gentle finger gesture, unnoticed by anyone but her two sons. She evidently was prepared to let Bok's opinion regarding these events go unchallenged. As usual, Lok Hornbill acquiesced to his mother. He walked up to Bok and slapped him on the back in comradely fashion. The People feasted that night.

Despite the show of reconciliation, Lok knew that Bok had mounted the first serious challenge to his authority. He displayed a new wariness of him. Lok introduced Bok to the hut that was reserved for him. To his own surprise, Bok rather liked the feeling of privacy, as he stepped in and looked about. He nodded to Lok as though accepting a compensatory gift.

A walk around the Village the next morning convinced Bok the construction was not mere willy-nilly. He also overheard what might have been the first world's first NIMBY complaint: "I would never have moved here if I'd known another hut would be built right next to me. It shouldn't be allowed." His impression of a plan was confirmed, on a brief visit to Alee's hut. On the flattened ground inside, she had sketched the layout she wanted for the Village.

Alee's master plan revealed radical social engineering. The King's hut was to the north, flanked by quarters for unattached men on one side and Bok's hut on the other. Alee's hut was towards the south, flanked by quarters for unattached women and their children. To east and west were homes of couples and their children. In the center was a large common area for the campfire and assemblies. She was using architecture to further break down the natural communality of the tribe into individuals and families.

"This is bad," Bok objected to Alee. It will make us less the People, and more . . ." he groped for a word, "just people."

"Very perceptive, Bok, but there is nothing bad about it."

Realizing Alee would never understand, Bok marched off and gathered together his hunting team. He planned to work off his frustrations up in the mountains.

Unaware Bok was on the other side of a thatch wall—Lok had entered the hut from the other side to look for two of his hunters. Lok approached his mother, and Bok overheard them speak.

"Bok will give us more trouble," Lok warned.

"Yes, but he has promise for all that. Bok is not at all stupid."

"I know. That is what worries me."

Alee laughed. In truth, she was proud of both her sons, even though she and Lok were closest in thought. "Although he just doesn't like any change, and he can be quite innovative in how he fights it, his way has value too."

"Does it?"

"Once the Village is built, he will defend against any change as fiercely as he now fights its construction. That will be useful someday. There are times when preservation is more important to survival than new things."

Lok considered this. He changed the subject to a technical matter. "I'm not sure we can expand the huts for me and you, as you suggested. The roof gets shakier, the bigger it gets."

"It is important for . . . status. You'll find a way."

Lok thought out loud. "Maybe with a center pole I can double the diameter."

"That will do nicely."

Bok left the Village with his hunters, while Lok examined the Village wall with some pride. The encircling fence of thorns and brush was scarcely sufficient to keep out a determined predator or attacker, but even Bok had allowed it would slow one down. Lok had also devised a movable wooden barrier to close off the Village gate at night.

Bok's hunt went well, and his mood lightened. In the course of the next moon cycle, Bok fell into the Village routine, and he began to think he could learn to live with the new order. Unfortunately, Alee never knew when to let things rest.

Her next round of meddling started with honey. Noticing that honey remains fresh indefinitely, Alee tried mixing it with grains and roots and fruits to keep them from going bad. She added water to soak them thoroughly. She hung up the skin containing the mixture to age. After letting the skin alone for longer than it usually takes fruit to rot, she examined what she had created. The skin poured forth a syrupy substance with a strong smell.

To her credit, she experimented on herself. She sipped a little. Then she tried more, and then more. At first she grew talkative, and then she fell asleep early. She was ill the next day. For some reason she did not regard her experiment as a failure. Instead she made more—lots more. She passed skins of the stuff around during the next of her celebrations. She described it as "a gift of the moon."

Bok tried it once. He enjoyed the strong taste and the warm feeling it gave him, but he felt so terrible the next day, he came to hate the moon.

The "Moon Drink" became a regular part of the People's rituals. The syrup helped the People to be more receptive to the storytellers who provided the songs and music on festival days.

The storytellers spoke in a rhythmic singsong as they told the history of the People. One of the men in particular had a talent for rhymes. Some of the stories became popular, and the People demanded to hear them again and again.

Life in the Village was growing more unnatural every day, and Bok was at a loss as to how to fight the self-feeding trend.

More years passed. The rituals Alee had devised came to seem normal to almost everyone but Bok. Somehow, too, the music and dance had more resonance within the Village than they had at open campsites. Somehow the walls formed a little world of their own, in which the doings of the People were magnified in importance.

The beginnings of the tribe's first true religion stirred. Alee was at the center of this, too, and Oho, grown into an exotic but reserved beauty, served as her apprentice. Bok made a point of not understanding the details of the religion, designed as it was to enhance the power of the two women who officiated over it. It all had something to do with the Moon and what Alee called a triple Goddess of birth, love, and death. It all sounded both foolish and dismal to Bok, yet the People took to it. Bok suspected most just liked the related ceremonial occasions and the opportunity to imbibe Moon Drink.

Lok and Bok were mature young men in their full power, and they were much in demand by the ladies. Alee had refrained from pairing either of them permanently with women, though she intervened readily with any other young man who seemed slow to take a bride.

This suited Bok.

Alee advised Bok and his brother, "Cavort as you like, but keep it casual. I'll declare no offspring to be either of yours. Being available bachelors has helped your mystique. Very soon, though, we'll make you suitable matches. They need to be special."

Bok noticed Alee's quick glance at Oho, who was some distance away. Oho was more and more at the fore of the religious ceremonies, and Alee dressed her provocatively. The thought of mating with Oho revolted Bok, but he saw the political possibilities if she were someday to assume Alee's mantle. Paired to his brother Lok, she could be dangerous. Paired to himself, she could be controlled.

The time came when, heeding its passing, Alee felt she could put off the marriage of her sons no longer. She announced her intention for a double marriage on the next full moon. Bok objected vociferously, but Alee insisted she could not demand proper family behavior from the People, if the royal family itself did not set a proper example.

"There is no need to rush! I like living alone!" complained Bok the communalist.

Lok offered him a solution: "Suppose I add another room to your hut."

"Another room?"

"Yes, it's an idea I had. If we build another hut right next to your own so the walls meet, we can put a door between them. You can live in one and your bride can live in the other."

"Maybe," Bok conceded, "but then everyone will want huts with second rooms."

"So let them. Anyone ambitious enough can add to his hut. I'll add one to mine and Alee's too, so you are not the only one."

"Thank you." Bok almost felt guilty for his ongoing plotting against Lok. Almost. "Then I will marry Oho."

"You are fond of Oho?" asked a startled Alee.

"'Fond' is not the point, is it?"

"It is a point, Bok. Regardless, I have someone for you. Oho is for Lok."

"But . . ."

"Oho is for Lok."

The double ceremony was an elaborate, all-night affair with feasts, Moon Drink, drums, and storytelling. Lok and Oho posed, looking regal. Bok's new mate was the Village mute. She was pretty and seemed intelligent enough, but she simply never spoke. Instead of despising her, as Bok always had, most of the People treated her with awe and even some fear. Bok didn't even know her name until the ceremony. He forgot it afterward. Alee thoughtfully had chosen someone he could ignore easily, while adding to what she called his "mystique."

Lok and Oho consummated their marriage noisily in his hut. Bok faced a similar unpleasantness with his bride in order to avoid snickering by the men the next day. He got through it by thinking of his current favorite among the hunters.

The union of Lok and Oho deeply disturbed Bok. They were the wrong people to wield power, and together they would wield too much. Bok recommitted himself to saving the People from the unnatural leadership corrupting them. He would be patient, but not too patient.

Bok treated his wife the mute as a non-entity, but she didn't especially mind. She was happy enough with her royal status. Besides, there were other men, and Alee's new rules on fidelity added the spice of outlawry to her relationships with them. So it was rather more to Bok's surprise than his wife's when, despite the paucity of attention from him, Bok's bride indicated she was pregnant. She bore a daughter before the end of the year. Alee chose the name Alu for the newborn.

Despite the rather more active proclivities of Lok and Oho, the reigning couple didn't produce an offspring until more than a year later. Alee named their new son, and heir apparent, Lekkek, a kind of remembrance of old Lek, who had sought the place where the sun sets.

Bok disliked his nephew's name. Two syllables had a feminine ring to them, despite the masculine consonant ending. It was a disadvantage in life for the boy. He was surprised Alee hadn't understood. She was slipping in her old age.

The People prospered more than ever in the following years. The population grew to an unprecedented size—more than any tribe Bok had ever known or heard about. Bok's daughter, Alu, grew to young womanhood faster than he thought possible. Bok found himself generous to Alu and spoiled her, often to the irritation of her mother. There were a few rewards to this "family" business of Alee's, after all.

Lok, like his mother, never knew how to live with victory. He was restless. He found reasons to be concerned by the very success of his reign. Prosperity and population growth worried him as much as their absence would have done. In truth, the sheer number of the People was straining the local resources. Sanitation was an obvious problem within the walls of the Village. The hunters had to range ever farther to bring back sufficient meat, as the animals learned to avoid the People.

Occasionally, Bok would mention to whomever would listen that food shortages wouldn't occur if the People would just follow the game, instead of staying in one place, but no one ever took this option seriously anymore, not even Bok's special band of hunters.

Lok explored ways of procuring a more stable food supply. He experimented with fish from the Poison Sea, as an alternative to bush meat. He tasted fish himself and survived. He even liked it, but he couldn't interest many others. He knew it was a possibility for the future, though, if times truly got tough. It was this quest for new food sources that brought, at long last, Bok's great opportunity to discredit his brother.

Lok continued to train warriors. He kept them busy repairing the wall and accompanying him on his various explorations. As he directed the warriors' repair of the Village wall one day, an idea came to Lok.

Perhaps the enclosure was good not only for keeping things out, but for keeping things in.

Lok went off to the hills with four warriors. He was gone for two days. This was not uncommon, so no one in the Village was concerned. Lok and the warriors returned with a live young bush pig, tied to a pole.

Bok was surprised.

"Where did you find the pig?" he asked. "They like wet land."

"There are wet valleys to the East."

"It was smart to bring it alive. It will be fresh."

"It will be fresh in a week too."

"You can't keep it tied to the pole for a week!" objected Bok.

"I don't intend to," Lok responded. "Close the gate," he told a warrior.

Lok untied the pig. It charged, squealing, frantically around the Village. The children were variously terrified and delighted. The women were either curious or disapproving. The men were perplexed.

"What do you think you're doing?" asked Bok.

"I have the same question," snapped Alee, who had been nearly knocked over by the animal. Alee leaned on her staff. Age made her feel frail.

"We can keep animals inside until we need them!"

"It will just die, unless it eats," Bok reminded him.

"So, we feed it."

Oho joined the discussion. "Lok…"

"Oho, do you see what we can do? There's no need to hunt all the time. We can get them to breed in here."

"You are so stupid!" exclaimed Bok in a blunt release of a long-held opinion.

Oho was annoyed by Bok, but on this issue she suspected he was right. She knew that women brought in most of the food. Raising pigs, too, would cost women more labor than it would save men. Lok had been too clever.

"The women won't like it," Oho explained gently. "It will mean more work for them, and the animal is dangerous to the children. Breeding pigs is risky, even if it is possible. They are too big. The males are aggressive."

"It doesn't have to be pigs. Some gentler animals eat grass. We can enclose a large grassy area, outside the Village."

"A village for animals!" scoffed Bok. "You will only feed lions, drawn by the game."

Lok had not expected such fierce resistance from within his own family. Resignedly, he backed down and offered the creature to his brother.

"The pig is yours, brother Bok. Kill it for your family."

"No." Bok saw a political opportunity. This was the first time Lok had done something so foolish, and he intended to capitalize on it. "This event is unnatural. It is not right. In here is in here, and out there is out there. To kill the pig in this enclosure is an offense . . . an offense against something."

"So kill it outside."

"That would be wrong too. The pig is tainted. Something bad will happen. We must let it go. Lok, you have endangered us. The animals and the land will turn against us."

Bok heard a murmur of approval from the growing crowd of onlookers. Alee's Moon ceremonies were coming in handy after all. They had instilled superstitious ways of thinking into the People. Bok was not simply playing to their fears. A part of him felt what he was saying was true.

"Don't be ridiculous," Lok responded. "What difference does it make whether you kill a pig as soon as you catch it, or kill it later? What difference does it make where you kill it?"

Calling the People's concerns ridiculous did not go down well with them. Bok replied, "The hunt is the way of nature. The walls are the way of Lok."

Lok was dismissive, but the crowd was firmly on Bok's side. The hunters in particular nodded approval. Of course, their livelihood and sense of identity were threatened by the domestication of wild animals.

"I said, the pig is yours," Lok replied roughly. "Do with it what you will."

Bok strode to the gate and opened it. The pig did not cooperate. It hid, among the huts. No fewer than four hunters were needed to chase it outside. Once beyond the walls, it was in no hurry to leave the area. The pig stayed near the Village the rest of the afternoon.

Bok approached Alee. "Tonight is one of your Moon ceremonies."

"It is your moon too."

"Whatever you say. I demand to be heard before the People. It is time to talk about this pig. There must be a council."

Alee turned to her other son and asked, "Lok?"

"I don't fear the words of my brother." He nodded his assent to an open council.

Oho looked alarmed. She whispered something to Lok. Alee, Oho and Lok went to his hut to consult in private.

That night under a full moon, Bok stood by the fire and addressed the crowd.

"I blame myself. I have stayed quiet for too long, while nature has been repeatedly defiled by our reckless and impious King. He has offended the spirits of the land, the spirits of the animals, and even the spirits of the trees. Do not think we will escape their wrath. They wait, as our evil festers, but the longer they wait, the more terrible their justice will be. Now Lok has tempted an immediate retribution. He entrapped an animal whose nature is to roam free. Its nature is to be hunted, not confined!

"The offense is so dire, I can see only one hope for the Village to escape or, at least, to delay punishment. Lok must leave, so his evil leaves the Village with him. It is either this, or we all must leave. This hilltop is now accursed.

"I still remember the old days—and some of you do too—when the People were pure. The People were free. They judged for themselves. The Chief was not a "King," but he was merely considered first among equals. Yet Lok has confined you and subjected you to his arbitrary whims, just as he confined the pig. Reassert yourselves as a free People. I love my brother, but I love my People more! So I plead with you, I beg of you, for your sake and the sake of your children, remove Lok. Expel him."

Bok sat down among his hunters.

Lok stood up. "You know me. I have no excuses to make. Bok speaks rubbish. I do not fear the judgment of my own People. Choose between Bok and me."

Lok's confidence, a product of years of popular good will and deference, was misplaced. Bok's hunters began to chant, "Bok! Bok!" They had no wish to herd pigs. One by one, women joined in the chant. "Bok! Bok!" They had no wish to see their hard-won gatherings go to feed pigs. Others joined in out of fear of angry spirits.

Motives of self-interest and fear aside, Bok also had tapped into the old instinct of crowds to turn on their leaders over trivial or trumped-up charges. Only a minority, including Lok's warriors, remained silent.

Bok did not expect Lok to abdicate. He would not, if he was in Lok's place. In truth, Bok did not expect to so inflame the crowd. He merely intended to undermine and weaken Lok for a later attack on his leadership. So what happened next stunned him.

Lok waved at the crowd to be quiet. Silence returned slowly. Though visibly taken aback, Lok remained self-possessed. He spoke soberly:

"This night has brought forcefully to our attention a problem that has been bothering me for some time. Our Village is outgrowing itself. The hunters are traveling further and further for game, which is why I suggested bringing game here. Moreover, our numbers invite conflicts that we find difficult to resolve. We have factions that are larger than our entire clan once was.

"A majority of you supports Bok's way. Some of you, I assume from your silence, support me. I don't agree with Bok, but his solution is correct. The Village must divide."

Bok shook his head. He hadn't proposed dividing the Village.

"I shall leave. I ask anyone who wishes to join me to do so. I leave the disposition of the Village leadership to Alee."

Bok couldn't believe Lok's capitulation was a sudden impetuous decision. Had Lok been proposing such a thing to Alee and Oho for months? Had the three of them once again maneuvered Bok into helping them achieve their ends? No matter, so long as Lok and Oho left, it was all for the good. If Lok took disloyal Villagers with him, it was better still. Bok figured he could handle the aging Alee on her own. He was hardly willing to leave "the disposition of the Village leadership" to her.

"Who will follow me in a new adventure to a new place?" Lok asked. "Who will found a new Village with me?"

After some shuffling, the warriors and their families lined up beside Lok. Aside from these, Bok was pleased to see only the mentally defective men and women joined him—the ones with dreamy expressions, their heads in the clouds. Bok was convinced the Village was better off without them. Oddly, Oho did not stand up by the fire with Lok.

Alee arose, and her smile did not escape Bok's attention. She was up to something.

"I am too old to join Lok, or I would consider it," she announced. "But I have a job here too. My first task is to fill the vacuum created by Lok's expedition. I declare Bok shall be King."

Bok relaxed. He had won everything without a fight. His objection to the title "King" was forgotten.

"However," Alee continued, "Lok's son Lekkek shall stay here with me and Oho. He will be in line to be King after Bok. Oho will follow me, when the time comes, as Priestess of the Moon."

Bok nearly called out an objection, but he held his tongue. Village authority was being handed to him. Bok reasoned Alee was not immortal. There would be time enough to deal with Oho and her weakling boy Lekkek. After Alee was gone, he could expel the two of them and make his own daughter, Alu, the Moon Priestess. If Bok didn't produce a son, and the means to doing so were disagreeable enough to make this likely, he would choose his own successor. He would wed his choice to Alu. The fact that Bok's plans employed every major element of Alee's social revolution—the ceremonies, the positions, the Village itself—bothered him not at all.

"Where will you go?" Bok asked his brother. He wanted to be sure it was somewhere far enough away.

"Far west. Beyond the flat mountain."

"Our father never came back from there."

"Maybe he found something worth staying for. Besides, I have seen the edge of the world in the south. Now I want to see the western edge where the sun sets."

His young son Lekkek heard him, and asked, "What about where the sun rises?"

Lok laughed. "I leave that to you. I'm also giving these to you." He handed Lekkek his ivory blade and the lodestones.

Bok was outraged. He didn't care about the lodestones, but the ivory was a symbol of power that rightfully belonged to him. With effort he held his tongue.

Lok set out with his followers before the end of the next day. Alee organized a farewell celebration. After the festivities, Bok confronted Alee in private about the symbolic ivory given to Lekkek.

"This is ludicrous. The boy is only half grown. He is one of the stupidest boys I've ever seen. He doesn't ever see you approaching him. His attention is off in the distance somewhere. He spends hours playing with rocks and water and stripping apart leaves. There is something wrong with him. He is scrawny. If he becomes a man, he is likely to get someone killed on the hunt when his attention wanders at a critical moment."

"I have made my decision," Alee answered. "You are King for now. Be happy with that."

Oho added no comment, but cast a murderous look at Bok.

Alee grew more frail in the months that followed. She passed more of her duties to Oho. Then, one day, much to the surprise of Bok (who was beginning to think she was immortal), Alee died. The timing was all wrong. (Even in death, Alee had thwarted him.) His daughter Alu was not yet old enough to become Priestess, and he was not yet ready to challenge the beliefs of the People altogether. For the time being, he would have to tolerate Oho as Moon Priestess.

Alee was cremated in a great ceremony, this, too, was a new thing. Oho handled the timing of the event well. At the most emotional moment, as the funeral pyre blazed, Oho revealed to the People her elaborate vision.

"We live in this world," she began, to the rhythmic beat of drums, "but there is a shadow world alongside of ours where Alee goes."

Moon Drink was passed around as the flames leapt high into the night.

"Now is the time for me to tell you of the two worlds. They are not entirely distinct. They overlap and influence one another, and the shadow world is greater than our own. The parts of the shadow world that we see in this world are the sun and the moon, but there are spirits, too, who move between the two worlds. These now include our protector, Alee.

"The essence of both worlds is the male and the female. The male is the Sun, which from now on we will know as "Lok." The female is the Moon (because the Moon controls the cycles of women), and from now on we shall know the Moon as "Alee." Lok walked to the Sun, and Alee returns to the Moon tonight. As Alee is the mother of Lok, the Moon was the mother of the Sun, and it is the true ruler of the World.

"The Moon has its phases. It waxes, shines full, and wanes. The woman brings life, the fullness of love, and rules death. The new Moon that ends the light brings new life, as well, in the cycle of existence. These are the three aspects of the Goddess Alee, and it is my duty as her priestess to interpret her wishes."

"Now Alee is a Goddess," mumbled an irritated Bok to himself. He understood the term, murkily, to mean a sort of a higher spirit with powers over the others. Bok had no doubt the moon's wishes would correspond to Oho's wishes. To her credit, in a stroke she had made her boy Lekkek the son of the sun. She herself wielded the authority of the Moon. If Bok wanted to challenge them he would be taking on the religion of the tribe.

Oho turned her attention to two concentric circles of stones, newly laid out in front of the pyre. "Before she returned to the Moon, Alee, in her earthly form, gave us a gift. Every day for years past, she watched the phases of the Moon and the cycles of the Sun, and she showed me how they can be represented in this way. We thank you, Alee, for this final contribution to the People you loved."

Bok considered this newly-created calendar to be Alee's final act of foolishness. Who needs to look at rocks when one can simply look at the Sun or Moon, themselves?

Lekkek and Oho had to go, but patience had worked well for Bok in the past. He had found the right moment to overthrow Lok and he had outlasted Alee. The chance would come when this troublesome twosome could be shunted aside too. His daughter would be his instrument.

— *5*—

The past weighed heavily on Bok as he watched Lekkek dawdle beneath the tree by the stream. Reckoning soon would be at hand! The time was nearly ripe for Bok to restore the People, at long last, to their primordial, natural, strength and beauty. On the morrow, Lekkek surely would embarrass himself with a pathetic performance in the ritual manhood hunt. Afterward, getting rid of the sod would be all the simpler.

Something seemed to dominate Lekkek's attention. Bok decided to investigate. He noticed his daughter and his very favorite young hunter, Tup, playfully following him toward the stream.

— *6* —

As he sat by the bank, Lekkek was absorbed in fashioning the image of a zebra from blue clay he had scooped from the stream bed. Sculpting clay into representational forms was an art form he had developed on his own. To his knowledge, no one had ever done such a thing. He saw no harm in it, but he kept his creations secret, because he knew Uncle Bok was not fond of innovation. For this reason, Lekkek worked at sculpting with his back to the Village.

He had upset Bok with his experiments in clay once before. His attention had been drawn one day to picking pebbles from the stream that seemed suitable for fashioning into spearheads, cutters, and scrapers. The texture of the stream bottom intrigued him. He scooped some clay out, played with it, and molded it into free forms. One of the shapes could hold water. He made a larger version. He left the bowl to dry in the sun. He filled it with water and offered it to his beautiful cousin Alu, but Bok seized it from his hands, and smashed it.

"You must not do that!"

"Do what?"

"Idiot! Imprison the water!"

"Why?"

"The stream will not like it."

"But we carry water in skins. What is the difference?"

"Skins are natural. The animal drinks water and the skin holds it. We hunt the animal and may use the parts as we see fit. This is unnatural. The stream's spirit will be offended."

Lekkek was skeptical. The idea of the spirit of the stream liking or not liking something was foolish. As the son of a Priestess, he did not take the notions of spirits seriously. He was sure Oho did not either. It was not the first time Lekkek had dismissed Bok's authority in his own mind. He never challenged it out loud, however, despite his own royal status. Oho had warned him against this.

Oho didn't share Bok's opposition to new ideas. When he told her what had happened, she asked him to make a bowl for her. She even improved it by setting it over a fire to dry it. The firing increased its hardness. After that, she used it for ceremonial purposes. When Bok saw the bowl he was angry, but he let the matter go.

As he worked to get the delicate shape of the zebra's ears right, Lekkek didn't hear his Uncle Bok approach. The little mosquito girl, Ulee, tried to warn him with a nudge to his arm, but Lekkek pushed her hand off with a twitch of his elbow. She chose not to try again. Lekkek didn't even notice the shadows cast by his uncle, Alu, and the young hunter, Tup, as they came up behind him.

Tup was older than Lekkek. He was tall, muscular, and assertive. He carried the name "Tup Gazelle," from his initiation kill of a gazelle the year before. A hunter had to stalk a gazelle to within a single human stride in order to have any chance of bringing it down, so his success bespoke great skill. The horns, an impressive trophy, he had given to Alu. Oho once warned Lekkek to keep in mind that Bok had a special relationship with Tup. Lekkek wasn't sure how the information was supposed to help him. By comparison to Tup, Lekkek was short, slight, and clumsy. Prince or no Prince, he felt unequal to Tup in the contest for Alu's affections.

Lekkek counted on success in his own rite of initiation to help even the score. Lekkek forced his mind back onto the image. He deliberately had started sculpting the shape of his target in order to focus his mind. Nearly satisfied with his model, Lekkek set it down next to him and tipped it over with a finger.

He looked up and saw Ulee shaking her head, with a "Serves you right!" expression.

"Leave me alone!" Lekkek warned the little Mosquito.

His uncle bent down, smacked him on the ear, and grabbed the clay object. "This is an abomination! Are you stupid, boy?"

Tup laughed loudly. Alu giggled. Lekkek gaped wordlessly. He was mortified in front of Alu. About Ulee he was unconcerned. She had disappeared anyway.

"Not that your witchcraft would save you! Didn't you hear me coming? Didn't you see me?" Bok railed. "You are sitting by the stream where leopards drink, and you see nothing and you hear nothing! You will die on your hunt! I don't know why I bother to warn you."

Bok prepared to fling the model, but hesitated. Lekkek could see the question on his mind: Was throwing the essence of a zebra bad magic? At last, Bok bent over and pushed the object back into the clay of the stream, as though returning the stuff to where it came was the safest option.

Bok cuffed Lekkek again and stormed off. Tup laughed and followed. Alu giggled, smiled coquettishly and followed too.

Lekkek watched the well-formed Alu recede up the hill. He felt a constriction in his chest and a stirring in his loins. He fantasized about Alu every day and dreamed of her at night. She was unapproachable, however, until he had scored his kill. He knew that he was not as athletic as Tup, but he was the son of a King and heir to the Kingdom. Perhaps he would have a real chance with her after tomorrow. He was irked when he saw Tup slap her posterior. He couldn't imagine why she would allow it.

"She isn't worth it," Ulee said. She had appeared out of nowhere.

"Go away. Tomorrow I become an adult. Little girls shouldn't annoy adults."

"I'm not a little girl. I'm only a few months younger than you."

Lekkek glanced at her again. Even if what she said was true, she was small and undeveloped—and she was still a pest.

"Go away."

Ulee stood by. Lekkek tried to ignore her.

Lekkek turned his mind to his initiation hunt. Unfortunately, Bok had a point. He should learn to be more attentive. Letting his mind wander could get him killed. Lekkek, however, had some tricks of his own. Fortunately, Bok had not discovered them as he had the statue. He knew that one of his weaknesses was, literally, weakness. He was not as strong as some of the hunters, and it was physically hard for him to take down a large animal with a spear. Yet it had to be a large animal or his status would suffer. He regarded his own solution as clever.

He had heard the story of the handles that old King Lek had added to hand axes back at the Great River in order to cut trees. Lek applied the same idea to his spear. He effectively increased the length of his arm with a throwing stick carved from wood. It worked well, but it made his aim less reliable. He might have gotten better with more practice, but as he was sure Uncle Bok would disapprove, he was restricted to practicing when he could sneak off and improve his throwing secretly. As it was, close-range use would be best.

The second part of his solution was to prepare an ambush. For months he had scoured the mountains, often staying away from the Village for days. These excursions upset Oho, but she understood his reasons. He found what he wanted. Amid the hills was a valley that formed almost a complete loop. It was shaped, in fact, much like the outer rim of a zebra's hoof. On the grassy floor of the valley, zebras liked to graze. If he could stampede them at one opening of the valley, he could head them off at the other opening.

Lekkek had gotten the idea from the lions and gazelles he had watched from a distance. The lionesses hid in grass downwind. A big male loped upwind. His smell scared the gazelles, and they ran straight toward the females.

In the dirt Lekkek drew a relief of the hunt site.

"It should be longer," Ulee said.

"What?"

"The valley is longer than it is wide."

"You again! How do you know about the valley?"

"I was worried about you, and I followed you there."

"That was stupid. You could have been killed."

"And you, as well."

"I suppose you're going to tell Bok about this, too?"

"I didn't tell about your clay zebra! I tried to warn you. I didn't tell about your throwing stick, either."

"How...? Let me guess. You followed me."

He was embarrassed that Ulee knew of the stick, and he was horrified she might tell Alu about it. It emphasized his weakness. Annoying him seemed to be Ulee's primary occupation in life. What he had done to her to earn her everlasting wrath was beyond him.

"You're going to chase them down the valley." She had seen his strategy at once. "What if they don't run? You're not very scary. And if they do run right around the loop and back to you, they could trample you to death." she added.

"They'll run."

He had a plan, and for once, Ulee hadn't found it out. All animals fear fire. He fingered his lodestones in the pouch hanging from his neck. They were relics passed onto him through four generations from the time of the Egret. By playing with them, he had quite accidentally discovered a new use. When struck together, they made sparks. Embedded in the tips of sticks and struck sharply, they could start a fire almost anytime and anywhere, with little labor or trouble.

"As for getting trampled, I can manage. I'm not a dullwit, despite what Bok says."

"Sometimes, you are."

"You are not the one I wish to impress."

"Which means you do wish to impress somebody. Are you still rutting after that sow, Alu? She'd spit on you before spreading her legs for you. Don't you know that? You are a dullwit!"

His nemesis marched back to the Village in a huff. He knew she would be back to torture him again. She was a mosquito that departed, only to return.

Lekkek made sure his throwing stick was well hidden in the branches of the cedar. He then walked back up the hill toward the Village. He needed his rest for the initiation.

Oho spoke to him after dusk. "I know you have eyes for Alu. You are right to see in her big political advantages."

Her political advantages were the last things on his mind.

"However, she is much too dangerous. Bok will fight you openly. Besides, she would not be a good wife to you."

"Who would you suggest? Ulee?" he asked mockingly.

She let the sarcasm pass. "You could do worse, but she has no connections to help secure your position."

"Why should I need help?"

"You need help. Be careful, son. This is a dangerous time. Bok is up to something. I don't know what, but it isn't good."

Oho and Ulee saw Lekkek off at the break of dawn. Though the King normally wished the initiates luck as they began their solo hunts, on this occasion, Bok slept in.

Lekkek hoped Ulee wouldn't follow him. He followed the path to the cedar tree and pulled his throwing stick from its branches. Thus armed, and also including a hand ax, a spear, and a javelin, he headed for the hills.

The valley was more than a full day's travel away at a hard trot. Nature seldom co-operates fully with human plans, so it was no surprise that the valley was empty of prey. Lekkek camped for three days and began to consider abandoning his ambush in favor of whatever game he could find. Just as he resolved to leave, a small herd of zebras moseyed into the valley to graze.

Lekkek descended into the grasses and approached the animals. Like most herbivores, zebras have a wide periphery of vision but poor depth perception. Hence they catch the smallest side to side motion but often fail to see something coming straight at them. Cats know this instinctively and stalk accordingly. Lekkek deliberately copied the strategy of cats. The wind was at his back, so the grazers caught his scent. Every now and then their heads bobbed up sharply and looked his way. The wind was ideal for what he would do next. Using dry straw as kindling and his lodestone spark makers, he started a series of small fires across the mouth of the valley.

For a time, the zebras ignored the fire, which gave off more smoke than flame. At last the wind blew enough smoke their way so that one animal, either alarmed or annoyed, began to run. The others followed, and the herd picked up speed. Lekkek hurried to the other opening of the valley. He was barely in position when he heard them approach. He waited until they were almost upon him, fixed his javelin to his throwing stick, stood, and threw. The javelin entered one beast's chest and it fell at his feet. The other zebras thundered around him. Then it was quiet. Lekkek drove his spear into his prize just in case there was still life in it. Then he began to cut away the rear haunch with his stone hand ax. The tail would be next.

Lekkek came home according to tradition waving the tail of the kill. He carried zebra meat over one shoulder. Children saw him from far away and ran inside the Village gate to tell the others. Initiations had become such common events that in most cases they no longer aroused the interest of the whole tribe, but Lekkek was a royal. Lekkek could hear the drums before he reached the gate. He knew most of the Village would be assembled there.

Ulee stood nearby just outside the central common area. She wore a grass skirt she had made, or acquired somewhere in a silly attempt, he supposed, to look sexy. Lekkek tried to ignore her, but in fact she did catch his eye. It was the first time he had thought of her as anything more than an annoyance.

"I was worried about you," she said as he approached.

"You needn't have bothered. I'm not incompetent."

She drew herself up at the rebuke of her concern. "Just a fool."

"Go away."

"Isn't that tail for me?" she teased.

"Shush!" he ordered as he passed her.

He approached Oho and offered the haunch. She nodded on behalf of the tribe.

"You are 'Lekkek Zebra,' man of the People," she pronounced.

He placed the haunch in front of the central Village fire and held up his tail trophy. He walked to the right of Uncle Bok and presented the tail to the beautiful Alu. Alu almost laughed, but then she stopped herself when she saw the impression the gift was making on Tup. She smiled at Lekkek and accepted the tail.

Lekkek turned and caught Tup's glare. It was the first time he had seen anger, rather than disdain, in the young man.

Lekkek strode away happily.

"Lekkek, you are a dullwit!" enunciated Ulee much too precisely as he passed her again.

He wished everyone would stop saying that.

Lekkek returned to his favorite cedar tree by the stream. The air was sweet, the sky was blue, and the water gurgled pleasantly. At the base of the tree, he dug into a hollow where he had hidden a secret treasure. The zebra had not been his only attempt at image-making. His personal favorite, and the one he had saved, was an image of Alu. With painstaking care he had carved, re-carved, and smoothed the clay into a graceful, diminutive likeness of her full-bodied form. Just handling the object aroused him.

Bok appeared behind him again and pulled the image roughly from Lekkek's hand. This time he did not cuff Lekkek or yell at him. He looked at the image and then back at Lekkek. Holding it, he strode back to the Village.

Lekkek spent the day by the stream brooding. The stream flowed to the sea. His father had hypothesized the sea girdled the world. Lekkek wondered how long it would take to walk completely around the shoreline. The thought of Alu seeing the statuette was embarrassing enough to make him consider the journey. On the other hand, he reconsidered, maybe she would be flattered.

Lekkek heard a clatter by the Village gate. He saw Bok emerge with all his favorite hunters. Tup was among them. The band crossed the stream at the stepping stones and proceeded toward the hills. Lekkek saw they carried loops of rope. This was unusual equipment for a hunt. He wondered what Bok had in mind.

Lekkek returned to the Village. Near by the Village center he saw Alu, but she paid him no attention. He doubted she had seen the image. Ulee made a point of walking past him without the eye-catching grass skirt. She feigned indifference, but Lekkek knew it wouldn't last. She would return to torturing him soon. Oho waved him over.

"Bok worries me," she confided seriously. "He left with a big party and a bigger attitude. He said they would be gone many days. He seemed . . . determined. I don't think it's a good thing. I think we should elevate you to King, now. You are of age."

"The People won't stand for it. They don't think of me that way."

"The People will think what I tell them—except for Bok's hunters, and they're gone."

"But they'll be back. You will provoke them to be violent. Why not let time take its course?"

"Because Bok won't. We can arm everyone, man and woman. Defend the walls. We'll let his hunters back inside only if they accept your rule. We don't allow Bok back at all. We'll tell him to go find his brother Lok at the western edge of the earth."

"No. We could get people killed."

"Are you refusing your title?"

"I'm deferring a title for the sake of peace."

"You don't understand. Maybe Bok is right when he says this easy land softened us. You have lived at peace too long. You don't realize that peace and war are as natural cycles as day and night. You are trying to prevent the night by not provoking it with a campfire. Night will come regardless."

"No."

"If Bok is gone, you can have Alu."

This time the word caught in his throat, but he forced out another, "No."

"Very well. Maybe Bok really is just hunting an elephant, and nothing is wrong. I hope you made the right choice."

Lekkek hoped so too. Oho's instincts rarely were far wrong. He resolved to keep watch for the return of Bok. He would ask Oho to have the small foraging parties, which left the Village every day, hurry back with word if they spotted him. In case something was amiss, Lekkek wanted advance warning of the band's return. He walked back toward the gate. On the way he passed Ulee, whose indifference had been replaced by a look of concern. It didn't surprise him she had been listening.

Bok hadn't lied. The band was gone for the better part of a month. It was Lekkek, sitting beneath his tree, who first espied Bok on his return. A tiny dark figure, he emerged from a grove of trees on a hillside up and beyond the stream. He was alone. Lekkek went to the stepping stones to greet him.

"Where is the band?" Lekkek asked.

"They will be coming. You be at the Council tonight, just after dark," ordered Bok gruffly.

*   *   *

The fire burned brightly under a starry sky. The People were assembled in and around the Village center. They were expecting a feast from a successful great hunt and hoped one was soon in the offing. Oho stood in her customary place. Tup had appeared, and he sat next to Alu. The rest of the hunting band were still somewhere outside the Village. Ulee looked about for Lekkek. He was not in sight.

"All right, Bok," prompted Oho. "You seem to have something to say."

"Where is that little runt of yours, witch woman?"

"I know no one fitting that description. I am Moon Priestess."

"You are a vagabond. Even the Cog tribe from which you came discarded you. You were rescued from the mud by a woman who should have known better. I remember when you couldn't even talk."

The People listened to the exchange in silent fascination. Their leaders never before had sparred openly in such a fashion. Ulee quietly sidled to Oho's hut and slipped inside.

"And your runt, Lekkek, is a half-Cog half-wit. I cannot allow this farce to continue. He cannot lead the People. He is not a hunter. He is not a man. His 'initiation' was a fraud. He didn't kill his prize like a man. He used witchcraft, learned no doubt from you."

"Nonsense, Bok! What witchcraft?"

"Address me as 'Bok Lion,' woman!"

"What witchcraft, Bok Lion?" she asked in a mocking tone.

"The day before the hunt, I found Lekkek making a zebra from clay. He used it to bewitch a real zebra to impale itself upon his spear."

"Do you hear what you are saying? A zebra from clay?"

"Then I caught him with this." He held up the clay image of his daughter that he had taken from Lekkek. "You all saw Alu accept the zebra tail from that runt. You all know she wouldn't talk to him before. He turned his evil witchery against her to make her do his bidding. He uses witchcraft against me . . ." Bok pointed at the crowd and swept his finger over them saying, "and he turns his evil against you!"

The crowd stirred. The magic statuette truly frightened them.

"I cannot allow this evil to contaminate the tribe any further. Lekkek must die."

"That is enough, Bok! As Moon Priestess, I remove you as King. Lekkek is of age. Lekkek is King."

Bok laughed. "You have no authority. You are no longer Moon Priestess. Alu is truly of the People. She is now Moon Priestess."

Alu stood up, with much less than full self-assurance. Tup stood by her side. He radiated confidence.

"I cannot allow the disease that has infected our tribe for generations to proceed any further. It ends here. It reverses here. We are returning to nature. We are taking back our ancient strengths. The power and brains of our true ancestors will flow in the blood of our people once again. The era of weakness is over."

"What are you talking about, Bok?" Oho stood her ground in her customary spot. Alu made no effort to displace her.

Bok's special band entered the gate and approached the Village center. They escorted fifteen Others in a line, consisting of thirteen females and two males. Ropes stretched from neck to neck of each creature. There were gasps among the People. They had heard of these disturbingly human-like beasts, with their fierce features and coarse hair, but most were not old enough ever to have seen one before.

Oho would have laughed had she not been so appalled. "If I understand you correctly, you are utterly sick!" Oho exclaimed. "The games you hunters play out in the field among yourselves are one thing. This, Bok, is unspeakably perverse. Why not romance with baboons? Or are they next?"

"Step aside, Oho. Your influence is ended."

"Your rule is ended! Lekkek is King," she insisted.

Bok nodded at Tup. Tup threw his spear right through Oho, and she fell wordlessly. Lekkek stepped out of the shadow of a hut. Expertly snapping his throwing stick, he sailed his javelin across the open center. It ran Tup through the neck. He died quickly, but gruesomely, choking on his own blood.

"Kill him!" order Bok to his hunters.

"I don't think so!" warned Ulee. She held the Egret's ivory sword to Alu's throat. "Let us go," she quietly demanded.

Bok took a step forward. Ulee pushed the blade gently until a trickle of blood appeared on Alu's throat. Alu squealed and Bok stopped. Ulee couldn't read his face. Was the expression really amusement?

"I'm prepared to sacrifice my daughter if I need to."

"I don't doubt it. You don't need to. I'm not trying to undo your 'Revolution.' You have won. I just want to leave, alive and with Lekkek."

"The witchcraft of that dullwit will end up destroying you both."

"Then you will get what you want."

Bok considered his options. "Fine. Let Alu go and leave," he granted. "Never come back."

"No risk of that. But I'll let Alu go only when we reach the stream. Don't follow."

Lekkek, Ulee, and Alu walked through the People toward the gate. The crowd parted for them. Lekkek half-expected to feel a spear enter his back at any moment. He saw the frightened, hairy Others cowering at the bloody scene into which they had been brought as captives.

When they reached the stream, Ulee roughly pushed Alu away.

"Can I go with you?" she asked.

"Go back home!" ordered Ulee. "I'm sure your father has picked out another husband for you. Maybe that big hairy Other tied up at the very back of the line."

Ulee raised the ivory sword in threat. Without enthusiasm, Alu returned to the Village.

"Disappointed with your new bride?" asked Ulee as they reached the foothills.

It took Lekkek a moment to realize she was talking about herself.

"No," he replied. It wasn't entirely a lie; he had resigned himself to the mosquito buzzing around him for the rest of his life.

"I know, you still wish I looked like Alu."

"No." This was entirely a lie.

"Here—I made something for you remember her by."

Ulee reached into a pouch tied to her waist and pulled out a figurine made from the blue clay of the stream. It was similar to the image he had made of Alu, except the figure was hugely exaggerated. The sexual features were gross and disgusting.

Lekkek laughed.

"Now you can worship her from afar," added Ulee.

"I'll never think of her the same way again," he answered truthfully. Perhaps there was magic in the statues after all.

"Where do we go?" she asked. "West, after your father?"

"East. I want to reach the coast. I want to see where the sun rises. Maybe afterwards we can go see the edge of the world in the north too."

"That would be fun." She went silent for a few moments. "About our kids…"

"Our kids?"

"Yes, you dullwit, our kids! Are you going to tell them that we were unwelcome misfits who barely escaped from our tribe with our lives, or are you going to make up some story about how we were brave adventurous explorers who chose our own destiny?"

"I'll tell them the truth."

Ulee accepted the ambiguity without comment.

"The Others may kill everyone as soon as they are cut loose," Lekkek speculated. "They are stronger than People, and they're probably pretty angry. Even if they don't, whether the Others stay or run away, under a totally unrestrained Bok the Village will be gone in a year," Lekkek predicted. "Savagery to savagery in three generations."

"It was a promising idea, though."

"Breeding with Others?"

"No! Building the Village. People will try it again one day."

"It may be a long time," he conjectured.

"Let's worry about our own time," she replied.

—Richard Bellush, Jr.

SOLITUDE

TOO YOUNG TO RETIRE

I'm just lying around thinking.
There's no one I want to call.
Sometimes I just go out cruising
but I don't see a thing I like at all.
I've just got no motivation
no way to break my fall.

I get so bored with the losers,
but man, those winners are worse!
I don't want no disco action,
with a gigolo eyeing my purse.
No, now I just want a dark moon rider
without any conversation first.

I don't like anyone to drive me
like I was a souped-up car.
Don't want anyone to shake me
like a mixer in a cocktail bar.
I want to find a lone ranger
from Atlantis or a two-tone star.

I want an extra-terrestrial
with a black leather software machine.
A true desolation row angel
sporting a laser gun, know what I mean?
I want to turn it on to intense
like the kick of an espresso bean.

You know when I break loose
I leave all the jockeys behind.
I own the speed that I need
but there's no one I can find.
I'd rather run Kamikaze
than slow down to a low-grade grind.

Anytime I get tied down
it's never as good as I'd thought.
Now all the Don Juans are faded.
They can't deliver on the lines I bought.
He looks too young to be jaded
but I know for certain he's been caught.

I guess the thing that I look for
is the hell and back look in his eyes
the black light aura
from the face that asks no reasons why.
I've gotten confused explanations
that make me crazy when I try.

Tonight I'm staring at the ceiling.
There's no one that I want to call
so I go out driving in my car.
But there's nothing going down at all.
The roadhouse isn't appealing
and there's no one at the shopping mall.

—Sharon Bellush

LITTLE GREEN WOMEN

Mandy stared up at the sky. The night was exceptionally crisp. For weeks, dust had obscured everything. At ground level the wind had not settled down even yet, but at high altitude there must have been a dramatic change. Dust particles had settled out rapidly. As she stood on the flat plain of Hellas Planitia, sudden gusts of up to 100 kilometers per hour pelted her repeatedly with granules of sand. They stung. Earth, currently an evening star, gleamed a bright blue near the horizon. It was close enough for the disk to be visible to the naked eye. The constellation Cassiopeia poised like a butterfly net ready to scoop up the planet.

In Mandy's case, "naked eye" was a term needing some qualification. Her eyes were covered by tough transparent keratin that formed protective goggles. If scratched, they would, like fingernails, grow back.

Mandy smiled, though an unmodified human might have had trouble recognizing the expression. She recalled the passage in Orson Well's *War of the Worlds* in which Martians looked longingly at earth. Now here she was, doing just that.

Appropriately enough for a Martian, her skin was green. Humans had found no little green men, so they had to invent them. The first of their kind was a woman, not a man. The color was not cosmetic. During the day, her dermal chloroplasts, which gave her the green hue, busily turned sunlight and CO_2 into energy and oxygen. Although the Martian atmosphere had only 1% the density of the terran one, it was more than 95% carbon dioxide. On earth, carbon dioxide made up only 0.03% of the total. In consequence, the air of Mars was even more congenial to photosynthesizing organisms. Mandy's chemistry had been altered to make use of the nitrogen in the atmosphere (2.7%) as well. The project scientists didn't find a use for the 1.4% argon or the trace gasses.

Something distracted her attention from earth. She stared at a point in the sky where something seemed to move. She wasn't certain she interpreted what she saw correctly. Then she was certain. A dim red dot at the limit of visibility moved slowly in an eastward arc. It had to be some sort of craft on an orbital track. Even if it was only a robot probe, as was likely, it was still the first interest earth had taken in Mars since she had been stranded there so long ago.

Mandy couldn't contact the craft. She couldn't contact earth. She herself had smashed the radios during a temper tantrum many years earlier. The act of destruction, prompted by rage and despair at her abandonment, was foolish, but it had made her feel better. She was not enough of an engineer to repair them, despite having built a radio as a childhood project. Her homemade device had been an educational kit with big clunky capacitors, resistors, and transistors. The components of real world radios were tiny blocks of semiconductors. How was she supposed to rewire those? She wasn't even sure there were parallels to capacitors and resistors in the devices. Besides, back at the base known as Martian Gardens, the miniature atomic power plant was malfunctioning, so she had no electric power anyway except for a few worn and sandblasted photovoltaic cells.

Nevertheless, Mandy strode determinedly NNE in the direction of Martian Gardens. When humans returned to the surface, they surely would want to inspect the site of the last expedition, even if they didn't expect to find anyone alive. It was the logical place to go. She wended her way through a patch of Cactus Pods. As it was nighttime, the outer shells were shut tight and they resembled reddish eggs. When they opened in daytime and spread out, the internal leaves being a traditional green, they looked like skunk cabbage. She suspected some of the genetic material for them came precisely from those plants. The taste of them backed up her supposition. Most of the insects that fed on them spent the night inside the closed pods.

For more than a century, humans had dreamed of terraforming Mars to make it habitable. Though even the most ambitious schemes would have left oxygen levels far too low to be breathable for earth-adapted humans, it was marginally plausible to raise average surface temperatures significantly. It was hoped that eventually a person in the open on Mars would need, in addition to his oxygen mask, no more protective clothing than a resident of McMurdo Base, Antarctica.

The centerpiece of every such plan was atmospheric engineering. The idea was to raise the volume of greenhouse gasses in the atmosphere to capture even more heat. Once started, the trend toward warmer temperatures would be self-reinforcing. Plenty of CO_2 was trapped in the polar caps. If it could be unfrozen, the atmosphere would thicken and temperatures would climb higher yet. On paper, the numbers seemed to work, though the project would have a budget as gargantuan as the scale of the effort. Moreover, it would take centuries to accomplish.

Another option became available in the 21st century. As years went by, ongoing advances in biotechnology made it tempting. Rather than terraform the entire planet of Mars, wouldn't it be easier and vastly cheaper to Areform a small number of people to survive on Mars in its present condition? They then could reproduce to populate the planet. The Martian environment was a daunting challenge to earth-bred biota, to say the least, but even unmodified simple life forms stood some chance of surviving there. The planet was not so alien as all that. Purpose-engineered humans could be designed to live in the bitterly cold temperatures. Body chemistry could be altered to conserve heat, resist UV light, and reduce the need for oxygen. An entire artificial ecology of plants and animals could be bioengineered to withstand the punishing Arean conditions. A group called the "Martian Colonial Society" investigated the matter serious and concluded the project was not only feasible, but cheap enough to be funded privately.

The deed had been done. Mandy was the prototype sentient Martian and, as far as she knew, still the sole working model.

Earth, at which Mandy continued to glance repeatedly as she strode across the plain, was as inhospitable to her present form as Mars had been when she was a natural human. To survive on earth's surface, she would need a sophisticated environmental suit, any minor failure of which would be deadly. Without proper protection, Mandy's own tough layers of bio-insulation, well suited to the average Martian temperature of -40C, would cause her body to overheat rapidly in the temperate zones of earth. Even on Mars, the tropics could be blisteringly hot for her at mid-day. On rare (very rare) occasions, temperatures at the equator could reach 20 degrees C, the same as a summer day in Maine. Only the thin atmosphere, which transferred heat poorly, saved her from death on those occasions. In the Martian tropics she preferred to stay in shadows until the blazing sun settled low in the sky, and the temperature dropped to a more comfortable -10 or -40. Even with her adaptations, Mars also could get uncomfortably cold at night, but she could manage with -200 for limited times, and sometimes she had to do so.

Then there was the crushing atmospheric pressure back on earth. Natural humans needed vast quantities of oxygen, but for Mandy such quantities were more than unnecessary. They were corrosive, even poisonous. She did, in fact, use oxygen produced by her chloroplasts (she didn't simply discard the stuff as did ordinary plants), but these relatively small quantities were adequate for her. Her energy equation was based on a very different chemistry. She breathed, after a fashion, with a bio-mechanism more similar to a roots blower than lungs, but just to absorb carbon dioxide and nitrogen.

The alternative to an environmental suit, if she wanted to walk again on the planet of her birth, was radical reverse bioengi-neering. Yet, even if she were to undergo such a procedure, the odds were not good she could be made fully human again—some Arean features likely would persist.

Mandy mentally corrected herself. She was fully human. To be human is not to have two legs, two arms, and opposable thumbs. Any ape fits that description. Many accident victims do not. To be human is to be self-aware: not only to know, but to know one knows. To be human is to share in the long evolutionary and cultural heritage of the one undeniably sentient lineage on earth. Body type is irrelevant. Humanity had struggled long enough to get past the notion that real humans came in only one shape and color. Actually, as Mandy's plight demonstrated, they were not past it yet. Though many on earth would disagree, Mandy was fully human, despite her name, which she always thought better suited to a fox terrier.

These thoughts led Mandy to consider the boundaries of humanity. Nature had worked quite a lot of changes into human body types all by itself over the past two million years. Mandy wondered at what point was the humanity threshold. Was old Homo Erectus human? She decided he almost certainly was, even if a living copy would have trouble on his SATs.

Mandy wasn't feeling too bright herself. After all she had volunteered for the Mars mission. The project funded by the Martian Colonial Society was given the name "Martian Gardens," apparently referring to a pun on one of the properties on the Monopoly board game. The Society offered her an incredible opportunity to pioneer a new world, to be a founding mother of a new civilization. At first the proposal had struck her as too bizarre to be taken seriously, but on reflection it had a weird sort of appeal. What kind of life could she expect on earth? Most likely, after 30 more years of routine flights into orbit to repair or retrieve satellites, she would retire to a cottage by the sea and drink tea with her neighbors. There was nothing very horrifying about the prospect, but all the same, it struck her as dreary.

Mandy had chosen to investigate the Society's offer. The computer images they showed her of Areformed bodies were scary. They put her off the project for a while longer, but the idea still didn't let her go. At last she asked herself, "Why not?" After all, she never again would have to worry about hair, fashion, wrinkles, or any of the other superficial concerns she didn't like to think about anyway. She never had been one to paint her nails or fluff her eyelashes. Her rare attempts to use cosmetics had induced well meaning friends to suggest she remove them.

Then there was the matter of family and children. She wasn't good at intimate relationships. Since the age of fifteen she had dismissed any desire for or expectation of marriage. She did not intend to reproduce either. There already were plenty of people on earth, and she didn't want to complicate her life. Yet, she found the idea strangely compelling in a Martian setting. Though her own conversion to Martian type would be a laborious undertaking, her zygotes would be altered to allow her and the other colonists to breed true. Mars was empty. Having and raising kids was not only possible but part of the job description.

Having children meant having a partner. The bioengineers had elected to keep the traditional two sexes rather than try parthenogenesis. Sexual reproduction was genetically healthier in the long run and probably psychologically too. Sexual identity was too much a part of the essence of being human for the project managers to abandon comfortably. Even those who reject traditional gender roles make the rejection itself elemental to their identity.

Mandy wondered how Martians would choose mates. With appearances so different from those that humans instinctively found attractive, would aesthetic superficialities be stripped from the Martian dating games? If so, this certainly would be a change for the better.

Mandy signed on for the project.

No sooner had Mandy signed the release forms than the biotechnicians set to work. Much of the procedure was fascinating to watch, in a grisly way, and truly awful to experience. Her DNA was grafted and sculpted using the new nanomachines, which, after decades of false promise, finally were capable of fine and extensive molecular work. She felt as though she were being eaten alive from the inside out, and in a sense she was.

Because she was an adult being with her existing organs already mature and in place, many of the adaptations required surgery. Changing her genes would not sufficiently alter her body type. The next generation after her simply could be born and grow up naturally. However, her body needed (not only figuratively) a hammer and chisel. Her own stem cells were utilized for the surgeries. They were altered to carry the new genetic code, and then they were used to grow new organs. The organs then were transplanted into her one after another as her strength allowed. Skin, fortunately, is made up of relatively undifferentiated cells anyway, so her epidermis was modified while still on her body. It transformed visibly day by day into a tough armor. This was unpleasant to see in the mirror, but it was not particularly painful.

Far worse than the medical procedures themselves, was the growing isolation they caused. The more Martian she became, the more constrained and artificial the environment she needed to survive. Soon, her only direct human contact was with medical workers in pressure suits. The more alien her appearance became, the more these same few workers, no doubt unintentionally, treated her as a lab animal rather than as a member of the team. They often talked about her progress with each other while in the same room with her, but they forgot to include her in the conversation.

She recalled one worker, whose face she never saw except vaguely through the tinted visor of his helmet, had the name "Batlia" taped to his suit. He asked Fredrika, who had been one of the people who initially invited her to join the project, "Do you think she feels cold, now that we've dropped the temperature another 10 degrees?"

Fredrika shrugged.

"Why don't you ask her?" said Mandy, referring to herself in the third person.

"What?" came a puzzled response from Batlia.

"No! She doesn't feel cold!"

She had little choice but to see the treatment through to the end. She was hardly free to walk out. After the first few months of modifications, even a short excursion out of her deep freeze chamber would have been fatal. Though she knew her trip to Mars would be solitary and would be followed by at least two more years alone on the surface, she looked forward to launch. At least she would be out of her glorified meat locker.

It seemed as though the torture would go on forever, but one day her new body was finished. After a few months of healing from her surgeries, there was only one more test to perform. She awaited results anxiously. When they came back, they were positive. The genetic modifications encoded into her cells were fully present at the zygote level. She was fertile. She was ready for Mars.

Unfortunately, Mars was not quite ready for her. There were seven more excruciating months to wait as Earth and Mars crawled into the proper positions for launch. Crawl, they did, and at the end of the wait, it was with eagerness that she sealed herself into the environmental pod to be transported to the Mars rocket. She saw little on the trip to the launch pad. The glass window of the pod frosted over almost at once. Some worker was kind enough to give the window a wipe just before she was placed on the gantry elevator. The insertion of the pod into the craft was eerily evocative of a foil-wrapped TV dinner sliding into a toaster oven.

After the outer door sealed behind her, she waited until a buzzer announced the ship's environment was adjusted. She opened her pod and took command of the Artemis. The interior atmosphere was set at Martian pressure and temperature. Any of her handlers would have died in minutes, but Mandy felt quite cozy.

She reflected that the ship wasn't aptly named. Artemis was a virgin goddess, often associated with the moon. Mandy's duties eventually would require a bit more active social life. Aphrodite, Ares' lover, might have been a better name, but then again Aphrodite was cheating on her husband Hepheastus. The Martian Gardens project managers probably rejected the name for PR reasons. The public had unpredictable bouts of prudery. There was political resistance enough to the project despite the private funding. Most of the money came from the Martian Colonial Society's most dedicated member and donor, a computer software mogul who was once one of the top ten richest men on earth. Thanks to the expense of Mandy and the Artemis, he was reduced to being a mere multimillionaire, barely flush enough for his remaining planned time on earth. He had bought one more privilege: he was one of the men scheduled to be Areformed and sent to Mars after Mandy.

Four unmanned ships had been sent to Mars ahead of Mandy that contained tools, food, water, power, and construction materials, and self-contained factories and laboratories. There was one more batch of cargo, and it was the most important of all: frozen spores, lichen, and insects engineered to live on Mars.

She would keep herself busy building the outpost and introducing life to the surface during the first two years alone.

Mandy knew the reason for sending her off to Mars without companions was political. The project managers tried to put a different spin on the decision. Before endangering more than one life, they told the press, they wanted to be sure the new biological designs could, in fact, live on Mars under real conditions. No earthbound simulation was truly an adequate test. While this was true enough, Mandy knew the managers were less concerned with individual lives than with the overall success of the project. Making more Martians would take time. If a launch window was missed, another two-year wait would follow. Meantime the risk of a restraining order continued to increase.

The opposition to Martian Gardens came from an unlikely alliance of political action groups on Earth. Some were opposed to all GM (genetic modification) science. The reasons were variously religious, environmental, and philosophical. They were joined by those who opposed GM being applied to humans specifically. Many people who had no objection to cooking up a better pig in a laboratory petri dish rebelled against doing the same to people. The objections usually were phrased in ethical terms, but Mandy suspected many of the opponents simply were worried about being outclassed by engineered *Ubermenschen*, a possible development that couldn't come too soon to suit Mandy. She believed humans could stand improvement.

Then there were the "spatial preservationists" who argued that neither Mars nor any other celestial body should be "despoiled" by humans, regardless of what physical shape they took. The preservationists' demand was to classify Mars a public park. Though the anti-GM people agreed on little else and were split between two main political parties, together they were likely to win a marginal majority in Congress sometime soon. Most UN member governments were already more or less in the anti-GM camp, and a number of resolutions to restrict research in the field were before the Assembly for consideration.

Mandy agreed with none of the arguments of the opponents, though she knew their opinions to be visceral and sincere. She didn't see why evolution was a fine enough thing to let happen by accident, but unacceptable when done by the application of human intelligence.

Mandy's first flight window came one month before the elections in the United States. The Martian Gardens promoters figured if they presented the public with a fait accompli, they would be unstoppable. Even an antagonistic public and Congress, they assumed, would balk at leaving Mandy stranded alone on Mars and unable to return. The only humane choice would be to allow the project to continue, though perhaps to limit it to Mars. Colonization of other planets might well be put on hold indefinitely. To the project managers, Mars was planet enough for a while.

Early in the flight, Mandy read the news beamed to her from earth. The U.S. election results were mixed. The House had a solid anti-GM and anti-Areform majority, but the Senate was evenly split with a mildly pro-GM Vice President casting deciding votes. The President refused to take a stand until he had proper time to "consider the matter." Until Messieurs Gallup and Harris gave him a clearer signal of what to consider, she figured he was likely to continue sitting on the fence. For the Martian Colonial Society the results were tantamount to a victory.

One long year passed by. The Artemis assumed orbit around Mars. The ship separated in two. The orbiter would remain in are-synchronous orbit, where it would provide the first segment of a planned global communications and weather station network. Mandy's landing craft fired its thruster in a series of short bursts and descended. The lander was small, as all the necessary supplies for the mission already were waiting on the surface.

The braking came in four phases. First the atmosphere itself helped slow down the craft, though the thin air of Mars was of limited help in this regard. Next, the parachutes deployed at 35km while the heat shield broke away and fell free. The rare air limited the value of the parachutes. At 3km the parachutes were released and the landing rockets kicked in. The deceleration in the third phase was more radical than Mandy had expected. Her stomach sank. The craft slowed nearly to a hover. At .25km the rockets stopped firing. Mandy's stomach flipped as her weight

vanished in an instant. The balloons deployed. This was a
technique first used with the *Pathfinder* Martian rover at the end
of the last century. The inflated balloons totally surrounded the
craft in order to cushion the final landing. Within moments
Mandy was jolted as the balloons made contact with the surface.
She could feel herself tumbling head over heels, as though in
some carnival ride, as the craft bounced and rolled along the
ground. Finally, movement stopped, although her head
continued to spin. She felt tipped to one side. The balloons
deflated and the lander righted itself.

When her illness from the ride passed, Mandy unstrapped
herself. She was long past fear. Donning no life support
equipment and wearing nothing more than light synthetic fabric
(because of the human habit of wearing clothes), she reached
for the door latch release. There was no sense of pressure change
as the door swung open. There was no unusual sound. It felt the
most natural thing in the world to clamber down to the Martian
surface.

The craft had come to rest less than a hundred meters from
one of the robot cargo vessels. The other two cargo ships were
visible as well. So was the ancient Viking 2 lander, which had
arrived in the 1970s.

The Utopia Planitia site, at the rather northerly 48 degrees
North latitude, had been chosen largely because of the Viking
probe. Not only was the smooth surface suitable for landing, but
the probe's photographs had shown frost, presumably water ice,
forming in winter. Water was a limiting factor in Martian
colonization, and the more of it there was at any given location,
the better.

Mandy bent down and picked up a rock. It felt oddly light in
the gentle Martian gravity. She threw it as though pitching a
baseball. Despite her weakened condition from months in space,
had the site been a ball field, she would have thrown the rock out
of the park.

Mandy's work schedule was ambitious. Almost at once she
began the task of unloading the cargo craft. In the months ahead
she would construct shelters. Aluminum frames would hold up
composite fabrics. The tent-like buildings in the end would

resemble Quonset huts. She would build similarly shaped warehouses next to the factory craft in order to store properly their products. The driller attachment to Cargo Vessel 2 already had tapped into a subsurface medium of sand and ice. The ships internal nuclear-powered machinery was ready to begin turning the ice into water and, through electrolysis, into fuel. Mandy needed to expand the collapsible containers for these and other products and put the factories into production. Her most important task by far, however, was to start a garden.

The project scientists had engineered a variety of plants. Several species of lichen had been adapted to Mars. In addition, there were no fewer than eight species of large crop plants. Due to the extreme conditions they faced on Mars, once the engineers came up with a successful design they tended to repeat it. Therefore, the crops looked very similar in shape to one another, but they were different enough genetically to make for a robust ecology. All began their life cycles as very sizable spores. When released, they would drill fine tendrils into the ground until they tapped subsurface ice. The plants would collect and channel heat from the sun to the tips using a photoelectric effect just powerful enough to liquefy the ice at point of contact. Adult plants had the shape of bifurcated pods. All of the pod species were designed to resist the bitter cold of night by shutting up tight. In daylight they would open and reveal tough cabbage-like leaves in order to photosynthesize. Each species had been designed for a distinct range of water availability, soil composition, and temperature.

Animal life had been designed for Mars too. Mandy would unfreeze insects, the largest resembling grasshoppers, after the crop plants began to sprout. Since they were designed to withstand Martian temperatures, "unfreeze" simply meant removal from liquid nitrogen. The role of the insects was to aid fertilization and to decompose old plants. Some of the plants were designed, in turn, to eat the grasshoppers.

By the time the follow-up ship of five colonists arrived in two years, the two women and three men would have homes, factories, and crops waiting for them. This, at least, was the plan.

Plans have a way of being overwhelmed by random events.

The random event that ran over Mandy was a misstep in the love life of the junior Senator from Pennsylvania. He inadvertently left classified documents in the possession of a DC dominatrix who was being watched by the FBI. She happened to be a spy. The Senator, after a period of fruitlessly denying the allegations in the face of FBI photographs and audio tapes, resigned as part of a deal to avoid prosecution. The Governor of Pennsylvania appointed the head of the State's Department of Environmental Protection to finish the Senator's term. The replacement Senator was solidly anti-GM, and she tipped the scales in Congress.

Sensing a shift in public sentiment toward the anti-GM camp, and guessing that Martians wouldn't vote in politically significant numbers for many years to come, the president came down finally and firmly on the anti-GM side. In a flurry of legislation, not only was future genetic modification of humans made illegal, Mars itself was sanctioned due to its contamination. Whatever sympathy might have been expected for Mandy's plight was undermined by a skillful PR campaign depicting her as a willful enemy of humanity and nature.

The UN firmed up its own measures, as did most of the member countries, thereby removing the possibility of moving the earth base of the Martian Gardens project to another suitable location. The hope and expectation among the spacefaring nations was that the Martian contamination, small and isolated as it was, would die out without further assistance from earth.

Mandy chose not to cooperate by dying out. She proceeded with the base construction and the establishment of life on the surface. Governments come and go, she reasoned. Political winds change. She would be ready when they did. Besides, she didn't have much else to do.

For the next few years, she continued to report back regularly with "I'm still here" messages, even though Earth (after a final order to her to desist in all further contamination) had stopped answering her calls. She deliberately omitted describing the flourishing state of her garden in her reports. The thought had occurred to her that evidence of success might prompt an actual attack against her.

The engineers had designed their crops well. The *siliqua frigida* species, which she preferred to call simply "frost pods," were slow to get started, but once they popped the surface they grew quickly. She tested her first meal of frost pod cabbage six months after the initial planting. Supposedly she had been fed samples back on earth from plants grown in special environmental rooms with UV light, but the chefs must have processed and seasoned them extensively. What she had eaten on earth wasn't bad, rather like collard greens. The taste of the Martian grown plant was vile. She re-named the dish, "skunk cabbage salad" for its smell and taste. However, she did manage to keep it down, and it seemed to be as nourishing as intended. She now was sure she could survive on Mars after the ship supplies ran out.

Mandy was almost embarrassed to be so conventional as to go through the four classic stages of grief when faced with abandonment by earth. In her denial phase she redoubled her efforts at building Martian Gardens. She even went so far as to collect local fieldstone to construct a dome, which looked in the end like a pink igloo. She used frost pod leaves and ice for mortar. During her anger phase, she smashed the radio and camera equipment, feeling if Earth didn't want to speak to her, then she didn't want to speak to Earth. This was followed by months of depression during which she did little more than watch her garden grow. She chewed the skunky cabbage, taking perverse enjoyment in its awful flavor. Finally, she snapped out of it and, for no particular reason, she was in a good mood. If she was stranded, well then, she was stranded and there was no use moping about it.

With this new acceptance of her fate, Mandy decided to make the best of it. She was still a pioneer on a new planet. She decided to explore Mars. The solar-powered rover, which had been brought by one of the cargo vessels, could travel only several kilometers at a time before it would stop and need to recharge its batteries, but she was in no hurry. The rover was a stripped down affair looking rather like a monster truck with absurdly big inflatable balloon tires designed to cross rough terrain and moderate-size ditches. The vehicle was lightweight, especially in Martian gravity, but it had a large bed. She loaded it up with canisters of spores, frozen insects, and lichen. While she explored, she would plant life, acting like a Martian "Janie Appleseed." When people returned to Mars they would find a living world waiting for them, even if she herself did not survive to greet them.

As she traveled, she flung a mix of spores wherever the soil seemed loose enough. At least one of the species usually took in each location. Though the adult plants did generate new spores, which the insects were intended to spread, they grew even more rapidly from root to root, forming stands like Martian birches.

"I was once myself a slinger of birches," she said to herself.

Mandy traveled southeast toward Olympus Mons, the highest volcano in the solar system and one of the natural wonders of the planet. Olympus Mons was an extinct shield volcano, a hugely oversized version of the type that had formed Hawaii. For reasons still unclear to scientists on earth, the Martian volcano's gentle slope from the summit ended abruptly in cliffs, which surrounded the base of the mountain. Mandy spotted the escarpment as it nudged above the horizon, but the scale became obvious only as she came close. She looked up from the bottom. The cliffs loomed kilometers high above her.

Mandy sent the rover around the cliff by itself to the other side. Its onboard navigational computer was quite capable of keeping the machine out of trouble. She knew it had a better chance of reaching the other side than she did. Mandy worked her way up the wall with a backpack of supplies. Only twice did she have to backtrack and pick a new route upward. She spent the night on a ledge. Much to her surprise, she made it to the top on the second day. Once atop the cliffs, the walk was long but easy. The grade was a mere 4 degrees. It was, however, 275 kilometers to the central caldera. She rationed her backpack provisions carefully.

Braving what even Mandy felt to be the bitter cold of nights on the mountain, Mandy eventually reached her goal. The view from the summit was spectacular. The mountain rose 25 kilometers above the surrounding plain. The caldera was 70 miles across. She tossed plant spores and insects into the crater, hoping to begin a park like the Ngorongoro crater on earth. Bugs were not as impressive as lions, true enough, but who could tell into what they would evolve someday?

She skirted the edge of the caldera and descended the opposite slope. When she reached the cliffs at the far side, she radioed for the rover, only half expecting an answer. The rover answered immediately and homed in on her signal. She climbed down the cliff and found the machine waiting like an anxious puppy.

"Well, at least the machine likes me," she muttered to the rover affectionately. "They at least could have sent me more like you."

She leisurely traversed Tharsis Ridge and then turned south to the enormous Valles Marinaris canyon system. Often called the Grand Canyon of Mars, it actually was far bigger. Transplanted to earth, the width would have spanned Arizona and the length would have stretched across North America coast to coast. She was surprised to notice striations in the rock walls. Given the supposedly limited sedimentary history of the planet, she was at a loss for an explanation.

She turned NNE to the Viking 1 landing site at Chryse Planitia. Finding the craft, a twin to the Viking 2 at Utopia Planitia, was like seeing an old friend. If she still had had tear ducts she would have cried.

To the east she traveled to the gouged regions bearing the scars of some primeval catastrophic flood, proof that water had once flowed on the surface.

Green spread across the surface of the planet following in Mandy's wake. So also spread crawling Martian roaches and bounding grasshoppers. Occasionally Mandy would double back, harvest her crop for food and collect more seeds. Then continue on. Well into the second Martian year of her journey, it was with surprise that Mandy realized she was enjoying herself, and that she had been enjoying herself since she left Martian Gardens. She was so accustomed to thinking of herself as despairing that she hadn't noticed her own happiness.

Eventually, her circuit returned her to Martian Gardens. She scarcely recognized the place. The plain was covered with frost pods and teemed with insects. After a few relaxing weeks, Mandy had another bout of depression. The trip around the world had given her a mission and a goal, but now she seemed simply to be wasting time.

She snapped herself out it by giving herself a new mission. Actually, it was her original mission: the human colonization of Mars. The GM experiments evidently were over on earth, at least insofar as humans were concerned. She concluded the next humans to reach Mars, whenever that might be, would be standard form humans living in domes and pressure suits. So be it. A rose is a rose. She would adjust her building techniques to accommodate standard humans. Mandy believed she still had a chance to be the mother of her planet's civilization.

Mandy decided the best place to start building a city for her future stepchildren was not at Martian Gardens, a rather dreary plain that was only slightly improved by the stands of frost pods, but the cliffs at the base of Olympus Mons. She loaded up the rover with tools and set off for the mountain again. Only a few kilometers from the cliff base, the trusty rover finally stopped permanently, but it had outperformed its design by far, and she held no grudges. She hauled the supplies the rest of the way on foot.

Inspired by Chaco Canyon, which she had seen as a child, she built living structures in the recesses and shallow caves of the cliff face. She dedicated herself to the task, carving out stairs and erecting multi-storey dwellings out of stone. There would be some way, she was sure, for the newcomers to make use of the structures by making them airtight with interior linings or perhaps by encompassing the whole construction with a half-dome.

Years went by. Then more years. Then decades. The cliff city took shape, looking in the end like a pink Oz. There was one five storey tower of which she was particularly proud. From the roof she could reach up and touch the ceiling of the cave. She loved to sit there and look out over the fields of pods below.

As the decades stretched toward a century, Mandy, quite unexpectedly, remained physically unchanged. Had the bioengineers inadvertently discovered the secret of youth while adapting her to cold and CO_2? Unfortunately, memories of the old 1950s SciFi movie The Wasp Woman kept coming back to her; she felt like she bore a passing resemblance to the eponymous character.

On the hundredth anniversary of her landing, Mandy rewarded herself with a vacation consisting of yet another world tour. It would be entirely on foot, but she was in no hurry. By this time, life had so spread across Mars that she scarcely needed to take supplies. She headed south, as she had given the southern hemisphere short shrift on her last excursion.

It was on this southern trip that she spotted the orbiting spacecraft. Whatever Luddite phase had gripped the earthlings must be over. Humanity was reaching out to Mars again.

Mandy footed back to Martian Gardens as fast as she could. Once there, she tidied up the site as she awaited for a robot lander or even, she dared to hope, a live human being. She was eager for the opportunity to lead someone to Olympus Mons and show off "Pink Oz."

In little more than two years, the day finally arrived. A bright spot in the sky caught her eye. It grew to a streak. The streak vanished but soon she saw four white dots, presumably a craft and parachutes. The three outer dots broke away and light flared from the central one. The dot grew into an unmarked silvery cone that soft landed several meters from the ship in which she had arrived so long ago.

The cone's skin unfolded, much like a metallic version of a frost pod. Inside was a hodgepodge of mechanical arms, cameras, power cells, and cables. An arm reached down to the soil and scooped up a sample. It retracted into the craft to perform an analysis. A ramp dropped, allowing a small rover about the size of a cocker spaniel equipped with its own arms and camera to roll to the surface.

Mandy had expected the first landing to be by a robot, so she wasn't surprised and only mildly disappointed. She made sure to keep within view of the rover's camera. The rover seemed to take surprisingly little interest in her, but it may have been acting according to a pre-installed program. It did take samples of the plant life and carry them back to the lander. Mandy watched as machinery on the lander processed the plant matter in some way and turned into a kind of oil. The machine then spat the oil into a cup, which retracted into a box. A tiny puff of smoke escaped from the box. Apparently the lander had tested the pods as a source for fuel. The idea made sense of a sort, at least of a rather mechanical sort. Mandy assumed the findings of this craft would result in a major expedition soon.

Mandy was right. In only four years the sky lit up with a swarm of re-entering vehicles. One after another, silvery cones landed around Martian Gardens. When they unfolded, they disgorged a bewildering variety of insect-like machines. Almost immediately the machines began to harvest the pods. Mandy assumed at first they were processing them for food, water, and fuel for the still to come humans, but as she examined the new ships and rovers, which continued to display a profound disinterest in her presence, a new suspicion grew in her. The machines were making only lubricating oil and fuel. They were not preparing the way for men at all. There would not be anyone to whom to show off Pink Oz.

She understood. People successfully had avoided the fate of being replaced by genetic mutants. Instead, they had replaced themselves with machines. Mandy decided to move to the Olympus Mons caldera. She realized she belonged in a wildlife preserve.

—Richard Bellush, Jr.

WHAT YOU ASK FOR

BYE, BYE, LADIES' MAN

Hey baby, don't you give me that ginseng jive
'cause you ain't keepin' my love alive.
You're like peeking inside my Grandma's purse,
a nunnery or live with you?
Couldn't say which was worse.

Gonna leave you honey.
Gonna move to the city,
where sweet-looking dudes
gonna tell me I'm pretty.

Heartless androgyny.
It's not funny.
Just want to stroke you
then steal your money.

Just want to show you a funky time.
Don't want to hear no punky line.
Come on.
Give it to me.
Give it to me.
Give it to me.

—Sharon Bellush

THE PERFECT GIFT

Barton MacPherson parked his car on Blackwell Street. It was the main thoroughfare of Dover, a town of moderate size, for which he had nearly missed the exit off of Route 10. Most of the downtown buildings dated to the 19th and early 20th centuries. He was surprised to see Dover had not yet fully shared in the gentrification overtaking most town and village centers of central and western New Jersey. He guessed it would come soon. All the surrounding municipalities flaunted the usual well-trimmed, suburban planned developments and townhouse projects; they looked much the same as those in any other part of the country. Although at a nearby McDonald's he had overheard locals complain of the bland uniformity of new construction, he figured at heart they must prefer it, since their own strict zoning ordinances allowed nothing else.

Barton strolled along the sidewalk looking for a gift shop with the odd name Croakers. He hoped his long years of research finally were about to pay off. Barton decided Blackwell Street was too prominent a location. Somehow it seemed much more appropriate for the shop to be tucked in a side street somewhere. He couldn't call for directions. The store had no Yellow Pages listing, and its telephone number was unlisted. Fortunately downtown Dover wasn't as big as all that.

He explored only two side roads before he found the shop on North Essex Street. He nearly walked right by it. A glass window, painted black on the inside, announced "Croakers, Novelties and Gifts" in gold letters on the dusty surface. Had the sunlight struck the glass at a different angle, he wouldn't have noticed the lettering at all. Barton pulled on the heavy six-panel oak door next to the window, half expecting it to be locked. It opened and he walked inside.

His eyes took a few moments to adjust to the light, or rather to the paucity of it. Most of what there was came from a blacklight florescent tube above the counter. The ceiling, walls, shelving, floor, and furnishings were black. In racks in the center of the space, Halloween-type costumes ranged from princesses and sailors to goblins and former presidents. Along the walls, shelves held vampire teeth, rubber monster gloves, Ouija boards, Tarot cards, adult party games, and plastic swords. Behind the counter under the black light, stood a high-school-aged girl with impossibly red hair and long white fingernails. Somehow, she was managing to read a paperback novel in the gloom. She didn't even look up at him.

"Hello, miss. I'd like to speak to the owner."

Still without looking up, she answered, "He's not available."

"That is not the same thing as not being here."

"He's not available."

"Tell him I went to a lot of trouble to track him down."

"He is still not available."

Barton pulled a sheet of paper from his inside jacket pocket. He unfolded it and dropped it on the counter. The young woman diverted her eyes to it briefly. It was a list of names and international addresses.

"Please give the gentleman this. It is a gentleman, isn't it?"

"If you mean as opposed to a lady, yes."

"What time do you close?" Barton asked.

"Six." The young woman turned the page of her novel.

"I'll be back at 5:50."

The young woman shrugged almost imperceptibly.

Barton left. He found a restaurant called Fred's Fish Market on Blackwell and had an early supper of blackened Cajun catfish. The chef's temerarious use of spices suited Barton well, though he needed three refills of his water glass. He settled up the tab, and then he walked again around the corner. Barton nearly collided with the redhead in the doorway of Croakers. She was on her way out.

"Excuse me."

The redhead didn't respond but simply hurried past. Barton reentered the gift shop. He waited again for his eyes to adjust. When they did, he saw a short man with a indistinctive but pleasant face standing behind the counter. The man's face had no wrinkles and his hair was brown without a trace of gray, yet somehow he gave the impression of advanced age.

"Hello, Mr. MacPherson," the man began. I have read your list. It puzzles me, I must say. I'm not sure what you want, but I very much doubt there is anything I can do for you."

"Permit me to disagree."

"You hardly need my permission for that."

"How should I address you?"

"Mr. Green will be just fine."

"Alright, Mr. Green, if that is what you want to be called. I have pursued you in every city on that list, and more besides. Always I have found your store location only after you closed up your shop and moved on. Sometimes I missed you only by days. I've spoken to everyone person on that list, and more besides, who hired your services. At last I followed a lead based on a shipping order from Uruguay, and I have tracked you down here on North Essex Street in Dover, New Jersey."

"Would it help for me to say I don't know what you are talking about?"

"No. Please don't play games with me Mr. Green. You were Mr. Vert in Paris, Zelyoni in Ekaterinaberg, a Miss Midori'iro . . ."

"Miss Midori'iro?"

". . . in Kobe, Mr. Rangi-ya-majani in Nairobi, Miss Verde in Montevideo . . ."

"Mr. MacPherson, do you have any idea how ridiculous . . .?"

"Yes, but it is not ridiculous, is it? Look, Mr. Green, I didn't come all the way here to cause you trouble. I merely want to employ your services."

"'Merely?'"

"You can see, from what it has cost me to find you, that money is not an issue. I'm willing to pay you any fee you may ask."

"If what you believe is true, you must know that money cannot be the primary influence with me."

"Then anything. I am a determined man. What can I do to persuade you to help me?"

Mr. Green looked his visitor over carefully. At last he said, "Come. You can come into the back room and have a cup of tea. It is already brewing. I want you to tell me about yourself, and how you came to have these curious notions of yours."

Barton followed Mr. Green through a black door and on into a back sitting room with pine paneling that was so old that the unstained wood had darkened to a deep brown. A frayed, but expensive Persian carpet, mostly green, covered the floor. The ceiling was beamed and paneled. An antique walnut oval table occupied the center of the room. Even compared with the black-walled store area, the room felt dark. The only light came from the upper sash of a north-facing window that looked out on an alley; the lower sash was blocked by a half curtain. The room was warmer than Barton preferred, but it was cozy. The aroma of burning wood rose strong but not overpowering. He assumed a wood stove was at work somewhere in the building.

"Please, have a seat, Mr. MacPherson."

Barton sat down by the table in a wooden chair with a faded fabric seat. The chair creaked, but it seemed in no danger of collapse. Mr. Green disappeared from the room for a few minutes and returned with two steaming cups of tea. The china cups matched neither each other nor their saucers. He did not bring with him or offer cream or sugar. Green's chair creaked, too, as he settled into it.

"Now, tell me your story, Mr. MacPherson."

"Yes . . . Well . . . My! This is very good tea."

"Thank you. You told me something of how you got here. Now please tell me why."

Barton paused, composed himself. "Dissatisfaction."

"There is much of that going around."

"Mine started early, when I was a child. Perhaps if I'd come from a family with strong religious views and so-called traditional values, things might have been different. I might have just accepted all that and been content."

"You are free to do so now."

"No, I'm not. I can't make myself believe it, yet I feel my life lacks a purpose as a result.

"Need life have a purpose?"

"Now you sound like my parents. They liked to call themselves 'latitudinarians.' They were open-minded people with an open marriage. They were strictly secular, and they deliberately kept me from indoctrination, as they put it, with sectarian views. They said it was important for me to make up my own mind about such things, when I was old enough. I shouldn't simply be brainwashed. They were the sort of people who sue local towns for funding Christmas displays using tax money."

"Well, that is a point of view with its own integrity, much as it galls many folks. Some people might admire them for it."

"I'm not sure I don't. It's just that it left me somehow empty. My parents seemed able to live full and happy lives in a world devoid of meaning and purpose, but I have always felt lost. Here I was in a temporary world for a limited number of days or years, and then... I would be gone. For what? Whenever I tried to motivate myself to do anything, whether it was to get good grades, win at sports, choose a college, or pursue a job, the same question kept haunting me: What's the point?"

"Some would say you should pick your point, rather than accept one from another's philosophy."

"You sound like my parents again. For a while I tried to interest myself in philosophy and then in traditional religion, but I'd received too much of a dose of skepticism at home to take any of it very seriously. I didn't find what anyone had to say very credible. For a while, though, I got rather a lift from poetry."

"Poetry?"

"William Butler Yeats."

"Really? That would have surprised the old boy. Much as he carried on about a coming cultural cataclysm, he wasn't much in the saving business."

"Quite so. In fact, he may have tried to contact me about it, though—just as he describes in his book, A Vision, about his wife's connection with other worldly spirits—the 'Frustrators' got in our way."

"Uh-huh. Let us try to keep our conversation to this plane of existence, if we can."

"If you wish. Anyway, all the background research I did on Yeats for my high school paper made me identify with him. He grew up with a rationalist father, an experience that made him a skeptic—yet this take on the world left him empty too. He found the answer in the occult, through the example of the Order of the Golden Dawn. He encouraged me to follow in his footsteps."

"Tell me, how was it that your so-called skepticism didn't forbid you this option?"

"Because the Order has a much more open-minded world view than those of conventional religions. We accept there are forces at work in the world beyond those we can touch with our fingers, but no one of us pretends to have all the answers. I explored many aspects of the occult in depth, both in and out of the Order. I joined several magical organizations and did my best to learn what I could about the larger universe."

"Alright, I won't argue religion with you, but if you found the meaning you were after, why are you still dissatisfied?"

"For a time, I wasn't. While I was learning about higher beings and forces and how to channel their energies in this world, education alone absorbed my interest. But eventually I came to feel I was making no progress on more fundamental matters. The mechanics of magic were just that, mechanics. They were, to use your words, a 'how' but not a 'why.' More than that, suspicion began to grow in me that all my occult learning had an element of self-deception to it. I began to question my own magical precepts."

"That is a risk of the skeptical turn of mind. Eventually it turns on everything, even itself. As for fundamental matters, Mr. MacPherson, perhaps you have to accept the possibility that you won't learn the answer to your 'why,' and that perhaps there is no answer to learn."

"Yes, well, that is why I'm here."

"I don't have an answer for your why, Mr. MacPherson."

"I don't expect you to have one. I am unhappy about it, but I have accepted the idea that no one can help me with this."

"I'm sorry you are unhappy, but what do you want from me?"

"I think you can give me something that's just as good as an answer. I first learned of you in London, you know. I was seeking out high-ranking magicians to teach me the more abstruse occult secrets. Several of them hinted that there was a very powerful magician about, who might know more than they did."

"I think you define 'magic' and 'magician' in a way peculiar to your occult training. If you think this so-called 'magician' is myself, I have to tell you I hold no rank in any occult organization, and my knowledge of such things is surely less than your own."

"So I discovered—or you would have been easier to trace through the secret societies. My first real lead was in Paris. I met one of your clients, Miss Benet, a very beautiful woman. I followed her directions to your shop, but it had closed years earlier. It took months for me to get another lead.

"Finally, research into shipping records showed a Russian destination. The trail led me to Ekaterinaburg, where again I found your location after you'd closed your shop. However, I had the good fortune to meet a Mr. Ostrogorsky, whom you helped. Following hearsay, hints, phone records, and shipping documents, I journeyed to India, South Africa, Thailand, Japan, Ecuador, and other places too. Always, I was a step behind. Now, at last, I have found you!"

"Disappointed?"

Barton looked around him. "No. It is very like a powerful magician to be discreet."

"Is a magician what I am?"

"I don't know what you are, to be truthful. Please tell me. Are you human? Are you an extension of a being from another dimension? Are you a little green man, and are the various lingual variations of your name a private joke?"

Green softened, abandoning his pretense of humoring Barton's eccentricity. "I am here as a refugee, of sorts. You need know no more than that. But I am very fond of this world and its amusing and tragic people. In return for my pleasant exile, I wished to give something back, in a low-key sort of way. Yes, I sold gifts, but I'm retired. Now I sell knick-knacks."

"You made people gifted."

"Perhaps once. No more." face showed resolve.

"Why have you stopped, then?"

Green sighed. "Just look at the list of people you have showed me. It represents a small fraction of the number to whom I've sold gifts, by the way. Do they have anything, that you can detect, in common?"

"From what I can see, they all got their hearts' desires."

"They are all miserable, Mr. MacPherson. Far more so than you ever have been. I wasn't able to help them at all. Mind you, I never tried to play pranks or teach them some moral lesson by granting gifts with a wicked twist. I truly intended to provide my customers with what they wanted. I kept the gifts within strict practical limits, of course: just one to a customer and nothing so extraordinary as to bring unwanted attention either to the customer or to me.

Green raised an eyebrow. "You met Miss Benet in Paris, whom you described as a beautiful woman—and so she is. She wasn't, when I met her. She was plain and a pleasant person."

"She struck me as rather hostile. I thought I had done something to offend her."

"You did. You noticed her beauty. She is convinced no one notices anything else, and this conviction makes her quite irritable. I offered to change her back, but she would have none of it.

"It was the same story everywhere. In Turkey, a young man wanted to be lucky in love. Though women flock to him, he now complains his life is loveless. He is bored and pines to be left alone. The risk of failure in his pursuits was what had made the game fun to play. Yet he won't trade back his gift, either.

"In Russia, a man wanted a great intelligence so he could understand more of the world. However, the gift of understanding has made him quite depressed.

"In Morocco, many years ago, a woman wanted a long life. Now she has watched all her friends and family die before her eyes.

"In South America, a veterinarian wanted empathy with the animals. He found it was a two-way street. He had to give up eating meat, which he loved, because he can't stand the thought of eating his peers. Even plants cause him guilt, because farming denies the habitat to animals.

"In Australia, a fat man wanted to be able to eat anything, but still remain thin. He forgot that his entire biology wasn't indestructible. He gorged himself so relentlessly that he put himself, trim and handsome, in the hospital with kidney and liver failure."

"So that's it, Mr. Green. I get the idea. Your customers haven't been happy with their gifts."

"And yet, I never can get any of them to give them back. I really don't understand it. So you see, in order to stop doing more damage, I have just retired. Now I sell trinkets, Whoopee Cushions, and water pistols."

"There is a gift you haven't sold yet, and I want it, Mr. Green."

"Haven't you been listening to me, Mr. MacPherson?"

"Yes, I have. But all the people you have helped made a serious mistake. All asked for something they thought would make them happy. They thought happiness came from the outside. They were wrong. If you don't know how to be happy, a new toy won't help you. The only people who truly can enjoy riches of any kind are the ones who don't really need them."

"Precisely. The observation is trite, but then, most truisms are."

"What if I asked for happiness, itself?"

"Excuse me?"

"Suppose I asked you to make me happy. Happiness from the inside out."

"Every gift carries its own cost, Mr. MacPherson. It may not be one you wish to pay."

"I'll pay anything."

"Keep in mind, the other gifts we discussed were quite superficial. No one was changed as to the very essence of who they were. Even the fellow who became a magnet for ladies got so through only a minor alteration in chemistry."

"Pheromones?"

"Something like that. What you are talking about, on the other hand, would involve a total change in your personality. Arguably, 'you' might cease to exist."

"I really don't care. It's what I want."

"Very well, sir. I'll make one last sale."

"Thank you."

The next day, the red-haired teenager entered the store after school and was surprised to see a man in brown coveralls

sweeping the floor. Eyes aloft, he smiled and sang My Bonnie
Lies Over the Ocean, over and over, to the rhythm of the broom
handle.

"Excuse me, Mr. Green. Isn't that the man who was in here
yesterday looking for you?"

"Yes, I hired him as my janitor. I was pleased to be able to help
him out."

"What's wrong with him?"

"Barton's severely handicapped," he whispered. "He has the
mind of a six-year-old."

"Oh? He didn't strike me that way yesterday. If I'd have
known, I'd have been nicer to him. It's so sad."

"Not really. He's happy."

—Richard Bellush, Jr.